Praise for the novels of Robyn Carr

"Brimming with insight, tender sensuality, sympathetic characters, and family anxiety, this story blends painful realities with healing love in a strong, uplifting tale that will lure both women's fiction and romance fans."
—*Library Journal*, starred review, on *The View from Alameda Island*

"This novel of sisters and secrets…will please fans of Carr's Virgin River series. Themes of responsibility, forgiveness, and the agony and ecstasy of female relatives will appeal to readers of Debbie Macomber and Susan Wiggs."
—*Booklist* on *The Summer That Made Us*

"With strong relationship dynamics, juicy secrets, and a heartwarming ending, it's a blissful beach read."
—*Kirkus Reviews* on *The Summer That Made Us*

"A satisfying reinvention story that handles painful issues with a light and uplifting touch."
—*Kirkus Reviews* on *The Life She Wants*

"Insightfully realized central figures, a strong supporting cast, family issues, and uncommon emotional complexity make this uplifting story a heart-grabber that won't let readers go until the very end…. A rewarding (happy) story that will appeal across the board and might require a hanky or two."
—*Library Journal*, starred review, on *What We Find*

"Carr's new novel demonstrates that classic women's fiction, illuminating the power of women's friendships, is still alive and well."
—*Booklist* on *Four Friends*

ROBYN CARR

SUNRISE ON HALF MOON BAY

mira

Recycling programs
for this product may
not exist in your area.

ISBN-13: 978-0-7783-3148-3

Sunrise on Half Moon Bay

First published in 2020. This edition published in 2022.

Copyright © 2020 by Robyn Carr

This edition published by arrangement with Harlequin Books S.A.

For questions and comments about the quality of this book, please contact us
at CustomerService@Harlequin.com.

Mira
22 Adelaide St. West, 41st Floor
Toronto, Ontario M5H 4E3, Canada
www.Harlequin.com

Printed in Lithuania

MIX
Paper from
responsible sources
FSC® C021394

Also by Robyn Carr

Look for Robyn Carr's next novel
available soon from MIRA.

Sunrise on Half Moon Bay

CHAPTER ONE

Adele Descaro's mother passed away right before Christmas. While she missed her mother, Adele was relieved to know she was no longer held prisoner in a body that refused to serve her. It had been four years since the stroke that left her crippled, nonverbal and able to communicate only with her eyes and facial expressions. Adele had been her primary caretaker for those four years and now, with Elaine at rest, she could get back to her own life. If she could remember what it was.

She was thirty-two and had actually spent the last eight years mostly as a caretaker. *Mostly* because Adele had also helped to care for her disabled father for four years. Her mother had done much of the work and then, within just a few months of his death, she had suffered her debilitating stroke. Devastated by this cruel turn of events, Adele resigned from the part-time job she'd taken as a bookkeeper at a local inn and dedicated herself to Elaine's care full-time. There had been help from a visiting nursing service and from Justine, her much older sister. Justine was, in fact, twenty years older, now fifty-two.

Adele was happy she had made her mother's care her

priority, but was aware that in doing so, she had allowed herself to hide from her own life, to put off her own growth and keep her dreams and desires just out of reach. Now her opportunity was at hand. She lived in the comfort of the home she'd grown up in, had friends in her little town and the time to pursue whatever her heart desired.

Justine, a successful corporate attorney in Silicon Valley and the mother of two teenage girls, hadn't been able to pitch in much time so she contributed to the cost of Elaine's care and provided a modest income for Adele. She had made it a point to stay with Elaine every other Sunday so Adele could have at least a little freedom.

The truth was that for the past four years, or actually eight if you really thought about it, Adele had been fantasizing about how she would reinvent herself when the time came. Now that it was here, in the cold rainy months of a typical Pacific winter, she realized she had yet to come up with a plan.

Adele had left her graduate studies in English Literature at Berkeley to return home when her father was released from the hospital. "To help out," she told her mother. Her father, Lenny, had been a maintenance supervisor for the Half Moon Bay school district and had taken a bad fall while trying to fix a heating vent in the ceiling of an auditorium. He was in a body cast for months, had several spinal surgeries and spent years either in traction or a wheelchair. But the worst of it was his pain, and he became dependent on powerful pain medications.

Adele's mother needed her help, that was true. But she might still have continued her graduate studies. But Adele had another problem. She fell in love and got pregnant—accidentally. The father of her baby didn't want the child, so in addition to her pregnancy, she suffered a broken heart.

She'd intended to raise the child on her own but she'd suffered complications; her baby was stillborn and her already broken heart was completely shattered. The safety of her home was her refuge, even with her disabled father's condition casting a pall over life there.

Then, as if to drive home the fact that she was not quite ready to get on with her life, her mother had her stroke.

And now, here she was, still with no plan whatsoever. She gazed out the kitchen window. It was early March in Half Moon Bay, and fog sat on the beach every day until noon. It was like living in a heavy cloud. Adele had no motivation whatsoever. She found herself eating a cardboard container of lentil soup from the deli while standing over the kitchen sink, alone. She was wearing a lavender chenille robe and had slopped some soup on the front. She was not ready for bed early; she hadn't bothered to get dressed today. She could have spent the day reading great literature or better still, drafting a life plan. Instead, she'd watched a full day of *M*A*S*H* reruns while lying on the couch.

She'd been sleeping on the couch for months. She and the couch were as one. She had often slept there in her mother's final days so she could hear her in the night. Adele's bedroom had been little more than a changing room.

The doorbell rang, and she looked down at the mess on her robe. "Great," she said. She took another spoonful of soup, then went to the door. She peeped out. It was Jake Bronski, probably her closest friend. He held up a white bag so she could see he brought something for her. She opened the door.

"Hi, Jake. Sorry, but I'm just on my way out…"

"Right," he said, pushing his way in. "You were invited to a pajama party, I suppose?"

"Yes, as it happens," she said meekly.

"Well, you look stunning, as usual. Why don't you slip into something a little *less* comfortable while I set the table."

"I will if you promise not to clean the kitchen," she said. "It annoys me when you do that."

"Someone has to do it," he said. Then he smiled at her. "Go on, then."

"All right, but eventually this has to stop," she said, even though she had no desire for it to stop.

She went to her room, the master bedroom. It had been her parents' room until they each got sick and they converted the only bedroom downstairs, which had an adjoining bath, into a sick room. They were fortunate that her father had remodeled the house a bit before his accident since these old homes didn't usually have large spacious main floor bathrooms.

Maybe that was why she had trouble sleeping in her bed—it was her parents' when they had been healthy and happy.

She stripped and got into the shower. Jake deserved that much. She blew out her curly hair and rummaged around for a pair of clean jeans. Of course she came from that ilk of women who gained rather than lost weight in their grief. How was it you could barely swallow any food and yet gain weight? She sighed as she squeezed into the uncomfortably tight jeans and added some lip gloss.

When she returned, she found the kitchen had been cleaned and the table was set for two with place mats, good dishes, wine and water glasses. Jake had even put his offerings in serving dishes—tri-tip on a platter, Caesar salad, green beans sprinkled with pieces of bacon. On the counter were a couple of generous slices of cheesecake with berries on top. A bottle of wine had been opened and was breathing.

"Your mother isn't coming?" Adele asked.

"*Dancing with the Stars* is on," he said, by way of explanation. "What did you do today?"

"Not too much," she said.

He held her chair for her. "Addie, have you given any thought to talking to someone? A professional? I think you might be depressed."

"You think someone can talk me out of it?" she asked facetiously.

"What if you need medication?"

"Jake, my mother just died!"

"I realize that," he said. "But for the last few years we talked about the things you wanted to do when you weren't tied down anymore."

"That's true, but I didn't want her to die! And I think my grief is normal, under these circumstances."

"I couldn't agree more, but you're turning into a shut-in. You are free to live for yourself. You can finally get together with friends, get out, do things."

"Enjoy this wet, cold weather, you mean? Maybe when the sun comes out, I'll feel more motivated."

"You had a long list of things you were going to do. I can't even remember everything…"

She remembered. "I was going to remodel or at least give this house a face-lift so I could put it on the market, find myself a chic little apartment with a view, finish my graduate studies, date Bradley Cooper—"

He smiled. "I can help with the house," he said. "Anything I can't do, I can find you the right person. Have you seen Justine lately?"

"I don't see too much of her now that I don't need her to

help with Mom," Adele said. "She brought the girls down a couple of times after Christmas."

"She should do better than that," Jake said, frowning.

"I could just as easily go to San Jose and see her. She's not the only one in this relationship."

"I don't think she realizes how much you need her," he said.

"Well, we're not close. We're family. We'd never be friends if we weren't family. We're nothing alike."

"Lots of siblings say that about each other. I'm not close to Marty. If he weren't in constant need of money, I'd never hear from him."

The two of them did have that in common, Adele thought, but for very different reasons. Marty, short for Martin, was Jake's younger brother. He'd been twice married, had three kids from those two wives, presently had a girlfriend he was living with, and was not doing very well at supporting his extended family.

For Adele and Justine, the twenty-year age difference was just the beginning. They had never really lived in the same house. Justine was in college when Adele was born. Elaine had been in her forties when surprised by a second pregnancy. Then, probably because of her age and experience, Elaine made Adele the center of her universe in a way Justine had never been. Adele had been dreadfully spoiled, her parents doting on her every moment.

It wasn't as though Justine had been pushed to one side, but she certainly didn't get as much attention. Many times Justine had told Adele the story of her asking their mother to make her wedding gown, Elaine having been a gifted seamstress. But, according to Justine, Elaine had said, "How could I find the time? I have a small child!" When Justine pointed out that the small child was now in school,

Elaine had said, "But I have myself and Adele to get ready for the wedding!" So how could she find time to make a complicated gown for the bride?

It had ever been thus as far as Justine could see. Adele was the chosen one and Justine was expected to understand, step aside and worship her darling baby sister. Justine's great accomplishments, and there were many, were taken in stride while Adele's merest babble was praised to the skies. Justine used to claim, "If Adele put a turd in the punch bowl, Mother would say, 'Look what Addie made! Isn't she brilliant?'"

As Adele remembered too well, her parents didn't exactly respond that way when she came home from college pregnant, refusing to name the father. Her own father reacted like he'd been shot in the gut, and her mother cried and cried, wondering what miscreant had knocked up her pure and precious daughter.

When her baby boy had been born dead, Adele's father pronounced that now she could start over while her mother had called it a blessing. It was only Justine who had offered true and genuine support. "Having children of my own, I can't imagine what you must be going through. Anything I can do, Addie. Anything. Just tell me what you need."

That was probably the closest Adele and Justine had ever been. It was brief, bittersweet but meaningful. There would always be at least that bond.

"I think tomorrow night we should go to a movie," Jake said. "We haven't done that in years."

"Not years," she argued. "Maybe almost one."

"Let's get out," he said. "Not that I don't like our dinners in, but how about a movie. I'll sit and quietly eat popcorn while you ogle Bradley Cooper."

"You know the first time you rescued me I was about four years old."

"More like ten," he corrected. "Headfirst into the pool and you sank like a rock." Jake had been a lifeguard at the community pool. He was eight years her senior and like a big brother to her. After that incident he taught her to swim. Now she could swim like a competitor when she got the chance. They had almost a lifetime of history. Their families lived a block apart in an older residential section of Half Moon Bay, California. Mr. Bronski used to walk to his market every day, Mrs. Bronski often visited with Addie's mother and they both volunteered at the schools. Beverly Bronski remained Elaine Descaro's most frequent visitor until her death.

They'd remained close through so many monumental events. Thirteen years ago, Jake had married Mary Ellen Rathgate and within two years she'd left him for another man, breaking his heart. Ten years ago Max Bronski died of a heart attack. Eight years ago, Addie's father broke his back on the job and was disabled for the remainder of his life. He had barely left the bonds of earth when Addie's mother suffered her severe stroke. Since neither was close to their siblings, Jake and Addie had only each other to lean on for a long time now.

They cleaned up the dishes together and even though Adele had a dishwasher, Jake washed and she dried. They talked about the neighborhood, the people they knew in common, their families. Adele said Justine worked all the time. Jake's younger brother, Marty, didn't have the same history with the market that Jake had and only worked there when he was between jobs. "I think it's high time he grew up," Jake said, not for the first time.

When Jake was leaving, he told her to plan on a seven

o'clock movie the next night. Dinner might be popcorn, and if they were still hungry afterward, they could get a bite to eat. He put a big hand on her shoulder, gave it a squeeze and said, "It was nice to spend some time with you, Addie."

"It was. Thank you, Jake. See you tomorrow."

He gave her a gentle kiss on the forehead before leaving.

Jake had had a thing for Adele for years, but it seemed the timing was never right. When he first saw her as something more just a kid, when she was blossoming before his very eyes, she was still a teenager and he was a man in his early twenties. Then she went to college, and he fell in love with Mary Ellen and married her in short order. By the time Mary Ellen had dumped him, leaving him shattered and lonely, Addie was involved with someone at Berkeley so he put her from his mind.

But every time she was home in Half Moon Bay for holidays or just to spend a weekend with her parents, she became bigger than life and he was aware of a bothersome desire. Yet, she was involved with someone. Then he heard through her mother that her romance had failed, so he lectured himself on patience and gentlemanly distance.

When she enrolled in graduate studies, he was blown away by her brilliance. He loved talking with her when she was in Half Moon Bay because she was fascinating; he believed she knew a little bit about everything. He could sit in a mesmerized trance just listening to her talk for as long as she'd go on.

Then she confessed she was involved with someone. She didn't want to say too much about the new relationship. "But are you in love?" he asked her.

"Oh, I'm just a goner," she said. "But I'm playing it as cool as I can so I don't scare him away. This time I plan to take my time, not like the last time when I dove in head-first and almost drowned."

He couldn't help but think about how he'd been with Mary Ellen. She had been so beautiful, so sexy, it took him about five minutes to want her desperately, and once he claimed the prize, he found there was very little substance there. Mary Ellen, God bless her, was shallow as a bird bath. She cheated on him almost immediately.

He gave Addie a lot of credit for taking it slow.

Then she returned home. Not for a visit, but to stay. She said it was because her father was injured and facing surgeries, but Jake had known Addie for a long time and he could tell there was more to the story. Then he watched her grow before his very eyes and knew what the something more was. She was pregnant. And she did not have the love and support of the baby's father. She was alone.

Jake made sure he checked on her often, at least a few times a week. If the moment presented itself, he just might tell her that he was willing to be that man. He had come to realize how much he wanted to be with her. But he never found the appropriate time.

There was once a moment of affection that he thought might lead to intimacy. They had a conversation about everything she'd been through losing her baby, and it was intense.

It filled Jake with joy that she felt comfortable confiding in him until she started sobbing. Jake did the only thing he knew to do—he comforted her. He wrapped his arms around her and kissed her forehead before he found his lips on hers. They kissed, clumsily, and then she'd pulled away. She'd been through so much and apparently was ill prepared to deal with anything more.

He had been waiting five years for her to decide she had a little more to give. And he gave as much as he dared.

She wasn't the only one with fragile feelings.

A nice dinner with Jake the previous night and an invitation out for the evening had put Adele in a more positive frame of mind. But who better than her older sister to knock her off that perch. Justine called to say she was coming by because there was something she needed to talk to Adele about. It was Saturday, and she wasn't going to her office.

Justine was Adele's opposite, in appearance and almost everything else. She was a tall, slim blonde while Adele was a shorter, rounder brunette. They used to joke that they weren't from the same family. But Justine's hair was colored and she wore blue contact lenses, making her look more Scandanavian than Italian. And she was chic, but then Justine lived in a professional, high-income world and was expected to be chic. Adele, on the other hand, always thought she'd be a natural as an English professor, one who wore oversize sweaters and flat black shoes. And she usually pulled her hair back in a clip or pinned it in a boring bun.

They had very little in common, yet another reason they weren't close.

When Justine arrived, Adele eyed her stylish haircut. "How much does that supershort blond coif cost?" Adele asked. "Because I've been thinking about making a change..."

"It's pretty expensive, actually," Justine said, giving Adele a brief hug. "I'm thinking of letting it grow out... Scott isn't crazy about short hair."

"So what if he isn't? It's your head, right? And I think it's wonderful. Would you like coffee?"

"I suppose it's too early for wine," Justine said. "How are you getting along since the funeral? Are things beginning to fall into place?"

"I suppose," Adele lied. "Not nearly as quickly or neatly as I hoped. All those things I'd been looking forward to, like having the time and energy to lose some weight and get in shape, or maybe at least look at a university program catalog, go back to my studies... Day after day goes by and I haven't done anything. I suppose I'm a little depressed."

"There's a lot of that going around," Justine said dourly. "Listen, I have to tell you some things. It's difficult."

Adele didn't like the sound of that, yet she couldn't imagine what might be coming. Justine lived a charmed life. "Where do you want to sit to have this difficult conversation?" she asked.

Before she even finished the sentence, Justine had taken herself to the living room and sat on the edge of a wingback chair. That sight alone, her tall, lithe and lovely sister perched, stiff and tense, in the old chair, emphasized to Adele that she hadn't even started her redecorating-remodeling project. Justine's house, though she was terribly busy, was breathtakingly decorated and picture-perfect. This old house was not only dated, it was threadbare. And her usually poised sister was very uptight.

"Let me cut right to it. Something has happened," Justine said. "There have been some changes in the company. My company. Serious downsizing and outsourcing. My job hasn't been eliminated yet, but there's no question there's going to be a major change. One that will involve an income adjustment."

"Oh no! Why is this happening?" Adele asked.

"A lot of complicated reasons that all boil down to profits and losses. We've merged with other software manufacturers twice, laid off employees and tacked a not very subtle For Sale sign on the door. They're paring down corporate officers to combine them since the latest merger. When two companies become one, there's no point in two VPs of Operation, two presidents, two general counsels. I've already been asked if I'm interested in taking over Human Resources since I have experience in dealing with many of their legal issues. I'm thinking about it, but it comes at a significant pay cut. It has forced me to think about other things."

Could one of them be asking your husband to get a real job? Adele thought. She kept her mouth shut about that. Instead, she asked, "Like what?" Wondering what any of this had to do with her.

"I'm planning to see a headhunter, look for another firm that's in need of general counsel. Since I'm experienced in corporate law, I could join a law firm but I'd be on the bottom rung. Or… I've even given some thought to private practice. My experience in Human Resources lends to a number of specialties. I have an open mind. I might be qualified to work for the state. Whatever, I have to be thinking now. I have a feeling, a strong feeling, my income is going to be severely impacted. Soon." And she wondered how Justine's husband was handling this news.

Justine started dating Scott in college, right around the time Addie was born. He was undeniably smart, though not a great student and not really motivated, except maybe on the golf course. Based on what little information Justine had shared over the years, Scott had never leaned toward ambition, but he was a steady, good man and devoted father. He got his degree in business, started out in sales for a big sporting goods manufacturer. He did pretty well, and while he was doing that, Justine took the LSAT and killed it. She went to law school—Stanford. Scott was very supportive of the idea. *Just make me a stay-at-home dad with a set of clubs*, he had said.

Since Scott traveled all the time in his first job, they settled in San Jose in a small town house. It was convenient for him as a base of operations and close enough to Stanford for Justine to commute. That was such a long time ago. Adele remembered that town house. She'd been there quite a few times as a little girl.

She remembered Justine had said Scott was excited that his wife was going to be a successful lawyer. "That's all we want," he had said. "She'll knock 'em dead in the legal world, and I'll take care of all the domestic details."

That transition had been gradual, but eventually it led them to where they were now—Justine, a self-made woman with a high-paying corporate job and Scott, a stay-at-home dad and husband who worked part-time in a sporting goods outlet. He had been a volunteer EMT, played a lot of sports, loved hiking, kayaking, scuba diving, boating.

"What does Scott say about this?" Adele asked.

Justine shrugged. Then she said, "He'll support my decision." She straightened. "I wonder how difficult it would be to find a small family law practice looking for someone like me. Or to start my own practice—a one-woman practice."

"Has it ever occurred to Scott to get a serious job?" Adele asked. "I mean, forgive me, since I haven't had a serious job in my life."

Justine smiled patiently. "Your jobs have all been serious, and without you we'd have been lost. If you hadn't dedicated yourself to Mom's care, it would have cost our whole family a fortune. We're indebted to you. And I agree it would help if Scott worked more than part-time, but I think that ship sailed years ago. He's only worked part-time since Amber and Olivia came along."

Adele adored her nieces, ages sixteen and seventeen. She was much closer to them than she was to Justine.

"I'm sorry you're going through this," Adele said. "I wish there was something I could do."

"Well, the thing is, the future is looking very uncertain. I might need your help," Justine said.

"What could I do?" she asked.

"Adele, I don't like to push you, but you have to get it together. We have to make some decisions about what you're going to do, what we'll do with the house. I realize what I've given you for your hard work hasn't been much, but I don't know how long I can keep it up—paying for the maintenance on this house, the taxes, a modest income for you... I don't want to panic prematurely," Justine said. "Maybe I'll be able to work everything out without too much hassle, but if I run into trouble... Money could get very tight, Addie. All those promises I made—that I'd help financially while you fix up the house, that I'd give you my half of the proceeds when and if you sold it... I might not be able to come through. I know, I know, I promised you it would be yours after all of your sacrifice, but you wouldn't want me to ignore the girls' tuition or not be able to make the mortgage..."

"But Justine!" Adele said. "That's all I have! And I was considering finishing school myself!" Though if she was honest, she had no plans of any kind.

Justine reached out to her, squeezing her hand. "We're a long way from me needing money. I just felt it was only fair to tell you what's going on. If we're in this together, we can both make it. I swear, I will make this all work out. I'll make it right."

But as Adele knew, they had never really been "in it together" in the past, and they wouldn't be for very long in the future. Addie's dedication to their parents allowed Justine to devote herself to her career. For that matter, it should be Justine and Scott shoring each other up. At least until Justine had a better idea. But where was Scott today? Golfing? Biking? Bowling?

Adele realized she had some difficult realities to face. When she dropped out of school to help her mother care for her father, she wasn't being completely altruistic. She'd needed a place to run away to, hiding an unplanned pregnancy and covering her tattered heart. She'd never told her family that her married lover—her psychology professor—had broken down in tears when he explained he couldn't leave his wife to marry Adele, that the college would probably fire him for having an affair with a student. For her, going home was the only option.

At the time Justine and Scott had been riding the big wave and didn't lust after the small, old house in Half Moon Bay. That house was chump change to them. So, they worked out a deal. Adele had become her mother's guardian with a power of attorney. But the will had never been adjusted to reflect just one beneficiary rather than two. In the case of the death of both parents, Adele and Justine would inherit equal equity in the eighty-year-old house and anything left of the life insurance. At the time, of course, neither Adele nor Justine had ever considered the idea that Adele would be needed for very long. But before Adele knew it, eight years had been gobbled up. She was thirty-two and had been caring for her parents since she was twenty-four.

Adele, as guardian, could have escaped by turning over the house, pension, social security to a care facility for her mother and gone out on her own, finding herself a better job and her own place to live. She wasn't sure if it was her conscience or just inertia that held her in place for so long.

"I just wanted to make sure you understood the circumstances before anything more happens," Justine said. "And since you don't have any immediate plans, please don't list the house for sale or anything. Give me a chance to figure out what's next. I have children. I'll do whatever I can to protect them and you. They're your nieces! They love you so much. I'm sure you want them to get a good education as much as I do."

Does anyone want me to have a real chance to start over? Adele asked herself. This conversation sounded like Justine was pulling out of their deal.

"I'll think about this, but Scott has responsibilities, too," she pointed out.

"He's been out of the full-time workforce for so long..." Justine said.

"Just the same, we all have to live up to our adult commitments and responsibilities. And you've had a highfalutin job for a long time. You've made a lot of money. You can recover. I haven't even begun."

"I need your help, Addie," Justine said. "You need to come up with a plan, something we can put in motion. Make plans for your next step, put a little energy into this old house, make suggestions of what we should do with it, everything. Let's figure out what to do before I find myself short and unable to help. I'm sorry, but we have to move forward."

CHAPTER TWO

Justine's visit and her ominous predictions created a pretty dark day for Adele. Her head ached from her brow being furrowed all day. She hadn't even begun to figure out what she wanted to do next before Justine threw a wrench into everything. Addie was lost in deep thought; she took a couple of hours with a calculator, looking over the numbers. They were pretty bleak. It had been a consideration to get a home equity loan to improve the property before selling it, but if Justine couldn't swing it, how was Addie supposed to? She was pretty sure one had to have a job before being approved for a loan.

Addie had no money, no income, just what Justine provided. There was a little saved from the insurance, but without money from Justine, she was going to run out soon. How could her sister do this to her now? While Addie cared for their mother, Justine and her family had been to France and Italy and Scotland, not to mention many long weekend trips here and there. They had all the sports equipment under the sun and lived in a very nice house. And now, after Adele had put in eight years, Justine was warning her that she might pull the rug out from under her? How could she?

She tried to remember that Justine hadn't had it easy as it all looked. Law school was a struggle for her, though in the end she graduated with honors. Then she worked long hours while Scott started to work shorter and shorter weeks. When Justine wanted a baby and didn't conceive, she saw infertility specialists and was thirty-five before being blessed with the birth of her daughter Amber. Then, like so many infertile women, she ignored birth control after Amber was born, thinking she just couldn't get pregnant. Olivia came eleven months after Amber.

Adele couldn't really remember all the details of Justine and Scott's early years together, but by the time her nieces were born when she was in high school, it was obvious that Scott made sure the girls got what they needed but he didn't go much further. Justine stopped at the store for groceries on her way home from work, sometimes at ten at night. She spent her days off doing laundry, and if she couldn't stay up until midnight working on briefs, she'd get up at four in the morning to work. And then Scott would criticize her for not working out and complain about the toll her long hours took on the family. But he somehow justified an expensive country club membership. Scott did most of the cooking, but it wasn't much of an effort. He didn't like labor intensive meals after a rugged day of playing golf. Adele witnessed a lot of those squabbles because she was a frequent babysitter when her nieces were little.

But none of that was Adele's fault! Now she feared Justine would go back on her promises and take advantage of her again.

She thought about canceling the movie date with Jake because she knew she wouldn't be good company, but she didn't have the heart after he'd been so sweet to offer. So she got dressed and was ready when he picked her up. "What are we going to see?" she asked when she got in the car.

"Anything you want. There are plenty of sexy leading men for you to choose from," he said. Then he grinned.

"Anything is fine."

So they chose the latest hit movie, bought popcorn and drinks, and she stared at the screen blankly. He asked her three times what was wrong, and three times she said she just had things on her mind. The movie was over before she'd really let herself enjoy it. Jake grabbed her hand and said, "Come on." He pulled her up and out of their row, out of the theater into the dimly lit hall that led to the lobby. "We're going to Maggio's. We'll get a dark booth in the back and talk. Whatever it is, it's better to get it out."

"What makes you say that? I'm a little moody, that's all. You've seen me—"

He was shaking his head. "You're not just moody," he said. "Any time you don't stare with big cow eyes at Bradley Cooper, the man you hope to marry, we've got us a problem. So, we'll go have a little wine. Maybe some pasta or pizza but wine for sure."

She raised a brow. "You think you're going to get me loose and talking?"

He nodded. "As only a good friend could."

They drove to Maggio's, a little hole-in-the-wall Italian pizzeria. It was one of his favorite places. Jake pulled his truck into a small parking lot behind the restaurant. They did a huge takeout business, but there was a small dining room with only eight booths. It was compact, each booth could hold six people so the maximum they could serve wasn't even fifty, and in all the years Adele had known about the restaurant, it had never been full. The front of the store, where people picked up their meals or pizzas, was always hopping, and there were a couple of tables on the wide sidewalk where people could sit outside in nice weather.

Adele and Jake entered through the back door because Jake knew the owners and most of the staff. People hollered "Hey, Jake" or waved a hand in their direction. They slipped into the restaurant and found a booth near the back. Adele loved that it was dimly lit and decorated with plastic grapes. They slid into the booth and sat across from each other.

"Hey, Jake," the waitress said, slapping down a couple of napkins. "Haven't seen you in a long time."

"It hasn't been that long, has it?" he returned. "You know my friend Adele, don't you?"

"Yeah, sure, how you doin'? And what can I start you off with?"

"A glass of cabernet for me," Addie said.

"Same," Jake said. "And we'll look at the menu for a while."

"I bet you know it by heart, Jake," she said, smiling prettily into his eyes. "I'll be right back."

"All the women in town like you," Adele said. "Why don't you ever take any of them out?"

"They don't all like me," he said. "And Bonnie, there, I think she's been married a bunch of times."

"Really?" Adele asked.

"Well, at least twice. Been there, done that."

Adele remembered too well—it was a scandal in the neighborhood at the time. Jake was in his midtwenties, Adele still in high school, when he married Mary Ellen. It didn't go well. Jake's mother complained to Adele's mother that there was a lot of bickering, and in no time Mary Ellen had become Jake's unhappy wife. Though she never missed a word of their mothers' gossip, the only thing she actually *saw* was that her friend Jake was suddenly alone, miserable, brokenhearted and inconsolable. Mary Ellen left him after a year, and they were divorced by two years. She had now passed her third divorce, been with numerous men she hadn't married and was said to be keeping company with a much older guy who left his wife of almost forty years for her.

"Yeah, I'd love to know what happened there, if only to understand it," Adele said. Jake was handsome, sweet natured, smart and most importantly, kind. His market was like the cornerstone of the older section of Half Moon Bay. He'd served on the city council for a couple of years and was greatly respected. By comparison, Mary Ellen was attractive but not very smart. But she must have some serious skills—she certainly had no trouble getting a guy though she did have short attention span. Adele suspected an abundance of pheromones. She also seemed to be cunning.

"Maybe when I understand what happened, I'll share," Jake said.

Their drinks came, they ordered a pizza to share and Jake went in for the kill. "How about if you tell me why you didn't drool over Bradley," Jake said.

She told him Justine had come by for a brief visit, complaining about having some job and therefore financial issues, and that she might not be helping out as much as Adele had expected. "It emphasized all the things I haven't done," she said. "I was going to change my life, you know—starting with a makeover of myself and the house. Neither has had much attention for the past few years. I was waiting for the inspiration to kick in."

"We've been over this," Jake said. "You have plenty of time for all that. And *you* don't need a makeover. The house could use a little paint, but other than that…"

"I haven't even made a list," she said. "I kept thinking

I was making plans but they were just fantasies. Plans require at least a list. Not to mention the purchase of a bucket of paint..."

"Well then, let's talk about what you'd like to do and you can go home and make a list, but Addie, stuff like this doesn't usually cause you to ignore a good movie. Or—" The pizza arrived just as he finished his thought. "Or ignore your best guy, Bradley." He peeled off a piece of pizza and gestured toward her plate. "I can help with this, you know. I remodeled my mother's house, and I've done a lot of my own work in my house."

"You're so busy," she said, chomping off a mouthful of pizza.

"Even if I'm not available to pound nails or paint trim, I know a lot of contractors, who to call, where to find them, and if you ever run into a problem—I know how to talk to them. You never saw my mother's house after I did the kitchen and both bathrooms. Damn good for a grocer, if you ask me."

"I'm sorry, Jake. I should have gone to your mom's to see your work. I'll be sure to go now. She always came to see my mom, to read to her."

"You know she enjoyed that," he said. "Sometimes she spends an hour at the store, visiting, talking to shoppers. I'd see one thing in her cart, but just couldn't get her to leave. I told her I could bring her what she needs, but walking to the store is good for her. I won't complain until she starts coming in five times a day, and then—"

His voice faded to a low buzz as something caught Adele's eye. The couple in the front left booth, sitting together so they faced the front door, backs to Adele, leaned their heads together for a deep kiss. The man's reddish-brown hair curled around his collar, just a little long. The

woman's short white-blond hair was teased up all spiky in
a slightly dated style.

Then Adele's brain started to play tricks on her. It looked
like Scott, her brother-in-law, his tongue down the woman's throat, his hand cupping the back of her head. They
broke apart, laughed into each other's open mouths and
she stroked his cheek briefly, saying something that made
him kiss her open mouth again. It *was* Scott. He must think
that even though Adele lived in Half Moon Bay, she would
never be out on a Saturday night, having a pizza. It was
a good bet, since that was a very rare occurrence. Adele
would have pizza delivered. And a date? Forget about it.

Then Scott and the unknown woman became other people as a very old and painful memory rose to the surface.
Hadley and his wife materialized in their place. Hadley,
her psychology professor, with whom she'd had a steamy
affair. She'd taken the class because he was so hot. Hadley,
the father of her baby. He had told her it was impossible for
him to leave the wife he claimed to hate, to marry Adele.
He told her the university might fire him for falling in love
with a student. They decided she would terminate the pregnancy. He would then divorce his wife, they'd have a fresh
start, begin to date as if the affair and the baby had never
happened. They'd marry and eventually have a family. Everything would be fine and they'd live happily-ever-after.
And she'd been naive enough to believe him.

She did what many a woman her age would do—she
drove by Hadley's house a dozen times a week. Then one
morning she saw what she should have known she would
see. He stood in the doorway with his beautiful blond wife,
an arm around her waist. She still wore a robe or dressing
gown. There was a small blond child holding on to his leg.
The child was also beautiful. Angelic. Hadley's wife had a

small baby bump. Hadley pulled her against him and covered her lips in a loving kiss. A deep and long kiss. One of his hands cradled her head while the other ran smoothly over the bump.

Hadley wasn't kissing his wife as though he was planning on getting a divorce.

Adele was supposed to have an abortion while Hadley got the gears moving on his separation and divorce. He said he'd try to scrape up some money for the procedure, but he couldn't be obvious about it or his wife wouldn't let him go. They would have to be discreet.

Eight years later, she still couldn't believe she'd bought those lies. She didn't go through with the abortion but her baby slipped away, stillborn. And Hadley never came looking for her. While she cared for her parents and mourned the loss of her son, she'd heard he was suspected of other affairs with students.

Scott and the woman he was with materialized again. The bastard was stepping out on her sister. She briefly thought about rushing over to them and pouring something over their heads, like a pitcher of beer. Luckily, she didn't have anything like that on hand.

She noticed out of the corner of her eye that Jake looked at her, looked in the direction of her stare, looked back at her. Her mouth was open and gaping, and a large piece of pizza drooped limply in her hand.

"Addie?" he asked.

"Shit," she muttered. She closed her mouth and looked at him. "Jake, I need a favor. Can we get a box for the pizza and leave? Right now? I can explain when we're in the truck."

"Something happened," he said. "What happened?"

"Shh," she said, hushing him. "Can you go back to the

kitchen, ask for a box, pay the bill and get me out of here? Quietly?" she whispered. "The guy in the front booth with the blonde—that's my brother-in-law. And that is not my sister he's making out with."

Jake couldn't resist. He looked again. "Whoa," he said, probably recognizing Scott at last. Then he slid out of the booth and made tracks to the kitchen. He was back with a box very quickly, and they transferred the pizza into it.

"I hope everything was okay," Bonnie said as they were leaving.

"Oh, it was fine, I just remembered I left the stove on," Adele said with a smile. By the time she got to Jake's truck, she felt weak. When he got in and closed his door, she was shaking. "That bastard!"

"What's he doing here?" Jake asked. "He lives in San Jose, right?"

She held out her hands, examining her trembling fingers. "He probably thinks no one knows him here, which except for me, maybe no one does. And he probably thinks I'd never be out for the evening, because what are the odds? While my sister is home worrying about her job, her husband is out deep kissing some woman—"

"Cat," Jake said.

"Huh?"

"Cat Brooks. She owns that kayak and snorkel shop on the beach. Cat's Place. It should make a killing, but it's been through three or four owners in the last dozen years. I think she owns it with her brother or something."

"Well, that makes sense," Adele said. "Scott works part-time at a sporting goods store in San Jose where he gets a discount on all the gear he can stuff into his car. That's what he does—plays. He loves to kayak. And golf and scuba dive and play ball and you name it. I bet his salary doesn't even cover the cost of his toys. Justine works such long hours, he complains that she works so much and this is what he does instead."

Jake put his truck in Reverse and backed out of the lot.

"And I'll have to tell her," Adele said.

"You have to?" he asked. "Why do you have to?"

"Come on!" she said. "I can't let Justine get caught unaware! Telling her now might not even help. Clearly he's into something serious, and he can't support himself and his fun times. Justine has been the primary breadwinner for at least twenty of their twenty-eight-year marriage! And he has the nerve to complain about her hours. As if the income would just materialize while she took time off to entertain him. Oh! I want to kill him right now!"

"Addie, don't do anything too soon here," Jake said. "I've seen it before. She might hate you for telling her."

"Now why would she do that?" Adele asked.

He took a breath. "It was Marty who told me Mary Ellen was cheating. I hit him in the face."

"Because you didn't believe him?"

"No. Because he ruined the illusion I had that I could make it work in the end. It was like a knife to the heart. It was in that instant I knew it was over. And it was going to get ugly."

"I'll tell you what's going to get ugly—me driving to San Jose."

Justine felt confident she'd made an impression on Adele. Surely her younger sister would finally get serious about getting her life on track so that Justine wouldn't feel obligated to support her forever. Just from looking at the comparable sales in the area, she judged the house to be worth roughly six hundred thousand, and it was paid off, free and clear. If she could get her own Realtor and decorator involved in cleaning up and staging the property, it could be worth more. She'd worry about how to scrape up the money to help in that effort later.

Adele would probably have to put off going back to school for a little while. She had to get a job. Justine was determined to make it up to her. Somehow. Eventually.

It was true that her company was struggling right now, downsizing here and there, and the stress was overwhelming. But she was hoping she could repair her real problem before she talked to anyone about it.

Scott had informed her that he didn't love her anymore. He was sorry but he couldn't help it. He didn't have much hope for the marriage; he thought it might be best if they broke up. He wanted to cash out. She was holding him back, expecting too much from him.

She was completely caught off guard. She had been asking him to apply himself a little more to what she thought had been a pretty satisfactory partnership. Their relationship was hardly perfect, but then whose was?

They'd been seeing a marriage counselor for three months, and she had no grasp of how that was working out. Some days Scott would say, *I think we're making progress here—I know I'm feeling better about things*. Other days he'd grumble that she wasn't really involved in the marriage, or their family life for that matter. He told her she was "emotionally unavailable" too often. "When was the last time you watched me play ball?" he asked. "When was the last time we went to a movie?"

Her work was very difficult and demanding, what more could she say? If she wanted to keep her job, she had to be on top of it. She worked sixty hours a week and brought work home, as well.

It was when he started saying things like, "I feel like I have a hole in my heart," and "I'm not really living, just existing," she began to suspect there was another woman. Those were women's words. Scott didn't say things like that. In fact, he had trouble sitting through a chick flick with dialogue like that. It made him roll his eyes. Now he was saying those things to her with a straight face.

In their thirty years together, two dating and twenty-eight married, she had suspected there were other women now and then, but there was never any clear evidence. Just a name that came up too frequently, that faraway look in his eye, a very unreliable schedule. He'd go MIA for a while. During their first decade of marriage, he traveled all the time while he was in sales. She'd had trouble getting pregnant and blamed his travel schedule. When she passed the bar, he was more than happy to take a less demanding, less lucrative job to improve their odds at reproduction. Seventeen years ago she had Amber and eleven months later, Olivia. He was a stay-at-home dad and she was so happy; her baby daughters were everything to her. She was a successful businesswoman with a supportive husband and two beautiful daughters. She didn't have a jealous bone in her body.

But she had to work. She was the bread and butter of the family. Getting home to her husband and babies was her reward for every hard penny she earned. She was successful, Scott urging her on every day while he stayed home and planned their vacations. In more recent years when he had so much time on his hands because the girls were self-sufficient and he only worked part-time, she never wondered where he was—he was busy every minute. They texted and spoke several times every day.

Maybe she should have worried sooner. Now she didn't

know what to do. She had asked him about other women and he'd said, "Don't be ridiculous." That wasn't a real answer, was it? Should she get a detective? It was a thought. She didn't know what she would do, how she would live. What would the girls say? Do? Would Scott try to take them from her? They adored him. Would they want to be with her, when she worked sixty-hour weeks?

At first she thought she couldn't let him leave. She didn't know how she'd get by. It never once occurred to her that her life might be slightly less tense without him constantly keeping score on her hours and familial contributions.

Now that she thought about it, Scott had always been a lot of emotional work. It wasn't easy trying to get a law degree while making sure she was always a good wife. True, she couldn't do all the wifely chores and work as an attorney, but a good balance was that she made enough money for a weekly cleaning lady. What she did do was never mention she was the breadwinner, never minimize his contributions. She took time to praise his every effort, compliment his mind and frequently mention how stimulating she found him, scream with joy during mediocre sex. It wasn't until he said he no longer loved her that she realized the enormous emotional weight of that effort.

Scott ran the house and made sure the girls got to school and every extracurricular activity, lesson or practice. Now that Amber was driving, he had even more free time. It took him roughly two hours a day to do his chores—she still did the laundry, stopped for groceries on the way home, cleaned the kitchen after dinner. The hours left over—some six or more a day—he could devote to biking, kayaking, working out, running, hiking, swimming or various sports training. He was a member of two bowling leagues and one baseball team. He watched hours of sports on TV, most of it re-

corded for later. He worked part-time at the sporting goods
outlet off and on, never more than twenty hours in a week.

How dare he not love me, she thought angrily. *If anything, I shouldn't love him!*

There was a time Adele was an adventurous soul, like
back in college and grad school. But for the past six to eight
years, she'd done little driving, staying close to home, rarely
leaving Half Moon Bay.

This was an old town, originally called Spanishtown and
settled before the gold rush, officially becoming Half Moon
Bay in the late 1800s. The history of the town was carefully preserved. It was a sweet town on the ocean that attracted tourists. This part of San Mateo County was known
for farming of vegetables and flowers, surfing and other
water sports, a quaint and quiet getaway filled with and
surrounded by beautiful state parks, redwoods and wonderful beaches. It got its name from the crescent-shaped
harbor just north of the city.

Addie thought of it as calm, sometimes too calm. Maybe
a little old-fashioned and stifling. When she was young,
she couldn't wait to knock the dust from that little old town
off her shoes, to get out and enjoy the freedom of college
in a bigger city. Now that she'd been held hostage there for
eight years, she was nearly phobic about leaving.

But leave she would, if only for the day. She wasn't
going to let Justine down, even though it appeared Justine would let her down. They might not be the closest of
sisters but if Adele had one shining trait, she was fiercely
loyal. She thought she was more loyal to Justine than Justine was to her, but that was okay. She believed that what
goes around comes around and she'd invest now, hope for
good things to follow.

Plus there was Amber and Olivia, and Addie loved them.

Adele called Justine first thing in the morning. "I know we just talked yesterday but I need to see you, in person, alone, as soon as possible. I'll drive to San Jose if necessary, but it would be better if you came here. I don't want to try to talk to you with the girls or Scott around. It's a very private matter."

"What's bothering you, Addie?" Justine asked.

Of course Justine would think it was Adele who had the problem, that it was something she was embarrassed to share or have anyone overhear. "We have to talk. It's urgent. Please decide where we should do it."

Justine sighed into the phone. It was clear she couldn't imagine Addie having a truly urgent issue of any kind.

"I have a lot to do today. Are you sure this can't wait?"

"I'm afraid it can't. Do you want to meet somewhere or what?"

"Can you come to me? Scott's playing golf and won't be home until after two. Amber and Olivia are both busy with friends, and I expect they'll be gone all day. If you come to me, at least I can get a few things done in the time I would have spent driving."

"Okay," Adele said in a shaky breath. She hated the freeway. And left turns. And other cars. She hadn't driven to San Jose, forty miles away, in years and she recalled it as traumatic. In fact, she hadn't driven out of Half Moon Bay in a couple of years. She was used to getting teased about it.

"Wow," Justine said. "This must be important."

"It is."

Adele thought about the one time Justine had really come through for her—when she was brokenhearted, pregnant and alone. Justine was supportive and nonjudgmental.

"These things happen, kiddo," she'd said. "But you're doing the right thing. Adoption is a good option."

"If I can make myself go through with it," Adele had said. "I feel him moving and I want to hold him."

"Of course you do. And women do raise their children without fathers all the time. But if you're serious about that, there are legal ways to make the father responsible. He can pay support. Just think about it. I can help."

But that option had been taken away from her when the baby didn't survive. It was Justine who showered her with sympathy, paid for the mortuary and cemetery costs, held her while she cried and encouraged her to grieve, get counseling and try to move on. For that compassion, Adele would be forever grateful.

She did love and admire Justine. She was also quite jealous, an emotion she fought constantly. It was just that until she saw Scott misbehaving, she thought Justine had everything, beautiful home, perfect daughters, happy marriage, great career. She had been so lost in thought that she was almost surprised when she pulled up to her older sister's house. She had managed the drive without incident.

She looked up and admired the place. It wasn't an estate or anything, but it was so much larger than the house they grew up in, plus it was relatively new—about fifteen years old. The kitchen was spacious, the great room was grand and welcoming and overlooked a small but beautiful pool and meticulously groomed yard. There were five bedrooms and as many baths, and the third port in the garage was stacked with sporting gear—skis, paddleboards, kayaks, golf clubs, et cetera. Justine and the girls also had skis and bikes and paddleboards, but the gear was by and large Scott's.

Now she wasn't sure what Justine was up against. Did Justine know her husband was unfaithful?

Justine opened the front door to greet her with a frown. "Oh jeez, you're pale. Come in. You know, now that you're officially off the caretaking job, you might want to broaden your territory. Do more driving, go farther, get your confidence back, put yourself out there."

"I will," Adele said, as she had been saying to herself for more than a couple of months.

"Let's go sit on the patio," Justine said. "I made a fresh pot of coffee and I have some cookies."

"I was going to give up cookies," Adele said. "Maybe I'll start tomorrow."

Adele sat at the patio table and let Justine serve the coffee, which seemed like the last thing she needed. She was jittery enough, and not from the drive on the crowded California freeway. Even on Sunday morning it was like bumper cars, but she'd managed it just fine.

"You going to spit it out?" Justine asked. "So we can spend what time we have figuring it out, whatever it is?"

"Scott is cheating on you," Addie blurted. "I saw him."

Justine jerked in dubious surprise, her chin lowering as did her brow. She frowned. "You saw him having sex?"

"No. I—"

"You'd better be specific. And very sure of what you're saying because this is serious."

"Oh, I know it is. I went for a pizza with Jake Bronski last night. Maggio's. Do you even remember it?"

Justine nodded gravely.

"Eight booths in the dining room. We went in the back door because Jake knows everyone there. We had just gotten a glass of wine when I noticed the couple two booths ahead and to the left. They were sitting side by side facing the front, maybe watching the front entry. They probably thought they were alone since we snuck in the back. They were kissing. Kissing like they couldn't stop. Like they really needed a room."

Justine was quiet for a long moment. "Kissing?"

"Powerful, desperate, crazy kissing. Like in the movies kissing. Mouths open, devour—"

Justine held up a hand to stop her. "Was there any evidence of an affair? Or was it just kissing?"

"Seriously? *Just?*" Addie laughed, though not in humor. "I never thought to follow them. You have a provision for movie-star kissing in the marriage contract?"

"Okay, thanks for telling me," Justine said, as if she couldn't bear to hear any more. "I can take it from here. And if you think of anything else…"

"I know who she is. Well, Jake knows who she is. The woman who owns that kayak rental shack near the ocean, down the bike path past the beach bar. Her name is Cat Brooks. She's not very pretty."

Justine seemed to wince ever so slightly. "Thanks."

"What are you going to do?"

"I don't know. But I know how this will turn out. Scott is caught kissing outside of our marriage and we're going to fight about it, quietly so the girls don't hear, then he's going to grovel, beg for forgiveness, make a lot of promises about his perfect future behavior, then things will be tense for a while and he'll invest a lot in flowers and maybe a little jewelry and then it will be over. It will pass."

"It sounds like you've been down this road before…"

"Except for the getting caught part. He's never been caught before, but we've had the discussion…"

"Why? He must have done something if you talked about it?"

"There were a few times I wondered if he was lying to me about where he'd been. You know—the timing was just off or his story would change. And he couldn't be reached... Didn't answer his phone. There was some texting with this woman or that—but I didn't see anything real damning. Still... It's not like I have a lot of time to chase him around, but if the girls can't reach him and call me... Don't worry about this. We'll get it straightened out."

"Do you think he's having an affair?" Addie asked, grabbing one of the cookies and taking a big bite.

"I suppose it's possible, but honestly I doubt it. Scott is very critical of men who step out on their wives. But believe me, I'll conduct a thorough interview. It's one of my particular skills." Then she smiled. Weakly.

"Where was he supposed to be last night?"

"A bowling tournament. He's in two leagues. I guess there's been some lying. I will find out how much."

Adele wasn't buying that smile. "You can talk to me, you know."

"Thank you, honey. That's very sweet. I'm sure we'll work this out quickly. And I won't tell him where I got the information."

Justine spoke as if Adele couldn't possibly be experienced enough to help her through this, to be a confidante.

"I suspect he was in Half Moon Bay because she lives there and he never thought he'd see me," Adele said. "I hardly leave the house."

"You're going to have to change that, Addie. It's not good for you."

"Yeah," she said, noting how quickly the subject changed to her. "I'll get right on that."

CHAPTER THREE

There was a vase containing a cheerful spring bouquet sitting on the breakfast bar. Scott had given it to Justine two days ago, a day after their weekly counseling session. "For you, Juss," he said. "I'm a very lucky man. I will always love you."

Had he told *her* about the flowers? About the declaration of love? Because according to Adele, who couldn't lie if her life depended on it, he'd been devouring the lips of another woman the next day, last night. Some woman named Cat Brooks who owned a kayak rental shack.

How was this possible? Justine had practically grown up with Scott. They'd met during their freshman year at Berkeley when they were mere children, just beginning to make their way into a future. They dated, fell in love, broke up a couple of times, but always came back to each other. By the time they were sophomores, they were exclusive. Right after graduation, they got engaged, though neither of them had two nickels to rub together. College costs, loans, very little help from their parents and only low-paying part-time jobs between them did not leave enough money for a wedding. The diamond in Justine's engagement ring could barely be seen with the naked eye, it was so small.

They lived together while they were in pursuit of decent jobs. Justine began teaching as a substitute, but before a year passed she'd acquired a permanent post teaching high school algebra. It took Scott longer to land a job in sales with a sporting goods manufacturer, but it seemed a good fit for someone as gregarious as Scott. By the time they were twenty-four, they could afford a modest but classy wedding with Adele as their flower girl.

At twenty-five Justine took the LSAT. She did better than just very well; she scored at the highest end of the scale. She'd always been a good test taker. Her biggest cheerleader was Scott. At twenty-six she began law school at Stanford, this not quite middle class janitor's daughter from Half Moon Bay. And she graduated from Stanford with honors. Scott had been so proud of her. But he also said he'd expected it.

When had he stopped being proud of her?

Through the years, through law school and two difficult pregnancies and a high-stress job in the legal department for a major software manufacturer, she'd always thought she and Scott were happy together. She was with her company through their first public offering, a killer project that yielded a handsome bonus and a big pile of stock options, setting her and Scott up for a tidy investment portfolio. From the time her little girls were four and five until now, even with the industry's ups and downs, she'd managed an excellent income.

And Scott had claimed to be a very satisfied house husband.

Now, after all of that, he was saying she hadn't been emotionally available?

Scott did contribute to the family income with a little part-time work on and off for the last seventeen years, but the days of his pursuit of a career ended with Amber's birth. "Me working will just put us in a higher tax bracket. I'm better off staying home and saving the cost of childcare," he had said.

It had seemed like a fair balance. Scott managed the money, the investments, the retirement accounts, the bills.

"I have to look at those accounts," Justine said to herself. The one thing she would never advise a woman to do, she had done. It was out of sheer want of time—she couldn't do it all. And now she had no idea what their true financial situation was. She had three credit cards, never worried about their balances, never wrote a check, never paid a bill. She earned the money, tried to be an attentive wife and mother, worked her ass off and had looked forward to a future of less stress and more fun.

Justine was fifty-two and had been with Scott since she was eighteen. And now he had another woman on the side. What would she do without him? They had always functioned as a team. She couldn't do her work and his work too! And although she had no problem being alone, she couldn't imagine having no partner. She thought she and Scott would grow old together, but now she would be alone forever. She didn't think that due to low self-esteem or lack of confidence, but when the hell would she find the time to even consider a new companion?

Scott, on the other hand, had nothing but time to screw around. He didn't have the pressure of bringing home a paycheck, for starters. His parents were healthy and strong and didn't need him for anything but the occasional visit, and they usually provided a dinner or picnic if Scott and his family planned to stop by.

Justine had had years of supporting ill parents and her younger sister, who shouldered all the care. The younger sister she had promised to reward for the commitment she'd made to care for their parents. Now she didn't even know what she would end up with for herself and her daughters.

She looked at the flowers. Was her life really this cliché? That he would cheat on her and then bring her flowers? To what end? To forgive him? To keep her from looking further into their problems where she would discover his lover? Did he in fact love that other woman?

Suddenly her arm shot out and swiped the vase and flowers off the counter, sending the container sailing across the kitchen and crashing against the cabinets. The flowers lay in the mess of shattered glass and dirty water on the floor.

She shook her head as she looked at the mess. It would not hurt Scott in any way, and now she would have to clean it up. At that moment she made a decision. From now on she would move with more precision and not do things that would only make her work harder. She would have to check her rage lest she make the situation worse for herself.

But she wasn't going to take this sitting down.

Driving back home, all Adele could think about was Justine. It was that much more upsetting because Justine did not seem the least bit worried about Scott's indiscretion. Even with her concerns about possibly losing her job, she'd been as cool as ever. Adele knew Justine had money and a good résumé, so she'd be all right. But what would she do about Scott? Because no matter what she said, Adele knew that her brother-in-law had crossed the line, been unfaithful, and she couldn't imagine Justine letting that go with an apology.

But she also couldn't imagine Justine without Scott. To be fifty-two and suddenly discover everything you believed in and valued most a lie? How devastating would that be?

Adele reminded herself that at least Justine had lived a rich life before reaching this crisis. In contrast, she had spent the last eight years treading water. And getting out of shape.

She was driving through town and toward her east end neighborhood when she passed a church with an adjacent building that held offices and a few classrooms. A sign in one of the windows said Weight Loss Clinic. She thought that maybe she could make that small first step toward reclaiming her life, so she went home and looked up the weight loss programs online and found the one at the church she had passed. They called themselves Emerging Women and met several times a week. It was just a few blocks from her house. She decided she could go to a meeting in the morning to check them out.

Like any woman more than ten pounds overweight, Adele had tried many diets, but none that had worked. Or maybe all of them could've worked had she lasted more than four days. This time, however, she read about the diet online and found it actually looked fun. They even had products available for sale both at the meeting and in the grocery store for those busy men and women who didn't have a lot of time for meal preparation. But everything she would need she could get at the local grocer.

Grocery store, not Jake's market.

Her first meeting was successful. The friendly woman who weighed her in, pronounced her as having thirty-six pounds to lose for her ideal weight.

"I would have guessed a solid fifty," Adele said.

"You'll be so surprised at the difference you see and feel in just ten," the woman said.

Adele listened to complaints and testimonials, heard advice and experiences, stayed late to get the instructions on how to calculate points for meals. She could even get an app for her phone so she could calculate the correct points for meals taken in a restaurant. Any place but Maggio's.

She went home from her first meeting, cleaned out her refrigerator and made a list for the grocery. After that, she cleaned out her mother's chest of drawers and half of her closet, stacking up the old clothes in either give away or throw away piles. Then she made a list of things she had to get done immediately. Topping the list was *JOB*.

She was filled with nervous energy, taking the first steps in starting over at last, unsure what the trigger had been. If she had learned Justine had a life-threatening disease, like cancer, she'd get it—don't waste another moment of your life on trivial matters. Live as if it counts! Be your best self! But what she had learned was not that. Her wonderful brother-in-law, whom she loved more than she realized, loved like a brother, was a scoundrel. Not to be trusted. And her sister, who loved him and depended on him, was headed for certain heartbreak.

Adele did not dare waste a moment more.

Justine was just scrubbing up the last of the shattered flower vase when Scott came home, looking over the breakfast bar at her. She was on her knees, sweeping small bits of wet glass into a dustpan.

"What happened here?" Scott asked.

"Oh, an accident," she said, her voice as pleasant as possible. "I dropped the vase and flowers. There were no survivors."

"Aw, that's too bad. There will be more, no worries," he said. He gave her a smile.

No doubt, she thought. Probably lots of flowers before all was said and done. She judged his rumpled golf shirt and shorts, but she didn't notice any sweat stains or grass stains, but then it was only March and there was a nice ocean breeze. Still, she'd like to ask to see a receipt for the round of golf. But instead she asked, "How'd you play?"

"Like crap. Eighty-six."

The rest of their day involved minimal conversation, consisting of routine issues like what to have for dinner and the needs the girls had for the coming week. Then, as had become typical, Scott went to bed before nine while the girls and Justine were all up until eleven. Justine had work from the office to complete before an early Monday morning start, and the girls were finishing homework they'd put off to the last minute.

Monday came and that meant work for Justine, and even with all the uncertainties in the company, she was anxious to get there. Once she got to the office she texted one of the detectives they often used for legal assistance. It's not like hers was a district attorney's or prosecutor's office— their investigations had to do with background checks on companies they might be involved with in business deals, contracts, that sort of thing. She texted a question.

I have a friend going through a divorce. Do you know a private investigator who does domestic investigations? I'd like to be able to recommend someone.

A name and phone number came back to her right away. She called a man named Logan Danner, a recently retired police lieutenant who worked for a private investigator's office out of San Francisco. She asked to make an appointment to discuss a possible job. She named the detective who had recommended him and said the issue was domestic. And personal.

"Thanks. I'll remember to tell him I appreciate the recommendation. Why don't you tell me when you're available and where I'll be researching if you hire me. Then I can suggest a meeting place."

"You don't have an office?" she asked.

"Sure, but it's better to meet in a public place that isn't too busy. That way you're not seen going into a PI's office…"

"I go into PI's offices from time to time, though mostly they come to me. I'm an attorney. However, in this—"

"Where and when, Mrs. Somersby. Let's make this easy."

She sighed. "I'm still just a little wobbly about doing this…"

"We'll talk about that, too."

"All right, you're the expert. Any day after four and before seven, and I suppose you'll be looking around San Jose and as far south as Half Moon Bay."

"Perfect. There's a great little Chinese restaurant in South San Jose called Chen's. Have you been there?"

"I haven't, no," she said.

"Then it's perfect. If we meet there at four thirty, it will be quiet. You can even get takeout for your dinner if you want to. Are you in a hurry?"

"Of course," she said, but she said it tiredly. "Today?"

"Today it is," he said. "Although it's possible there won't be many people in the place, I'm forty-eight and ordinary looking. Brown and brown. You?"

"Fifty-two, short blond hair, business attire."

"Lawyer attire," he added with a chuckle.

"I'm a corporate attorney," she explained. "I read a lot

of prospectuses. And contracts. And stock option proposals and documents filed with the SEC."

"Noted," he said. "See you a little later."

For the rest of the day, she fluctuated between anxious for some details about her husband and frightened of what this detective might find. She wasn't really sure if she hoped Scott wasn't found to be doing anything egregious or if she hoped he was nailed with a red-hot poker. After all, what Adele had seen was not benign. Passionately kissing someone else was not allowed in their marriage.

Perhaps it was forgivable and survivable, however. She wasn't sure how, but perhaps. However, was there enough love left between them?

She arrived at Chen's a little early. There was no one dining at the time, and she told the hostess she'd be meeting someone at four thirty. The woman said, "You want food? Of course?"

"Of course," Justine said, but she was thinking about what she could order that wasn't exactly a meal. Her appetite had disappeared with Adele's news. "A cup of tea for now, thank you."

What she said and did today could decide the rest of her life. It was not too late to change her mind, forget about hiring a detective. If Scott ever found out... *Wait a minute*, she said to herself. *He's kissing some strange woman! That's a worse crime than hiring a detective, isn't it?*

Her appointment walked in. Just his entrance alone was memorable. He spoke softly to the hostess, smiling at her. Then with an arm sweeping wide, the hostess indicated Justine. Logan Danner thanked her with another big smile and walked toward Justine.

"Mrs. Somersby?" he asked, putting out a hand.

"Yes. Thanks for meeting with me so quickly," she said, noting his firm handshake.

"I'm happy to. It happens I'm not working tonight, so there's plenty of time to talk about how I can help."

"I'm not even sure what I'm looking for," she said.

"How about I ask you a few questions to help us get there?" he suggested.

"Of course," she said.

"Infidelity?" he asked.

The hostess brought her tea and for Logan, a tall blond beer. For both of them, water. Then she left quickly.

"I suspect so. My sister saw my husband kissing a woman. She described it as passionate kissing. In a dark restaurant."

"Forgive the question, but is there any reason you know of that your sister would make up something like that? Some ax to grind. Family arguments, jealousies, anything?"

Justine shook her head. "Addie loves Scott," she said. "She told me immediately. She's outraged and hurt. I didn't get overwrought, at least for her to see."

"Who might he have been kissing?" Logan asked.

"I don't know the woman, but Addie was with a friend who said her name is Cat Brooks and she owns a kayak rental shop in Half Moon Bay. That's where I grew up. I've been gone for over twenty years, since college, only home for brief visits. Addie still lives there. She's quite a bit younger than me—twenty years younger."

Logan frowned. "Kind of ballsy, kissing some woman in his wife's hometown, his sister-in-law's town of residence…"

"Well, Addie lives there, but she has a very small circle of friends and doesn't have much of a social life. For years she cared for our parents who were disabled and in need of medical care. Our mother only recently passed away. Addie can finally go out with friends, if they haven't all deserted her by now. She was out for a pizza with a friend she's known since childhood."

"So, what is it you want me to do?" Logan asked.

"Let me tell you some things first," she said.

"Of course," he said. He took a swallow of his beer. Then he pulled a small notebook and pen from his pocket. "Take your time. Tell me what you think is important." Pen poised over notebook, he gave her a nod.

"I'm a corporate attorney for a major software developer. Sharper Dynamic. I have two daughters, age sixteen and seventeen. Scott has been a stay-at-home dad since Amber, my oldest, was born. We've been married twenty-eight years but started dating in college. And I've provided most of the income the last twenty years."

"Most?" he asked.

"When Scott didn't have the responsibilities of two babies or toddlers or preschoolers, he sometimes worked part-time. Usually sporting goods retail—he liked the discounts on his gear from golf clubs to high-end mountain bikes. Discounts for the whole family. One year he even gave me a profit and loss statement showing me how much money he saved the family with his discounts. Enough to take a great vacation."

She sounded ridiculous even to herself.

"And," Logan said. "I sense there's more."

"He managed the finances. He would ask my opinion from time to time. No, that's not right. He would tell me things like he was moving a little money to lessen our exposure in a volatile market. And I would say okay. But I rarely looked at a credit card bill or a phone bill or a bank statement. For all I know—"

"What do you want to know?" he asked.

"What do I want to know?" she repeated. "I guess I want to know if he's having an affair."

Logan leveled his gaze on hers. "I think you already know the answer to that. You just can't prove it. In your capacity as an attorney, you've had occasion to work with an investigator or two."

"On a regular basis, yes. But in quite a different way. Background checks, financial records, lawsuits, et cetera. I can honestly say extramarital affairs never crossed my desk."

"Unfortunately, there seems to be an epidemic. You've been married a long time. Have you considered counseling?"

"We're in counseling now. At Scott's suggestion. Do you suppose that means he wants to save the marriage?"

"Let me be honest, Mrs. Somersby—"

"Please, feel free to call me Justine."

"Justine. He might be trying to demonstrate he's made an effort when he has no intention of staying in the marriage. I suggest you acquaint yourself with the accounting just in case..."

"Right..." She suspected they both knew this could be the death knell of a marriage.

"I can surveil him, find out how and where he spends his time, ascertain if there's any inappropriate behavior that would suggest an affair, do a public records search of the woman he's involved with, that sort of thing. To get started, I just need your husband's full name and a license plate number. A picture would help. If the car he drives is registered in both your names, you can put a GPS tracker on the car. I can do that with your permission."

"All right. And yes, the car is registered in both names. How much time will that take?"

"A matter of days, depending on the schedule your husband keeps. But plan on a couple of weeks. That way you won't get impatient. A retainer and a very brief contract is required. It only states that you'll pay for my time and expenses and I'll deliver information to you and only you."

"What if what we learn is the worst-case scenario? What am I supposed to do?"

"I'm an investigator, Justine. I'm not a marriage counselor. I don't know the answer to that."

She took a sip of her tea. "I might be the primary breadwinner, but I'm completely dependent on him."

Logan didn't say anything for a moment. "If you have a business card with your email address and cell number, I can send you an attachment with our agency contract. You can also wire me the deposit through this cell number." He handed her his business card. "You'll want to stash this card in a secure place. Unless you have a lot of PI business cards already so this one wouldn't seem suspicious."

She reached into her purse, pulled out a business card and wrote Scott's full name on the back. Scott Rush Somersby. She texted a picture of the two of them. They were smiling confidently for the shot. There were pictures like that framed all over their house. So many people thought they were the perfect couple. "Here you go. I don't remember his license plate number, but it's a new Escalade, dark blue. I'll send it to you when I get home."

"Okay, then I can get started."

After a quiet moment she said, "Finish your beer. I'm going to finish my tea. And I promised the hostess I'd order some food."

"You'll feel better about making a decision after you have the information you need," he said.

"Oh, I don't think I'm ever going to feel better about this."

"Yes, you will," he said. "If I find what you expect me to find, you'll want all of the facts before you make a long-term decision."

"What makes you think I have an expectation of what you'll find?" she asked.

"You wouldn't have called me otherwise. And Justine, I doubt you're as dependent on him as you think."

Justine tried to remember when, exactly, she'd given up her individual power. It might've been right away, when Scott said, "I'll take the right side of the bed." Then he proceeded to give her a list of her advantages to being on the left side. She would be closer to the bathroom, would have the better reading lamp and when he turned on his left side toward her, he could caress her with his right and dominant hand.

He must have forgotten about the dominant hand lately. Or, more like for years. Because he wasn't ever in the mood anymore. That hadn't bothered her much, since she worked such long hours and was frequently tired.

The more she thought about it, the more she realized he chose the TV shows, the dinners, the vacations, managed their social life. He told her to take the LSAT. "You're a good test taker. You always have been. I know you like teaching, but you can make more money in law and I bet you'd like it."

"Why don't *you* take the LSAT. I'll help you study," she'd suggested.

"We both know that's not a good idea," he said.

He was good in sales, any kind of sales, because he was good with people. He was the fun and entertaining one. But it was probably when they moved in together, right after college, that she slowly began to give away any decision-making power in the partnership. And once she became a lawyer, she began to defer to him lest he feel that masculine bite from being the less successful of the two.

When she thought about it, he was quite eager not to work. She had always assumed they would both work and find a nanny or a reasonable day care. She had no problem after thinking about it. And in practice, it seemed to work. It seemed so modern and progressive.

Oh, but the neighborhood women loved him. He showed up at all the school events, was usually the only man to volunteer in the classroom, went on school field trips, had coffee with the stay-at-home mothers. They used to fuss over him, comparing him to their working husbands who never pitched in. Justine had wanted to say, "He has a cleaning lady, you know," but she said nothing. And Scott had many limitations—he refused to do laundry and he wasn't very helpful with homework. "You're the teacher," he always said.

So, what did he actually do? He took care of the kids and he was very good at it. He tidied up the house after they were safely dropped off at school. He paid the bills and managed their retirement funds. Those funds she now needed to get up to speed on.

Five years ago Scott had received a text at 5:00 a.m. and she'd wrangled the phone away from him to read, Coffee later? on the screen. It was from one of the elementary school teachers, a former teacher of Olivia's. They'd had a big fight over that. She told him he should not be texting with or meeting a woman for coffee. It was inappropriate! So he said, "Fine, I'll tell her. Consider it stopped here and now." Justine asked a few times if that nonsense had stopped, and he offered her his phone. She didn't take him up on the offer. She wanted to believe him.

Now, suddenly, she wondered if there had been inappropriate liaisons all along. She tried to envision Scott kissing a woman in a public place, and it made her sick to her stomach. She had to go home and face him. She'd talked to him twice today and he said he wasn't planning to go anywhere in the evening, so she'd have to wear a poker face. She could plead a headache. She was in the mood for a very large martini but she'd be careful; a too large martini could loosen her tongue and cause her to scream, "You've been cheating on me, you lowlife son of a bitch!"

There was no one to talk to about this. It was important that while Logan Danner did his investigating, she not tip off Scott. She knew a couple of women from work who had gone through messy divorces, but she hadn't paid close attention because she'd believed that was never going to happen to her.

She thought about Addie. She wished she could talk to her but felt she couldn't show any vulnerability or weakness to her younger sister. Yet the circumstances they both suddenly faced called to her. They had both become isolated—Addie because she chose to take care of their parents and Justine because she worked, worked, worked and let Scott decide how they'd spend their time. Even among their couple friends, she didn't have a lot of time to spend with the women.

Addie and Justine had become loners. For Justine it was almost twenty-five years ago, after passing the bar and settling into her job. But for Addie, just eight, when she came home from school with a baby bump and never went back.

Justine was overwhelmed by the feeling that she had failed everyone. She'd failed her daughters, who would be devastated by this family crisis; she'd failed Adele, to whom she should have shown more support. And she'd failed herself. Here she was, fifty-two and had never felt quite so alone. She had done nothing wrong and yet couldn't escape the feeling that everything was all her fault.

Scott was snoring loudly as Justine came to bed. It was something she had become used to over the years, but now it just hit her as the biggest insult under the circumstances. Circumstances that were very bad.

She had boldly paid Logan Danner's retainer with her credit card, confident the detective would have some news for her before Scott would notice. And indeed he did. It hadn't taken long for him to contact her to let her know that Scott had been a regular at the kayak shack on the beach for quite a long time. Any PI worth his salt knew that strangers would tell strangers anything. He reported to Justine that he had said to someone, "That guy, I think I know him. Dave Besteil?"

"Naw, that's not his name," said the young man putting up kayaks. "That's Scott Somersby and he's around here all the time. He's tight with the owner, Cat."

Logan texted a few pictures of passionate kisses and afternoon trips to the No-Tell-Motel. One picture was time stamped for Thursday when Scott had claimed he'd been playing ball. Instead, he was having dinner at an oceanside lodge, after which the couple went to a room. Scott left alone while the lady stayed on, presumably for the night. He was quite late getting home—he said he'd gone out for a beer with the guys after the game. According to Logan, he had not been on that team for a couple of years. It had not yet been determined if he was still part of the bowling leagues.

The woman Scott was seeing had quite an interesting history. Divorced twice, she had a couple of bankruptcies, was currently struggling with debt, but her late-model car was paid off. Oh, and she was married to her third husband. There had also been some police calls for domestic disturbances. "It's possible the woman is in an abusive relationship," Logan said.

"Would that explain her fishing around for a new boyfriend?" Justine asked.

"Well, I suppose it could. But typically abused women are afraid of the abuser and don't take those kinds of chances. There haven't been any assault charges filed, but people lie and cover up domestic violence all the time. You need to keep in mind that Scott might have gotten himself into an explosive dynamic."

Justine did not know exactly how long her husband had been involved with Cat. She could only assume it had been quite a while. Years, perhaps. It was possible she was just one of many.

Justine felt like a complete fool.

Logan Danner had given her as much information as she needed to move forward and said he would remain available if there was anything more she needed from him. But she could take it from here. She would need a court order to do a forensic accounting, find out if he had other bank accounts and credit cards. This was her wheelhouse. It's what she did for a living.

It played out at their next counseling appointment. Scott opened the session as he usually did by giving Justine her report card, as if this marital crisis had only to do with her behavior.

"Justine has been great about remembering to say thank

you. I think we're making great progress," he said, as if counseling a first grader learning to say please and thank you.

As if she should remember to thank him for warming up frozen burritos for dinner while he didn't find it necessary to thank her for working so hard for the generous paycheck that paid for that food.

When it was her turn to speak, Justine was very calm. "Scott has been having an affair with a woman named Cat Brooks. I'm not sure how long exactly but at least a couple of years. We have some urgent decisions to make. We have two daughters at very vulnerable ages, and I won't have them lied to."

The counselor, a thin, bald man wearing wire-rimmed glasses, looked shocked and off balance. But it was brief. He was about to speak but Scott reacted first.

"You're out of your mind! I'm only friends with the owner of the kayak shop because I love to kayak! And you know that!"

"I have lots of proof," Justine stated.

"And how would you come by proof when I haven't done anything?"

He'd know soon enough, when the credit card bill came. "Let's not waste precious time on you denying everything, Scott. There are pictures, receipts, witnesses, tons of stuff. We have to talk about how to face the future. We have kids. We have assets. I'm a lawyer and I know only too well, once lawyers get involved, we'll be sucked dry. You clearly don't want to be married to me anymore. And I can't be married to a man who cheats. So how do we resolve this?"

Scott stared at her for a long time, not speaking. His lips were as thin as a wire; his temples pulsed. His eyes narrowed. He sat there frozen, looking at her with silent hatred. At that moment more than any of the other moments before, she realized she didn't know him at all. At. All.

"This is all your fault," he finally said.

Justine couldn't cry. She wanted to release the valve, open the dam, scream out the pain of betrayal and rage. She'd been used! Every nickel in their portfolio and retirement accounts had been earned by her. The house they lived in—she qualified for and paid the mortgage.

She wasn't sure when it happened, but the ability to break down and cry had been trained out of her years ago. It was a feature of practicing law. While she might not be putting away hardened criminals, she was responsible for keeping the legal affairs of a corporation in order, protecting the jobs of hundreds of employees. Still, her job wasn't always dry and unemotional. There were times she felt the weight and pressure of the future of her company at stake, awaiting an answer from the Securities Exchange for example, and getting the wrong answer and knowing there would be grave disappointment, possible monetary losses, perhaps bankruptcy or in an extreme case, a hostile takeover. She held the legal aspect of the company in her hands, and of course she couldn't cry about it, no matter how scared or disappointed she felt.

Scott had never been sympathetic to the pressure she felt.

But when was the last time she cried over her husband or marriage? It was probably before the girls were born. In their attempts to have a family, there had been a couple of miscarriages—those brought her to her knees. And she was sure she cried tears of joy when Amber and Olivia were born...

Oh God, her daughters! They would be so devastated by this news. They adored their father, and while she was certain she had their love as well, they were closer to Scott. After all, he was the one available to seek out for permission, to go to for favors, to call if they needed a ride or wanted to borrow the car.

It was Scott who played with them. He took them to watch games—football and hockey were their favorite sporting events. Scott taught them to play tennis and golf. They often went biking or hiking together, most of the time leaving Justine behind if it was her day to stay with her mother or if she had work to do.

The girls needed their father. But there was no way she was leaving her home! They would be heartbroken to think of their father not being there. Especially Olivia. Her girls looked very much alike with their long, thick brown hair and dark eyes, but were as different as night and day. Amber was smart and strong and fiercely independent. Now that she thought about it, Justine realized it was rare for Amber to cry, as well. But Olivia was another story. She was sensitive and emotional and would probably fall apart at the thought of her daddy not being at her beck and call.

She would have to share her daughters with their father; she would have to take over as the primary parent. She would have to do all of the chores Scott routinely accomplished. Everything she'd become used to would change.

Right after Scott told her everything was her fault, he delivered a litany of complaints about her character. She worked all the time and didn't take adequate care of the family. He was never sure he could count on her—in her business something was always coming up to delay her or take up time at home. They didn't agree on anything. She was stubborn and pushy. She flaunted her success. She was cold.

"Wait a minute—I am not! And when did you expect me to earn that paycheck if I wasn't committed to the work I do?" she had asked. "If our genders were reversed and if you were a woman, a housewife for lack of a better word, you'd seem mighty ungrateful right now. And I think it's pretty well established, you're the one who is cold and unavailable! You've been with another woman. And looking back, I doubt she's the first!"

"Let's slow this down and talk about where this is going," the counselor said.

The man explained that if they wanted to try to save the marriage, he could offer counseling. But if they were going to separate and perhaps divorce, he couldn't counsel them individually. At least not both of them.

After talking and answering the counselor's questions for half an hour, it was Justine who said, "We should separate pending divorce. I'm not completely closed to the idea of saving the marriage but I admit, it doesn't look promising. I don't know that I can ever trust Scott again."

"Fine, then you leave," Scott said.

"I'd like to suggest we have a candid talk about what we can do and how to go about it. We should both have a look at our assets and discuss options for living apart. I can take tomorrow off so we can talk while the girls are at school. We also have to talk about what we're going to tell them." She swallowed, and her voice was not as strong when she continued. "They'll be very upset."

"To say the least," Scott said.

CHAPTER FOUR

Adele was starving. Maybe not exactly starving since she wasn't particularly hungry. There was plenty of food in her new program, most of which could provide a steady diet for bunnies. There were some things missing, however. Chips and ice cream, which she didn't think she ate much of until two whole days passed without a bite of either. Then she realized she must have downed them regularly.

Jake's mother, Beverly, called to ask if she might stop by for a little visit and another reality hit her—Beverly's cakes. At least one a month, sometimes more, she'd bring one over and Adele would eat the entire thing.

"I would so love to see you, but you must not bring a cake," Adele said. "I'm on a strict diet!"

"But you can have one piece," Beverly said. "No diet wouldn't let you have one small piece."

"I'll make us tea or coffee. But, please, no cake!"

It was hard but she stuck to it, and at the end of her first week she was pleased to discover that four pounds had disappeared. The Monday morning group warned her not to expect that kind of progress every week, but a good, steady and small loss would add up and before she knew it, she'd reach her goal.

That day, after the meeting, she walked all the way to the beach. It must have been ten miles. When she got there, she sighed in appreciation—she'd forgotten how much she loved the beach. The fog there was just lifting, the sun pale in the sky. It brought so much comfort. It soothed her. She had walked along the beach so little while her mother was sick. She had only ever left her mother for an hour or so, usually just enough time to run an errand, maybe park at the beach for fifteen minutes and soak up the view, but never for long.

Later, after going home, she drove back to the beach so she could check how far she'd actually walked and found it was a mile and a half. Almost.

The realization that her mile and a half felt like ten gave her another wake-up call. Taking care of her mom had been hard work but not the right kind of exercise, and she'd bolstered herself with lots of extra calories. She decided to make an hour of walking every morning a part of her day.

She called Justine more often than she ever had before because she had no idea what was going on in her sister's life. The image of Scott kissing Cat stuck like a boulder in her brain and she thought about it all the time, fearful that her sister's marriage might be in ruins, equally fearful that her sister would look the other way.

The first time Adele called, just three days after she informed Justine of the kiss, her sister merely said she couldn't talk about it yet because she was still in the fact-gathering stage. Only Justine would call it a fact-gathering mission when it had to do with a cheating husband. A few more days passed, and Justine said she couldn't talk about it yet because she and Scott were working out possible options. A few days after that, Justine couldn't talk to Adele about it yet because they hadn't discussed their situation with their daughters.

"What *is* your situation?" Adele blurted.

"It's still a little murky," Justine said. "It has been established that Scott has had some serious doubts·about the state of our marriage, but he is unclear if it can be saved or is doomed to fall prey to the statistics. We have to decide before we tell the girls."

"Are you sure the girls don't know?" Adele asked.

"They're teenagers and very self-centered. All Amber can think about is school getting out for the summer and that she'll be a senior next year."

Adele's nieces had been winter and spring babies, making them slightly older than the average student in their class. They had both finished their SATs, and Amber was making college applications.

"What about your visits to colleges with Amber?" Adele asked.

"Obviously we'll have a conversation about the changes in our family before we finalize plans, but some things won't change. My daughters will go to college, however that has to be managed…"

"Justine! Doesn't anything just throw you? Just knock you out?"

She was silent for a moment before replying, "Wouldn't we be in trouble if I collapsed right now?"

"What about Scott? Is he upset? Worried? Emotional?"

"He's very angry with me. For finding him out. It seems the kayak shack bimbo has been grooming him for a takeover."

"Holy shit!" Adele said with a gasp.

"Say nothing, do nothing, please stay calm. If I don't handle this well, it's going to be a full-blown crisis."

And so Adele, somewhat shaken by the idea of her older sister getting a divorce, just walked every morning, ate a lot of celery and countless chicken breasts, dropped four more pounds, then two pounds, then three pounds. She stripped the varnish off the baseboards and watched a number of videos on reupholstering, wallpapering, refinishing floors, and even remodeling a kitchen. She also called several of the local businesses, including resorts, and asked what positions they were hiring for. After she explained her circumstances, that she was halfway to her master's degree but had stopped to take care of her ailing parents for eight years, it was usually explained that she would start at an entry-level position for minimum wage until she grew in experience and could be considered for a promotion. She kept phoning and studying the online job sources, hopeful.

"But I was a teaching assistant in the English department at Berkeley!" she would protest.

"Eight years ago," was the reply.

Then she did something she'd done before, many times. She looked up Professor Hadley Hutchinson on the website of UC Berkeley. He was still there. It was an old picture. He would be over forty now. And still drop-dead handsome.

She sighed deeply and longed for cake.

Ultimately Scott admitted that he had strayed. That was his description of what had happened. He'd strayed.

"So, do you love her?" Justine asked.

"I don't know," he answered, sounding exasperated. "I enjoy talking to her. We have a lot in common. We're both obsessed with fitness, and you don't show much interest in that…"

"I work sixty hours a week to pay for your fitness program!"

"Hey, I cover that cost!"

"Yeah, while you didn't have to make a mortgage payment or save for college or pay for utilities or— Never mind that for now. Go on."

"We talked a lot. And I wasn't looking for a girlfriend, but one thing led to another..."

"You could have said no," Justine suggested.

"If you must know, I did. But there was something missing with us, with you and me. There was an empty place inside me and—"

"Stop that!" she yelled. "Stop feeding me those stale old chick flick lines. If there was something missing with us, you should have stopped going to that kayak shack and addressed the problem with *me*."

"I did. We've been in marriage counseling," he said.

"Much too late! You'd already been involved with her for a long time! Years."

"Not years! We were mostly just friends. She was someone to talk to. It's been fairly recent that we—"

"It's been *years*! And obviously we can't stay married. Or let me put this more succinctly—I can't be married to someone who lies to me and has another woman on the side. For YEARS."

"What are you suggesting?"

"I'm not suggesting, Scott. I'm not going to stay married to you. You're unfaithful and you're a liar, but most of all you've been screwing her while we went to marriage counseling! I can't stay with you because you have no interest in saving our marriage! You need to leave, and we have to tell the kids."

"Where am I supposed to go? I have no place to go!"

"Why don't you see if they'll set up a cot in the kayak shack."

"Funny," he said.

But Justine wasn't joking.

"We really don't have to change anything, you know," Scott said.

"Oh, are you suggesting we invite your mistress into the family?" Justine asked frostily. "Because yes, we do have to change a few things."

"Of course I'm not suggesting any such thing. And she's not my mistress."

"Oh. Sorry. Would you prefer *girlfriend*? *Side chick*? *Whore*?"

"You know, take your potshots at me if you want to, but she's a very good person. A good Christian woman."

"In her third marriage," Justine said. "Three marriages, two bankruptcies, no arrests that I know of, thank God."

"How do you know that?" he demanded.

"Scott. It's public record. I'm an attorney. And a smart woman. I looked it up. She sounds like a predator."

"Stop that!"

"Fine. We're getting a divorce because you have a girlfriend. We'll separate and settle our property. We can get it done cheaply or we can each get our own lawyer and spend a hundred grand and a year of our lives we'll never get back."

"Justine, where do you think I'm going to go?"

"What did you think was going to happen when I found out? You'll think of something."

"Why can't we live here together as roommates?"

She was stunned. Something about the look on his face said he was serious. "No! I'm having a hard enough time getting used to the idea you've been unfaithful. I'm not continuing to live with you as your wife. We'll tell the girls this weekend."

Justine took a couple of additional days off ahead of the weekend. She worked on her laptop, and Scott probably assumed she was doing legal work from home. In fact, she was doing something she should have done a long time ago. She was diving into their financial records—tax returns, online bill paying, credit cards. She needed to find out if Scott had any additional credit cards, bank accounts, cell phones, email addresses and so on. She put in a call to Logan.

"I've been wondering about you," he said. "How are you holding up?"

"I'm okay," she said. "I'm going through our financial records, but it would be helpful to have a little more information if only to see how deep and far back the lying goes. Scott is a fun, attractive man but still, given this woman's background, I wonder if he's being had."

"That could require surveillance," Logan said. "Would I be out of line to give a little advice?"

"Knock yourself out," she said. "I'm not feeling all that smart right now anyway."

"I'll be glad to do whatever I can to help you gather information, but the laws are clear. If you can negotiate half of your holdings and property and a reasonable support payment, you've done good. You can probably file the papers yourself. If you get the lawyers involved, they're going to get most of the money."

"I know," she said. "Let me know what you find. And if it's beyond your reach, please just tell me."

"Absolutely."

The conversation with their girls was not easy, but it was very similar to their discussion with each other. Scott started it off.

"As you know, Mom and I have been in marriage counseling because we weren't completely happy and we've grown apart..."

"I was completely happy, and I know nothing about this growing apart," Justine said.

Scott scowled at her. "There was something missing in the marriage for me. I wasn't happy and—"

Justine put her elbows on her knees and leaned toward them. "Look, this may be a bit hard for you to understand. While your dad was feeling whatever that growing apart business was, I was working. Often ten-hour days. I might be guilty of not paying close enough attention to him, missing something, but nevertheless, he found himself involved with another woman..."

"Dad?" Amber asked, her spine stiffening in shock.

Olivia was eerily quiet.

"It's true," he said. "I strayed."

That word again.

"I never have before and I can't believe I did, but there it is. I'm the guilty party. That's what your mother wants me to say, that I'm the guilty one."

"But are you sorry?" Amber asked.

"Of course!"

"And so she's gone now, right? The woman?"

"Not exactly," Justine said. "Your father is still involved with her. I believe he loves her."

"Do you, Dad? Love her?"

"We're good friends, that's how I can best explain it. If you knew her, you'd understand—"

"Oh, you did not..." Justine said. "She is the reason our marriage is falling apart and our family is torn, and you're going to argue that she's just too nice to resist?"

"But you can stop being friends with her, right? Because you can't still want to be friends now, right?" Amber's voice was pleading.

"Scott, please be honest with Amber. You and that woman are much more than friends. And you've made no suggestion that you'll stop seeing her."

There was a heavy silence in the room. Finally it was Olivia's very quiet voice that broke through. "Daddy, don't you love Mom anymore?"

"I will always love your mother, but I don't think I love her in the way I did when we were younger. We've grown apart. We don't spend time together. We don't have much in common. Your mother's work takes up a lot of time and is her priority. I don't blame her, I blame myself. But things have changed and sometimes that happens. Your mother and I are talking about a separation. Not immediately, but soon. We need some time apart."

"Are you getting divorced?" Amber asked.

"Honey, we love you very much, but—" Scott started to respond.

"Yes," Justine said. "This is not your fault, either of you. But yes, we're going to divorce. Because our marriage contract has been broken and can't be mended. If your father wanted to save our marriage, we might have a fighting chance. But he doesn't."

"But you're in counseling!" Amber cried.

"And the whole while, he's been seeing another woman. I'm afraid I can't fight that."

"Dad!" Amber said. "Don't you want to be married to Mom?"

He was quiet for a long moment before he said, "I don't know."

Amber's breath went out in a huff. Olivia stood quietly and walked out of the room.

* * *

April arrived, rainy much of the time and Justine's girls were crying a lot. If Justine thought her own heart was breaking, all she had to do was look at her daughters to see just how much Scott's affair was hurting the whole family.

Justine called the high school counselor to alert her that the girls had just been informed of their parents' pending divorce. Scott did not try to talk her out of it, but he did put a lot of energy into trying to negotiate some kind of living arrangement that did not leave him trying to find a hotel.

"I don't know why I can't just stay here," he said. "I'm the one who's been in charge of the house and the kids."

"Two reasons," she said. "One—you're not one hundred percent in charge. They get themselves up, drive themselves to school and half the time get their own dinner. I do their laundry, spend most evenings with them, help with homework and studying. And two—you're the one who *strayed*. You broke the marriage contract."

"And you don't even seem that upset," he said accusingly. "I haven't seen you shed a tear! I think maybe you're secretly glad to have a way out."

"But I'm not," she said. "Plus there is no other way out now."

It was true; she still hadn't cried. She felt like she was locked in a tight box with an iron band wound around her middle and her chest. She even asked herself a few times if it was possible she was having a heart attack. She considered going to see her doctor, who she thought of as a friend. If you met your doctor for drinks or a light dinner now and then, didn't it make you friends? She thought about asking her doctor if she was abnormal.

She did throw up frequently. She couldn't eat. Food didn't appeal, and when she did force something down, it stuck in her throat. She stocked up on yogurt and ice cream and went home from work early so she could be there for the girls when they got home from school. They talked endlessly, trying to get a fix on what their lives might be like going forward. Every single afternoon and evening was consumed with talking. She made them soup or pizza or sloppy joes or anything they had a yen for; the poor things didn't feel like eating either. She tried to reassure them they would still have both of their parents whenever they wanted them, but she did think it was a good idea that only one of them lived in the family home.

Justine had long heard about that rule of never saying negative things about the departing spouse and that was damned hard, given he was a jerk and a liar. But as it turned out, she didn't have to say anything at all. Scott was on another planet, free to be with his mistress. He didn't show up on time, didn't keep tabs on the girls, didn't talk to them about what their lives would be like, didn't try to explain. Didn't apologize. Instead of begging for forgiveness he merely said, "I haven't been happy. Don't you want me to be happy?"

Apparently, it was all about Scott's happiness.

It was also true there was no other way out, even if she forgave Scott, though he hadn't asked her to. How did you continue a partnership when one of the partners was capable of a long, insidious, remorseless betrayal?

But Scott just wouldn't leave. They didn't fight, though they did grind out a few terse words here and there. He had been banished to the guest room at night, and it felt like he was settling in too comfortably. He had stopped telling her or the girls where he was going, just dropping short sentences as he walked out the door like, "I'll be home by ten," or "I'll be out for a few hours."

"I hope you're thinking about a property settlement," Justine said. "The more we can work out amicably, the better for the girls. They won't be involved in our negotiations. If we're smart, we can get through this without doing them any more harm."

"If you're going to keep acting like this is my fault, there will be harm," Scott said.

"I'll do my best, but this *is* your fault. You took a lover. I did not."

And why not? she asked herself. She'd been lonely, too. Scott was busy with his activities all the time and didn't seem to need her. They spent a couple of afternoons a month as a family doing some activity, and they had dinner together once or twice a week. She was just starting to realize that it'd been a lonely way to live.

She hadn't taken a lover because there'd never been a temptation. Nor an opportunity! The fact that Scott complained that she'd been working all the time and that she wasn't interested in his life only added insult to injury because he'd had plenty of time to take a lover. Maybe if he'd been working, worrying about retirement and college tuition and paying the bills, he might not have had the time!

She spent a couple of hours with a friend who was an attorney who did a lot of divorces. The advice was familiar to her and exactly what she'd told a dozen friends and Scott—if they could agree on the division of property without lawyers, it would be cheaper and less likely to be contentious. Her friend warned her, "Your biggest problem will be alimony since you've supported him for so long."

"But he could have worked!" Justine said. "He loved not working and having all that time off! I asked him a hundred times if there wasn't something he wanted to do, even as a volunteer, and he said he'd put in enough hours of volunteer work as a dad!"

"It is assumed that every such decision is made in joint partnership, just as net worth is jointly shared."

She'd never thought about it because she couldn't imagine this happening to her, to them. There had been the rare time she'd said to Scott, "Have you heard about Char and Dennis getting divorced after thirty years of marriage? How does that happen? Please tell me that can't happen to us!"

"Us? The most married couple in the county? Impossible!" he'd said.

And she would let it go. After all, they talked or texted all day, every day. They were constantly in touch; constantly joined at the hip.

She told Adele they would be separating soon, filing for divorce. Despite the fact that Scott had a lover, apparently he had nowhere to go and was living down the hall.

Adele began to cry on the phone. "You guys were one of the only reasons I had faith in marriage."

"You can't imagine how sorry I am that this is another shattered image," Justine said.

So, staring terror in the face, she went to see the CEO of her company. She told him that her marriage was over and explained that none of the options she'd been offered in the restructured company were appealing to her and she wanted to offer her resignation.

"If you resign, there won't be an exit package," Wayne Holloway explained. "That's an expensive decision. Do you have another position lined up?"

She shook her head. "I suppose I'll talk to a headhunter," she said. "For years I had fantasies about striking out on my own, starting a private practice or joining one, maybe consulting, something that would be less stressful and give me more time to enjoy my kids before they're gone. But the demands of the bills were bigger than I was."

"You're right not to wait too long, Justine. Otherwise, you might end up spending your whole life trying to hold this company together."

"What was your fantasy, Wayne?" she asked.

He leaned back in his chair and said, "I'd like to play the piano in a jazz band. Seriously."

He was not known as a musical talent. "That's amazing. I never would have—"

"Can I give you some advice?" he asked. "As a man divorced twice?"

"I'd welcome it," she said.

"Be generous, don't try to punish him even if he deserves it, but know what your priorities are and set fair boundaries that are nonnegotiable. You'll be better off in the end if you can settle."

"He doesn't inspire my sense of generosity," she said. "He makes me want to fight for everything."

"I know. I get it. I've been the betrayer and the betrayed. Either way, just keep safe what means the most to you."

"That's easy—my girls."

"Be practical, Justine. Can you be a full-time caretaker and provider?"

"Women do it all the time."

"It isn't easy," he said. "And you wouldn't be happy without work, so balance the scales. Take some time to think about it. Walk on the beach. Talk to friends. Maybe get a little counseling or find a group for support. Or try church, if that's your bent. Come up with a plan."

"I have a little vacation…"

"Justine, take time off, forget vacation. We'll hold your decision about your future job until you've at least reached a preliminary settlement with your soon-to-be ex. Then let's talk again."

"You know what makes this hardest?" she asked her boss. "One of the things I've been most proud of was my marriage. I thought it was strong. Solid. I thought it had stood the test of time." Her voice caught. "I thought my husband loved me."

"Did you ever suspect him of being unfaithful before?"

"Not really," she answered.

Wayne touched her hand. "I have a feeling that when this is behind you, you'll be glad it went the way it did. Painful, yes. But worth it? Probably."

She took Wayne's advice. Maybe not to the letter, but she considered her priorities and struggled to push the need to kill Scott way down to the bottom of her list. She went over their books, soaking up the details. She walked on the beach. She saw the kayak shack and got a glimpse of the woman. Cat. She didn't get too close because she assumed Cat would be able to identify her, and right now her anonymity was important. Later, maybe, she'd let herself be seen.

She thought about her priorities, and Amber and Olivia remained at the top of the list. She barely slept, thinking of how to best provide for them. A picture of Wayne Holloway playing piano in a jazz band kept intruding, the image enough to make her smile if not giggle. He was a senior citizen now and should be thinking about his own retirement if being the CEO of a company constantly under siege didn't kill him first.

Scott noticed she was not going to work, that she was dressed in her yoga pants day after day. He asked her what she was doing. "Thinking," she said. "Trying to figure out what's to become of us." She assumed he wasn't asking a lot of questions because he wasn't quite ready to move out. And she was struggling with how to proceed.

Then it hit her. Putting her kids first wasn't only about money. Sure, they were comfortable in their house and needed funds for college, but they also needed two parents. Scott might be off his rocker right now, but he'd always been an involved father. The big question was—what about the woman? Would she interfere in Scott's ability to pay attention to the girls? Or even worse, would she try to win the girls over? Capture their affection?

How was she to know the true character of the woman who broke up their marriage?

She called Logan Danner again.

"As for her character, that's questionable," Logan said. "After all, this isn't the first time she's been the cause of a divorce. She twice met her next husband while he was married, and another time they lived together after he dumped his wife of many years. Giving her the benefit of the doubt, she might just be a sweet but stupid woman who keeps trying to better her lot in life by picking an upgraded man over the last man. As you know, she's twice divorced and twice filed for bankruptcy. This is not a rocket scientist. And she has domestic abuse issues in the current marriage."

"She must have some serious skills," Justine said. "I always thought of Scott as a very smart man."

"I think you can disabuse yourself of that notion," Logan said.

"You think he's not smart?" she asked, actually surprised.

"My opinion of him at the moment is not flattering," Logan said. "I think he must be an idiot."

"Will you please see if you can find anything…interesting?" she asked.

"Like?"

"Like—if she has a lot of debt, how did she pay for the new car?"

"Cars are easy. If you make the payments, you get the car. If you don't make the payments, they take it back."

"Just check, please," Justine said. "And see if you can figure out her income."

Justine spoke to Scott. "Let's spend tomorrow morning working on our settlement."

"Maybe we should just stay as we are," Scott said. "We're both here for the girls, we're not in each other's way, we can make this work. In many ways, it's not much different than it was."

"There are a lot of concessions I'm willing to make, Scott, but I'm not willing to earn the money while you spend it on your mistress."

"I'm not spending it on—"

"I know what hotels you paid for. Nice ones. Expensive ones. I can't trust you and I can't live with you. But there is a deal we can work out. If you're willing to talk it over."

"You can't know anything!" he said. "How could you know anything? There's no evidence of that!"

"Scott," she said tiredly. "They know you at the Oceanside Lodge. Come on, don't stack up any more lies. Not now when I'm willing to deal with you. Let's do this nicely and fairly for the girls."

In the end he relented.

She went for a long early-morning walk after the girls had gone to school. Forty-five minutes later she was sitting at the dining room table with a folder full of papers and her calculator. Before starting the conversation, she asked Scott if he had any ideas on how he would divide their property.

He barely paused. He pulled the yellow pad from the bottom of her stack of papers and began to list things, plus their approximate value, beginning with their retirement accounts, their savings and investments. He added in the equity in their house, all the toys in the garage, their vacation house in the mountains, their cars, their art. Her mouth fell open. *Art?* They had a few decorator paintings, not expensive and chosen strictly to enhance the decor in their home. She had purchased three from an arts and crafts fair in the park.

He went on, listing the approximate value of their china, crystal, silver, bric-a-brac and even linens and clothing. And then, if she wasn't already in shock, he added in the cost of law school.

"I had scholarships!" she said.

"And I supported you while you went to law school!" he shot back.

Then he crossed off all those household items on his lengthy list and said, "I don't have any real desire to go through the dishes and sheets. I just want to be able to live. I don't want to be selfish, I just want enough money to pay the rent and eat."

The girls' college funds, which were not going to send either one to Harvard but could cover the costs of California universities, had not entered the discussion, for which Justine was weirdly grateful. She had been afraid when it was all laid out on the table, he would pick at those remains like a bird of prey picked at the bones of a carcass.

"I think I was very generous here," he said magnanimously. "When you get down to it, what I am asking for is far less than half. The only thing to talk about is support, bearing in mind I always supported you, if not by working then by managing the home and family."

She wanted to shout at him, say something horrible to him, because he was leaving her for another woman! He effectively tossed her out and was done with her. Now the cheating bastard wanted to be seen as generous!

She tried to regain her focus. It took great effort not to lash out.

"I might have a better idea. A generous cash out." She turned the tablet toward her, wrote a huge number on it and turned it back toward him. "Also, I'll give you half of whatever I earn in the next five years. You're good with money, Scott. It would allow you to buy a house and, if you're interested, you could even go back to school and get another degree or an advanced degree. We can share the house with the girls. I'll want to have unlimited access and allow you the same, but we'll spend the nights on different nights. I'd like to see them almost every day. By the time they're in college, we'll both have figured out where we're going to settle. We can sell the house then, and I know I'll have space for them wherever I live. And I suppose you will, too."

He was clearly shocked. "You'd leave the house?"

"When I find something, but I'd want to be here for them often to help them make the adjustment. I'm sure that can be worked out, don't you think?"

"I…ah… Yeah. You mean you'd leave this house?"

"As I said, I'd want to stay in very close touch with Amber and Olivia, see them almost every day, help with homework, shopping, chaperone, et cetera. And it's bound to take at least a few weeks or months to get them used to the idea that we're going to live apart. That's certain to be as difficult for them as for me."

"Of course," he said, sitting up a little straighter. He grinned. He looked downright excited.

"I have only one condition."

"Name it."

"*She* cannot be in this house. *My* house containing *my* things. Never. Not once."

"Now why would you make that a condition?" he asked. "She is not the reason our marriage is ending. The blame is mine!"

"Of course the blame is yours and make no mistake, I'm willing to work with you even though I hate you. You've torn up my family! You destroyed our marriage. My daughters have been crying for weeks! Everything will be affected. Likely where they can go to college will be affected! But I ask one thing—she must never be in my house. She must not cook here, sleep here, celebrate here, watch the Super Bowl here or die here. In a couple of years, when we sell the house and you take your things and I take mine, do whatever you want. Until then, that's my condition. I'll get language in the decree that if you violate that condition, the house is mine, free and clear. If you want to fight it out, I'll get a lawyer. I can guarantee you it'll run up a bill of a hundred grand and take a year of your life you'll never get back."

"A hundred grand! How do you know that?"

She softened her voice and kept steady. "I'm a lawyer. We talk."

He rubbed a hand over his head, through his thinning hair. "Wow," he said. "How am I supposed to explain that?"

The way he said that, she knew.

"Oh my God," she said quietly. "She's already been here."

"No," he said, but he couldn't meet her eyes.

"Her DNA is in my house!"

"No," he said. "When we were remodeling, she was curious about the kitchen counters and stuff, so I showed her. That's all."

"God, I could kill you! Well, that's it—I can't believe anything you say." She shook her head. "When did you become such a liar?"

"You're overreacting. We were just friends until very—"

"Just shut up, Scott. Tell her I blame her as much as you. Tell her I'm not only a mean black-hearted bitch, I'm smarter than both of you put together. Tell her she took what was mine and I'm not giving her one more thing. And tell her to be afraid. Very, very afraid."

"I don't know about this," he said. "I thought we could work it out fairly, but—"

"We're going to the bank together, Scott. We're dividing the cash. I called Sal, the wealth management adviser. He put our funds in lockdown. You are free to consult an attorney, but that's on your dime. I'm not hiring an attorney and am willing to write this up, get your approval and file it, which will save us a ton of money. From now on, we keep track of every nickel. Decide what you want to do. You can make this neat and easy or difficult and expensive."

CHAPTER FIVE

Adele could feel the change in her sister, but she wasn't sure exactly what it meant. Justine, who had never called often, seemed to have put herself on a schedule, calling Adele at least two mornings a week. She reported only the most rudimentary information. "Scott and I have reached a settlement we can live with. The girls are adjusting with difficulty, but I have promised them that neither of us will abandon them, though we won't be exactly the kind of family we were. I'm writing up and filing the divorce myself with the help of a friend who is a divorce attorney."

There was a distant and controlled sound to Justine's voice that Adele had recognized from other times of trauma and uncertainty. When their mother was failing, when Olivia was having medical tests at age twelve for a possible heart condition, and now, as she was navigating a divorce. There was a deep, throaty sound to her voice, as if she was measuring each word.

"Do you have to get divorced?" Adele asked.

"I'm afraid so," Justine said. "How can I ever trust him again? He betrayed me. Now I am filled with doubt, unsure if this is the first time. I have to protect what I have left."

"But is your heart broken?" Adele asked.

After a moment she said, "In a million pieces. But I'm so angry at what Scott has done that I'm not sure it's for the love of him that I'm in pain. I think, God help me, it's the betrayal that hurts so much."

Adele had not seen Justine in weeks, not since that morning she'd driven to San Jose to tell her what she'd caught Scott doing in the pizza parlor. She felt almost as though she was going through a divorce herself, though it was not because she was terribly close to Scott and Justine. It had more to do with the fact that if she had ever believed in anyone's marriage, it had been theirs.

She went to her weight loss meetings, even adding an extra one every week. She was losing weight steadily, not rapidly. A couple of pounds a week. She amped up her walking, delighted in the fact that her thighs hurt. That held promise in her mind. Someone at one of her meetings said yoga was great for shaping and also would relieve stress, so Adele found a class where she was stretched and twisted like a pretzel to the point of farting. But she forced herself to go back anyway, still waiting for that feeling of spiritual renewal she'd heard so much about. Namaste.

In five weeks she had lost fifteen pounds and she noticed a difference; her jeans were loose. It was almost a religious experience. She couldn't remember the last time her clothes were loose. Summer was approaching, and she had fantasies of wearing a bathing suit for the first time in eight years.

Her other fantasy was getting a job. Any job. She had so much anxiety about not being qualified for anything, she had become discouraged after the first few applications. In one of her weight loss support groups it was suggested that she check into one of those reentry programs.

"My neighbor was widowed after eighteen years of being

a stay-at-home mom. It used to be called the displaced homemakers program for women who had been out of the workforce for a while and suddenly had no job or income or partner. But now I think it's called reentry and isn't just for women."

"I don't think I really qualify, unless they include displaced caretakers who were working on a master's degree."

"But do you have a job?" the woman countered. "Look 'em up and see if they can help."

Jake, who stopped by at least a couple of times a week, lately bringing things like salad or stir-fry, liked the idea. He pushed it as something to do, something to check off her list. When he was leaving, he remarked on how fantastic she was looking. It made her feel really proud that she'd finally started moving forward.

She looked up reentry programs and found several, all very much alike. They offered counseling, workshops on everything from résumé writing and interview coaching to escaping domestic violence. The websites always encouraged a visit to see which of their many programs would work best. But she called, only to have an energetic young woman tell her the same thing.

She was seeing Jake more often than before. She supposed it was for a combination of reasons. One, after her mother passed, he gave her some time to grieve before dropping in on her frequently. Two, he'd been with her when they sighted Scott and Cat, making out like rock stars in the restaurant, so they kind of shared the drama of that situation. Three, he was interested in her plans to remodel her old house, and he was a wealth of knowledge about that since he'd done it before. And four, she was not oblivious to the fact that Jake might harbor romantic feelings for her.

Adele dug around in her closet for something professional looking that actually fit her new body. Fortunately, black skirts and nice sweaters never went out of style. She went to the reentry program offices very early, feeling shy and trembly. There was something shameful about having accomplished so little in eight years even though what she had done had been unselfish and giving and had required fierce dedication. She knew she wasn't supposed to suffer shame. She also knew many caregivers who had put their lives on hold to care for a family member felt the same way. As though they should have been able to do everything.

No one was there, but the door was unlocked. She entered an office that was lined with chairs, a typical waiting room. A computer monitor sat on the only desk. There were a couple of doors, one of which opened abruptly. A woman who did not look entirely happy stood there. Her hair was salt and pepper, the coarse black threaded with steely gray, but her skin was young and creamy and Addie couldn't guess her age.

"Are you here for the part-time receptionist work?" she asked.

"Well, sure," Adele said. *It can't just be that easy*, she thought.

"Are you going to be able to handle that computer?" the woman asked.

Nonplussed, Addie went to the desk and turned on the computer. Up came the screen. It asked for the password.

"Everything you need should be in that notebook right there. I put it on the desk this morning, but at close of business make sure it gets put back in the bottom drawer. I changed the password and wrote it on the first page. In the bottom drawer are the intake forms and clipboards. It's not a real busy day, just a couple of small workshops. We'll have a few counselors coming in—their names should be on page five of the notebook. Go ahead and have a seat. There's coffee in the break room. Feel free to help yourself. I'm sorry. Forgive my manners. You are?"

"Adele Descaro. And you're...?"

"No one told you? Fran Costello." She finally smiled. "Also an Italian name. Maybe we're cousins. Just so you know, a lot of people wander in. Some will call ahead for appointments, and there's an appointment calendar on the computer. Acquaint yourself with the computer files and if you have any trouble, let me know and I can help. Hopefully it's all very self-explanatory." Then she smiled unexpectedly. "I'm really relieved you're here."

"You are?" Adele asked.

"Good grief, yes! I needed the help." She looked at her watch. "Take some time to get comfortable with the computer. People will start coming in soon. I have a few appointments and a couple of meetings. Felicity will be in later—she can conduct some interviews. She's a social worker."

Adele remembered the name. That was the woman she'd spoken to, the one who told her to come in and they'd decide together what she needed. "Is anyone going to interview me?" she asked.

"Nah, just do your best and ask for help if you need it. Check the appointments first—you'll want to direct people to the right place."

"Okay."

Adele opened the notebook, found the password on the first page and got the computer up and running. "I have a question," she said as Fran was trying to escape into what Addie assumed was her office.

"That was quick," she said, pausing in the doorway.

"What are the people who will be showing up today displaced *from*?"

"Any number of things—women who haven't been in the workforce in years and are suddenly widowed or divorced and just ready to get back to work and find their skills and experience rusty, maybe illness, a family member's illness, military men and women whose skills don't match the current job market or who have been displaced since active duty, homeless people trying to get on their feet, maybe drug addicts in recovery, migrants or refugees, anything that took them out of the job market for a while and they need help reconnecting. If you read any of the intake forms, please remember that information is confidential."

"Of course," she said.

"Don't give advice. Leave that to the counselors. Just be friendly, welcoming, ask them if they've been here before, if not give them an intake form."

"And should I answer the phone?"

"Of course! Answer Banyon Community College Reentry and Employment Counseling. I'll answer my own phone or if I can't, it'll go to voice mail. If a call comes for me on the general number, my extension is 515. Good?"

"Good," Adele said a little weakly.

Shortly, a few women began to trickle in and timidly approach her desk. Most of them looked the way she felt—scared and nervous and shy.

"Just fill out this intake form and then one of the counselors can help direct you to the best services," Adele would say.

They would invariably tell her what had happened to them.

"My husband left and I thought he'd come back but here I am. I'll have to work."

"My husband lost his job and can't find another, so I'm going to have to go back to work."

"I was a corporate administrative assistant until my first child came along, and I've been a stay-at-home mom, but—"

Then a woman came in who said, "My husband died and there's no money and I'm seventy. Do you think I can get a job at my age?"

Addie was frozen for a moment. Stricken. She'd been worried about her fifty-two-year-old sister, but seventy? People should be retired at seventy. But what if you couldn't?

"I'm not a counselor, just a receptionist," she said. "Go ahead and fill out this intake form and someone will help you."

A couple of counselors came in. She met Felicity who looked like she sounded, a slight, very young, freckled redhead. "Yay! Secretarial help!" she said as she greeted Adele.

Ross, an African American woman of about fifty, was not so chipper, which was somehow more appealing. "I'm Ross," she said. "I guess you drew the short straw. You getting along all right?"

"I hope so. It's so new," Adele said.

"Just ask for help if you need it."

At one point Fran stuck her head out of her office door and said, "Check your email. I set it up for you."

She looked. There was a message for her that said, "Will you please print this out for me? Fran." So she did, taking it to her. Then the printer displayed a low ink error message. Only slightly terrified of breaking something, Adele opened cupboards and pulled out drawers until she found a box of cartridges, and changed the depleted one. She printed a sample page and actually put a hand to her chest in ecstasy. She'd done it! When she was evaluated later to assess her job skills, she'd make sure to mention this.

It's a receptionist job, she reminded herself. *I was half-way to my master's! I may not be too handy with office work, but I'm way overeducated.*

A beautiful woman came into the office. She was dressed to the nines, too. She introduced herself as Carmon Fautz, an engineer. She was looking for work. Her husband, a doctor, had wanted her to stay home to raise their children, and now he was leaving her and she needed a job.

"But you're an engineer!" Adele said, forgetting herself.

"Have you ever heard of the half-life of engineers?" she asked. "The advances are rapid-fire, and a few years out of engineering put me way behind. I'm hoping for some new ideas. And I hope this is the place to find them."

"I hope so, too," Adele said. "Just fill out this intake form…"

From that point on, Adele greeted the most interesting people. A former minister, cook, factory worker, gym teacher, many office workers and many women who had not worked since high school. There was only one caregiver in the group—she had cared for her mother for three years. There were a couple of women who admitted to being homeless.

The one thing most of them had in common was having been abandoned by men, either when they died or divorced them. Adele had not thought it so common. But it took her thirty seconds to connect the dots—they were married to the breadwinner and when he died or left, their income was gone.

A couple of female military veterans came in, not together but separately. It was the same for them—they'd been married to the army and couldn't find civilian work.

Both told Adele they were thinking of reenlisting for that reason, though they couldn't bear the thought of going back to a war zone.

In the little time between clients, Adele organized the desk drawers and cleaned up the cupboards in the waiting room. She drank three cups of coffee and did the dishes in the small employee kitchen. When she went for her first cup of coffee, she ran into Ross.

"I hope you locked your purse in the drawer," Ross said while stirring cream into her coffee.

"I didn't know it could be locked."

"The keys are in the center drawer. Lock up your purse and put the keys in your pocket. These people are desperate. I make no judgment, but why tempt fate?"

"Thank you! I'll do that."

It was Ross who stopped by her desk later and said, "I'm going down to the supermarket deli for a salad. Can I get you anything?"

Adele had barely noticed that the whole morning had passed. It had been a rush and there were still people waiting. Felicity, Ross and Fran had all been seeing clients continually. Adele had stolen a look at the online appointment calendar to note that the names of the women they saw had filtered into other categories—various workshops, referrals, counseling sessions and the like.

She grabbed her purse and pulled out a ten. "Any kind of salad will do, no dressing. I'm on a diet."

"Will do," Ross said.

When Ross was back with their lunch, she offered to sit at Adele's desk for a while. "Go have your lunch in one of the empty conference rooms or the break room. I'll spell you for a while."

"What about your lunch?"

"I'll get mine when you're finished. Go now. I'm sure you crave a few minutes alone."

By midafternoon, Adele felt as though she'd managed that office for years. She was comfortable talking to the clients, responding to her email, doing whatever was requested. And she liked the people. A few more counselors and volunteers came in that afternoon—Jasmine, Carol, Marie, Susan and Paulette.

The office became even busier as people gathered for a couple of workshops. They were doing interview role-playing, critiquing résumés, looking through lists of employment opportunities. A couple of times it crossed Adele's mind that she had no idea what was coming for her. They might thank her kindly for helping out and tell her that their regular receptionist would be back in the morning. Should that be the case, she would ask if she could avail herself of the services offered in their program. Maybe they could help her get a receptionist or secretary position at Banyon Community College. After all, even though it had been a long time, she knew her way around a campus.

The women who had attended the workshops seemed so optimistic, so happy and animated. She could see that a little encouragement went a long way.

She did some typing for Felicity and Ross; she printed out a new workshop schedule that had been scrawled on a yellow pad by Jasmine. Glancing at the schedule online for the next day, she noticed several appointments, counseling sessions, new workshops and a counseling group session for women overcoming abusive relationships. There were also a couple of groups meeting in the evenings on Tuesday and Thursday, and if she was reading the schedule right, they closed for Friday afternoons.

She found herself wishing to sit in on these different

workshops and group sessions. Maybe if they let her come back as a client, she would. Any option they offered her, she would take it.

It was nearing four in the afternoon when the office began to thin out. And then Fran was standing in her office doorway again.

"Adele, would you please step into my office?"

"Of course," she said. She followed Fran inside and saw that Ross and Felicity were there, as well.

"Have a seat," Fran said. "I'm afraid there's been a mistake. I assumed you were the temp I called. About an hour ago I had a phone call from the agency apologizing for the fact that our temp hadn't shown up. Apparently she had a sick child and car trouble and a host of problems and didn't contact the agency to say that she wouldn't make it that day until after noon."

Adele was stunned. Of all the explanations she'd considered, that one had never come up. All she could say was "Oh."

"You didn't say anything," Fran said.

She looked at their faces. Ross looked a little angry, but then Ross seemed to look a little mad even when she was happy. Felicity looked confused. "I didn't know you were mistaken. I thought you were throwing me into a job to see what I could handle. I came here to get advice. On getting a job."

"You're a client?" Fran asked. "You were looking for a reentry program?"

She nodded.

"What's your story? Why have you been out of the workforce?"

She told them her story and why she had shown up there that morning.

"What about school?" Ross asked.

"I have a degree but no teaching certificate. I might be able to get a job in a private school. I haven't really looked. And I'm not sure my goals are the same… I'd like to say I'm going to change my course of study but the truth is, I'm almost out of money and…and I need to work."

"Would you like to come back tomorrow morning as a client? Fill out the intake form and sit with one of our counselors?"

"That would be very nice of you," she said.

"Well then—"

"Or I could come back and work as your secretary. Until your regular secretary comes back," she said boldly. "I would love to do that."

"Why?" Ross asked with a slight frown.

"It's a great job," Adele said. "I loved meeting the women. I didn't try to counsel them but I did talk with them. This is a very good place. I liked what I did today."

"But—" Fran began.

"It's the happiest I've been in a long time," Adele said. "I felt needed. I know it was a mistake, but it's the best mistake I've made in years. And if you need someone…"

"We usually do a background check, interview, check references…" Fran said.

"I'm not wanted or anything," Adele said. "I always pay my bills on time and haven't worked for anyone but my parents for eight years. My sister has always said I couldn't tell a lie if my life depended on it. Won't you think about it? I know it was an accident, but I think I did it well."

Fran seemed to be thinking this over. "Can you go back to your desk and give us a little time to discuss this?"

"Sure," she said. "I think I could do even better tomorrow. Really."

Adele sat impatiently at her desk, wishing she could be

part of the discussion happening in Fran's office. She had assumed Ross and Felicity were part of the management of this office; now she was sure.

She looked at her watch. Four ten. She got her phone out of her purse and turned it on to check her messages. There was only one text. I hope you're having a great day! Jake. It was four fifty before that door opened again. By now the office waiting area was empty, though there was one group session in progress in the back.

"Come on in, Adele," Fran said. "We talked it over. We need someone at that desk, and if you're willing to work for fifteen dollars an hour, we'd like to give you a try. Our receptionist isn't coming back, and the woman we hired to replace her didn't work out. But there's considerably more to do than those few office chores I gave you today."

Adele's smile was so big she thought her face might crack. "I'm pretty smart," she said. "And I'm not afraid of hard work."

"The receptionist has to double as the janitor," Ross said.

"My father was a janitor!" Adele shot back.

"I was kidding, kid. Except for the fact that we all pitch in to make sure the place is tidy. You know—wash your dishes, wipe out the sink, sweep up. You know—if you see a mess, clean up the mess. Right?"

"Right," she said. "I have a job?"

"You have a job. You fell into our laps and we fell into yours. Let's see if we can make this work. We'll get your paperwork done in the morning," Fran said with a smile.

"Thank you! Thank you so much!"

Maybe my luck is changing! she thought happily.

Adele wanted to tell someone, of course. Not Justine. What would Justine say? She wouldn't compliment Adele's cleverness. She'd probably warn her to do extra careful work to keep the job. Not Beverly; Beverly would want to bring her a cake. She texted Jake. Have you eaten yet?

Not yet.

Can you come to dinner? Stir-fry? Chicken.

Love to, what time?

Seven?

I'll be there.

She hurried home to chop her vegetables and set the table. She checked her makeup to be sure it was fresh, brushed her teeth and reapplied her lipstick. She wasn't trying to impress Jake so much as look like it wasn't a total accident they wanted to keep her. Then she decided on a sip of wine as she waited for him, and of course that first sip contradicted her toothpaste and made her pucker. She made the rice and had her chicken and vegetables ready to go. Finally, she heard the doorbell.

She threw open the door and there he stood, holding flowers. Jake had stopped bringing her food, so intent was she on her new eating program.

"You will never believe what happened! I have a job!"

"Well, that was fast."

She poured him a glass of wine and told him every detail of how it happened, from beginning to end, while she began to feed the chicken and vegetables into the wok. She explained how she wasn't sure why she just answered yes when Fran asked if she was there for the job. "I guess

I was there to get a job after all." And she told him all the possibilities she had thought might come to pass, like they might say, *Good, now that we know what you can do, let's look at the job openings.* "It doesn't work that way, I guess. But I didn't know that." She told him how much she enjoyed talking to the women, finding that they were all so different from her and yet so much the same. "They've all been held captive, of their own free will, of course, and yet when set free, they are lost. It didn't really matter if they were homemakers, moms, caregivers, whatever— suddenly they need work and have nowhere to turn. They all looked better when they were leaving—if not entirely joyous at least relieved. It's an amazing place, this office, this program." And in the end, when they explained to her it had all been a misunderstanding, she practically begged for the job. "And it wasn't because I so need a job. At least not totally. I really wanted to stay there. I wanted to watch what was going to happen next. I don't have any idea what their success rate is, but some of those women who were feeling so scared and hopeless are going to get work and get on with their lives."

"Like you," he said.

"Like me!"

While they ate, she told him about some of the women, not using any names or physical descriptions, of course. But she did describe some of their problems. "Imagine finding yourself broke and in need at the age of seventy! I can't wait to see how her story turns out. That's a real wake-up call. It really got me thinking—my mother could have been left with no resources and what would we have done?"

"Your sister would have stepped up…"

"My sister. I wonder if she even knows how lucky she is. What Scott has done to her is terrible, but she has a job."

"A job you said is in peril," Jake reminded her.

"I'd better check in with her tonight. How's your stir-fry?" she asked.

Jake put down his fork. "It's very good. Adele, you look wonderful, you know. I'm sorry if I haven't said so enough."

"I have a long way to go," she said.

"You'll do what you want, but I think you look wonderful. I thought you looked wonderful before."

"And better now?" she asked.

"Addie, I have a lot of admiration for anyone who works at being their best, but I've always thought you were beautiful."

"I'm going to have to get up very early to get my walk in and make it to work on time," she said, as if she hadn't heard him.

But she had heard him.

"Luckily the sun is coming up earlier, but the beach is still foggy early in the morning. And will be till ten or later. You be careful," he said.

"I'll be careful," she said. "But we don't have trouble around here."

"Mostly nuisance stuff. But I wouldn't want you to be the first one with real trouble."

"Nothing can scare me off my program," she said. "Everything about it feels better. And did I mention I have a job?" She couldn't stop smiling.

CHAPTER SIX

Justine knew work could be a beacon, a white light. The right kind of work even more so. Just the sound of Addie's voice was magical when she called to say she had a job. She sounded so much more filled with life than she had in years. As her sister had been consumed with responsibility, monotony and drudgery, Justine had wondered if Addie would ever break free from her isolation and come to life.

Such could be the plight of the caregiver. You wanted to do it because you loved the patient and felt personally responsible, but there was no harder work. And at the end of the day you had succeeded only when things weren't worse.

Without their mother at the house to check on, Justine hadn't seen her sister in weeks. They'd talked every couple of days, mostly so Justine could keep Addie apprised of the divorce situation. Her lawyer had filed, Scott had signed the settlement agreement and it could be over in as little as two more weeks. The girls were still very upset but they were hanging in there, and school would be out soon. They both had summer jobs, which would keep them busy and might help them rein in their emotions.

She enrolled them in counseling, which took a great

deal of time. They needed individual sessions—they were too different to attend together and their coping methods would not be anything alike. Amber went to the counselor on Mondays and Olivia on Thursdays.

Tonight Scott was planning to be home to make dinner for the girls so Justine decided to be absent. She didn't want to run into any neighbors so she went to Chen's since it wasn't too far from home. She ordered a glass of wine and was studying the menu, not feeling the least hungry when she heard a familiar voice.

"Justine?"

She looked up into the warm brown eyes of Logan Danner. She was so surprised her mouth hung open. "It's you," she said.

"It's me," he said with a smile. "I never expected to see you here but I'm glad I ran into you. I've been wondering how you're getting along."

"You could have called," she said.

"I would have, eventually. Once it was pretty obvious you were no longer a client. While you still might want my services, it's strictly professional."

"Will you sit down?" she said. "Let me buy you a beer? And you can tell me what you're doing around here."

He slid into the booth across from her. "I was in court today. Here in San Jose, testifying on behalf of a client." The waitress approached him and asked him if he wanted beer, and he gave her a nod and thanked her. "I guess you can tell this is a favorite place of mine."

"Big fan of Chinese cuisine, are you?"

"I like it, yeah. But one of the good things about this place is that at certain times of the day there's hardly anyone here. If a potential client isn't too far away, this is one of the places I frequent to meet them. I have a partner, Georgianna, who lives in Santa Rosa. We share an office in San Francisco, but we're only there a couple of days a week. Now, tell me about you. Will it be a divorce?"

"Absolutely. It's not what I want, but it has to be."

"Are you sure? People manage to work out all sorts of things."

"I thought about it, a lot. I thought about it for the sake of my girls, but in the end I'm not sure what I'd be teaching them by doing that. I look back over almost thirty years with the man, and I'm wondering if this is the first time. I can't live with a man who lies and cheats. Who could?"

"People have all kinds of arrangements..."

"I think Scott stayed for my income. He likes to buy things like golf clubs, scuba gear, bikes. He'd been talking about buying a sailboat. He would have stayed with me another couple of years for that sailboat."

"Wasn't he bored?" Logan asked.

"He's been very active," she said with a short, disdainful laugh.

"Is he a good father?"

"He's a very good father. I think we're both good parents. That's my biggest concern. Can we be good parents as divorced parents? Because I didn't realize how selfish Scott is. He's the fun guy. If I had to work late, he'd get a neighbor or babysitter to stay with the kids so he could play ball or bowl. He took very good care of the girls, but now I can see he always did the bare minimum. His free time was carefully guarded. And the girls don't need him like they did. In a year and a half Amber will be in college."

"Did I mention I'm divorced?" Logan asked. "No kids, though. And I've been a divorce spectator a lot. Too much. Here's what happens—the wronged party is very hurt and angry. There's no help for it—getting over that takes as long as it takes. Some people move on fairly quickly while others pick at it like a hangnail. I have a buddy who's been divorced for two years, and his eyes still tear up when he talks about it."

"Two years?" she asked.

"Over two years, actually. I have another friend who had a new woman in three weeks. That didn't work out very well, but he wasn't depressed for two years and sometimes he had trouble remembering which woman he was mad at."

"What about you?" she asked.

"My situation was unique," he said.

"Aren't they all?" she countered.

"Not as unique as this one. We hadn't been married all that long—just a few years—and we were always fighting. We never fought before we got married. She finally told me she wanted a divorce because she just wasn't happy. Because she's not into men. Your mouth is standing open... That's right—she's playing on the other team. She really loved me, she said. And she thought she could just make it work since we were such good friends, agreed on so much, et cetera. But I just didn't do it for her. Quite literally."

"Ouch."

"It hurt but we're back to being friends. In fact, she's my sister's best friend. She has a partner now and I am happy for her, even if it's a little awkward at times."

In spite of herself, Justine laughed. "Thanksgiving must be a hoot at your house."

"Life in general is a comedy. Here's where I was headed. This will be hard for you for a while, especially with you worrying about your kids and how they're adjusting. But they will be okay. Know how I know this? Because fifty percent of married couples divorce, the kids are always upset and the kids always survive. It might not be their first choice, but they adjust and ultimately get on with their lives. A lot of that depends on how you and your husband deal with the parenting.

"As for you," he went on. "At some point you'll start to look at what you have as opposed to what you've lost. I don't know what that's going to be—maybe freedom. Maybe an opportunity you didn't have before. Maybe a man who really appreciates you. Just don't rush that one, okay? Maybe, since you were always the breadwinner, it's financial independence. But your list will grow. You're a beautiful, smart, successful woman. Your husband is hooking up with a woman with a bad track record—not good at relationships, not good with money. Big mistake, Scott. She has none of the things you have to offer. She must be making him feel like a king."

She just stared at him. "And you said you're not a counselor."

"I'm forty-eight and single. My partner, Georgie—she's married to a firefighter and they have three kids and they're still crazy in love. I envy the hell out of them. If they ever break up, I might kill myself from disappointment. I'm obviously no genius when it comes to relationships. If I have any experience at all, it's from watching other people mess up. Now tell me something, Justine. How are you eating? Sleeping?"

She gave a helpless shrug. "Not great. Right now all I want is to wake up in the morning and have my cheating husband *not* be the first thing I think about."

"We're going to eat. Did anything on that menu look good to you?" he asked.

She just shook her head. In the end he ordered for both of them: egg drop soup, lo mein, beef and broccoli, chicken and vegetables. "We'll share," he said.

While they were waiting for their dinner he asked, "Who's getting you through this?"

"A girlfriend who is also processing the divorce. She wrote it up and filed for me. And you."

"That's not enough! You might want to call on a few more friends, Justine. They say this also takes a village."

Adele was up at six, excited for her day. She walked for an hour, the sun barely lighting the day through the fog. It was gloomy on the beach but not in her heart—she felt lucky and happy. She discovered other people on the beach, walking dogs or jogging or strolling, all, she assumed, getting in their exercise before work.

She felt as though she'd finally entered the grown-up world.

She made her lunch, showered and got ready for work. Given the way she'd spent the last several years, she didn't have much by way of office clothing. On the weekend she'd do a little shopping for her new life.

She was so eager, she was the first to arrive and the door was locked. She had to wait for Fran whose words of greeting were, "Good morning! I'll get you your own key today."

"Thanks. I was a little excited, I guess."

She fired up the computer, then put her lunch away in their refrigerator. She checked the cupboards to take stock of the supplies—office supplies, trash bags, glass cleaner and so on. With a large plastic bag in hand, she went around to the offices and conference rooms and collected trash. The kitchen looked pretty clean, but she hit it with some cleaner anyway to give it sparkle. Then she sat at her desk and read through the day's schedule. There were appointments and workshops and a group counseling session. She checked her forms and clipboards, and it wasn't long before someone came through the door.

"Good morning!" she said cheerfully. "How can I help you?"

And so the stories began. Women coping with death, divorce, abandonment, escape—so many fearful dead ends for women who had been out of the workforce for more than a couple of years. In her first official day on the job, she greeted thirty-two women between the ages of twenty and sixty-eight. Plus she began to learn that there was more to the reentry program than filling out an intake form. There was also fund-raising and grant writing going on because the stipends allotted from the county and state couldn't begin to cover the expenses of running an office of social workers. And there was a great deal of networking to do, connected with businesses that would take on a displaced individual who was starting over. Just before noon, Fran left for a professional businesswomen's luncheon where she would be the keynote speaker.

Adele desperately wanted to hear her speech. She found herself mesmerized even when Fran asked her to print something out.

After lunch she found Ross sorting through a stack of folders, envelopes and loose pages. Addie asked if there was anything she could do to help.

"I'm trying to organize these client files so they can be put in some order."

"Do they have to be filed?"

"And scanned so they can be saved. We're trying to go paperless. By now you've noticed we don't have enough space."

"How about I scan, file and save them to the cloud?"

Ross just looked at her, a little nonplussed. "For someone who hasn't been in the workforce in eight years, you seem to really know your way around an office."

"The computer and social media was just about my only connection to the outside world. At least my most dominant, since I could check in on the computer without leaving the house. I used to scan and file my mother's medical records and insurance papers. The computer was my lifeline."

Ross just pushed the piles toward Addie.

She took them eagerly. "What's your deadline on this project?"

"You have a front office to maintain. My deadline is whenever you can get it done. Thank you. This helps tremendously since I'm also in the middle of writing a grant proposal."

"I'd like to learn more about that," Addie said.

"You can count on it," Ross said with a smile.

At the end of the day Addie went home, exhilarated. She had so much to look forward to.

She went to a weight loss group meeting that night. She was going to have to switch over to evenings, since she'd be working during the day. She introduced herself, weighed in, her name was pulled up on the laptop and the group leader said, "Adele, you're down nineteen and three-quarter pounds! Congratulations."

I'm going shopping this weekend, she thought in a fever of excitement. *I always hated shopping, but this feels brand-new.*

That night she stood in front of her mirror in her underwear and turned this way and that. She was noticeably slimmer than she'd been in over eight years, trimmer than she had been even before she got pregnant. Then that thing that had been lurking in the back of her mind surfaced. She had had zero contact with Hadley. He didn't know about the baby, never sought her out to ask, just walked away without looking back after telling her he loved her. After telling her they'd start over together.

She intended to get some closure on that.

Justine closed her bedroom door. Olivia was practicing her guitar in her room; Amber was on the phone in her room. Homework was finished, dishes were done. Scott decided he was going out for a couple of hours. She couldn't wait until they were no longer sleeping in the same house. She found it incredibly annoying that Scott never asked if she had any plans. They barely spoke. She got the impression he'd go on like this forever.

She took a sip of her wine. She found a number in her directory, dialed and a man answered. "This is Logan," he said.

"It's Justine Somersby. I'm sorry to bother you," she said. "Do you have a minute?"

"Sure. Of course. Let me turn this TV down."

"If you're busy—"

"It's fine. I'm not working tonight. Nothing going on here."

"I wonder if I can use you for a sounding board," she said. "I've been thinking a lot about your advice. It's that business of focusing on what I have instead of what I've lost. Once the divorce is final, we will have divided our retirement funds. Also, there's a little savings. You mentioned looking for opportunities. There are a couple of things that interest me. But they're risky."

"Well now," he said, a little humor in his voice. "Looking for someone to run them by?"

"Yes, exactly. But first, our settlement so far. Scott will get half. And there's the house, which has a healthy equity.

The only things that are untouchable are the college funds. We'll remain co-owners of the house, each paying half the mortgage. And there's alimony. I've agreed to pay Scott half of what I earn for five years."

"I know you're going to get to the risky part pretty soon…"

"I'm thinking of starting a private practice. A neighborhood law practice. I would make very little money for at least the first couple of years, but I can live off my savings."

He was quiet for a moment. "Assuming you're a good lawyer, that doesn't sound all that risky. Sounds like you'd just have to budget carefully for a while."

"Scott wouldn't be getting much alimony."

"Awww… Didn't you say he has a degree? Is there some reason he can't get a job?"

"Yes, they don't need a stay-at-home parent anymore. They're self-sufficient. They've been in school the last ten years! Not that they haven't been in need of available parents, but I've participated in that almost as much as Scott. And yet…" Her voice trailed away.

"Justine…?"

"Sorry," she said, sniffing.

"Okay, take your time. Are you breaking down?"

"No! No! It's just that… I don't know how to do it, Logan. Even though I was doing it, I wasn't doing it alone. There was always one more adult on the team. Backup, you know?"

"I know," he said. "And there's a loud, tearing sound when they rip themselves out of your life. It's the betrayal, Justine. You have to take it slow. One step at a time. It's easier when you have food and sleep to keep you going."

"I know," she said.

"So, the divorce diet. How much have you lost?"

"Oh, just eight pounds," she said. "I can spare it. But I'm not used to this confusion... I walk into the grocery store and don't know where things are even though I've been shopping there for years. I don't know what to buy. No one has given me a list. And I've changed all my credit cards, but I'm still popping up on Scott's accounts or his name is still haunting mine. I'm used to being much more organized. I've always had a memory like a steel trap. Lately my mind is mush."

"It doesn't help when a vision of your husband with another woman pops into your mind. What a thought, huh?"

"You sound like you can relate," she said.

"Yeah, try to imagine the visions I was getting. That was a long time ago now. Listen, it's a process. I remember mailing my tax return to my mother. That was pretty embarrassing, but I regained my clear thinking and common sense over time."

"I'm so angry," she whispered.

"Of course you are," he said. "Hell, I'm angry for you! Sometimes talking about it helps."

"I'm leaning on you. I'm sorry," she said.

"Don't apologize. Tell me about this fantasy practice."

She leaned back against her pillows. "In my mind there are a variety of clients with varying issues. Property settlement, estate issues, divorce, lawsuits, business sales or closures. I think I could consult with local tech firms I've worked with in the past. It would be so refreshing to help people with things that will make their lives better. Adoption. Prenups. Partnership agreements. Family trusts. Charitable foundations. The neighborhood law office." She took a sip of her wine. "I could do other things, even that of a criminal nature. Arrests, DUI, custodial interference. Then there's personal injury claims. It takes a while to build a practice, but there's no shortage of need for legal services."

"Wow. Well, Georgie and I retired from the police department at the same time. We each had twenty-five years in, retired as lieutenants and went together to an existing PI firm. We had worked together as detectives for ten years, so moving to the same PI firm as a team worked for us. What's your first step? Look for space?"

"I suppose," she said. "I'm also looking at existing practices, just to get a feel for things. Small legal practices. Most that I've seen so far specialize in either personal injury or divorce or medical malpractice." She took another sip. "I'd like an office in an old building that maybe was built out of a restored office or house. There should be a kitchen. Best case scenario there would be a fireplace. That would add comfort on those cold, foggy days from November to April. I like old houses and buildings but then, why wouldn't I—I grew up in Half Moon Bay, one of the oldest towns on the coast."

"So, you've come to terms with your marriage being over?" he asked.

"I'm not done grieving, but I don't want that marriage anymore. The more I think about the last ten years, the more I suspect this woman is merely the most recent affair. Scott had a lot of time on his hands. He could afford to be bored and restless."

"If Scott has to go to work, it could be the best thing that ever happened to him," Logan said.

"You're right. He's only fifty-two, and what he'll get in a settlement and alimony won't keep him through old age. Maybe he thinks his new woman will support him."

"Not if the woman owns the kayak shack," Logan said. "Does any part of your fantasy involve things other than work? Your kids will be in college before you know it. What will you do for fun?"

"Funny you should ask. I've been thinking a lot about that because for the last twenty years I've been working too hard. I was well compensated. I have no regrets. But I wouldn't mind a little leisure time and entertainment. I rarely saw a movie because the only things Scott wanted to see either had a gun or a ball in it. The girls and I went to a few chick flicks, but it was rare. I love movies. There just never seemed to be any time. I spent weekends catching up on chores and work from the office."

"Building a law practice is not going to be a vacation, but if you want to succeed, you have to find time to do the things you like. What do you like?"

"I like to spend an entire afternoon on the couch or the chaise outside, reading. I like to garden. That takes commitment, but I've done it before. Long ago, sure. I like concerts..."

"There's live music in the parks everywhere," he said. "San Francisco has some great outdoor music all over the place."

"You do that?" she asked.

"I've been known to. In fact, I'm looking at a place in Carmel. Small, grossly expensive, old, close to the water. The only downside is tourists. Billions of them."

"Why Carmel?"

"Georgie is in Santa Rosa, north of the city, so I'm determined to find something south. I've looked all over the towns below San Francisco. When we get a case, I'll work mostly in the south and she'll do fieldwork north of the city. We see each other in the office or work together a couple of days a week. Otherwise we're in touch via phone or computer. And I like Carmel. Except, you know, all the tourists… What about you?"

"I'll stay where I am until I figure out where I'm going to work. And I'm not going to figure that out until the divorce is final. Scott and I might take turns staying with the girls. I mean, we might each get something small and efficient, then take turns in the big house with the kids. That could work, couldn't it?"

"Depends on what kind of closure you need."

"I hadn't thought of that," she said. "Closure. That's kind of hard if you have to keep seeing each other, sharing space even if you're not both there are the same time."

"Exactly," he said. "It could work as a good transition…"

"Hmm, yes." And then she thought, *transition, closure, focusing on what you have, not what you lost, the next challenge*… His common sense about divorce was very helpful. "Really, Logan, I can't thank you enough."

"Any time, Justine. Once you're in your next life, we'll get together for a drink or something. I know you're going to have big things to report. But meanwhile, you have my number. And I have yours."

Every morning Adele rose early, took her walk, then headed to Banyon Community College with great enthusiasm. She listened raptly to every client coming in the door, and if they didn't volunteer much, she would take a glance at their intake sheet to see if she could piece together their needs or purpose, even though that wasn't really her job.

She began to see repeat clients and welcomed them by name. "Hi, Alexandra. How's your mom?" Alexandra was a recovering agoraphobic whose mother had MS and was recently admitted to a nursing home.

"Hey there, Leslie. Any news on your college admission?" Leslie, formerly military and recently homeless, had just applied to community college. She also now had a modest place to live in a community devoted to homeless veterans.

"Rosalee, you look fantastic!" She was dressed in business attire she'd gotten from a charity that specialized in office appropriate hand-me-downs for women in need of such clothing.

"Today is my interview dress rehearsal," Rosalee said, smiling.

After ten days on the job, Addie felt as if her life had become an adventure. She was getting to know the clients, employees and volunteers, looking forward to each day's lunch hour as the time she spent getting to know her new friends. Fran was divorced and the mother of teenagers. Her ex-husband moved home to his native New Jersey and rarely saw his son and daughter. Addie didn't know why she was surprised, but she was pleased that Fran had a boyfriend. He was a cop, also divorced, and she talked about him with great pride, especially when mentioning how good he was with his kids as well as hers. Ross had an ex-husband and a couple of grown kids; she had raised them primarily on her own, finishing her college degree after they were born. But Felicity took the cake. She was thirty-five, slight of build and kind of fragile looking but brighter than sunshine. She was a social worker and had been with the center for five years. Adele learned that Felicity, so bubbly and happy and positive, had lost her young husband and five-year-old son in a small plane crash six years ago. Ross had whispered this to Adele. It caused Adele to look at Felicity with caution, wondering how one survived something like that, wondering what was buried beneath the surface.

Adele started her job ten days ago, making do with clothes she already had but they were hanging off her frame, so she went to the mall for some new, smaller outfits. Walking and the routine of working had even more of a slimming effect, and while she noticed it in the feel of her clothes, there were just so many things on her mind, she didn't know which change to give all the credit to. Everything in her life was different. She was working, she had friends, she'd lost weight, she was exercising and feeling healthier and her life, all of it, felt brand-new.

She was thinking about how good it felt to take control of her life when Justine walked into her office unannounced.

"Hi," she said, walking right up to the desk.

"Justine! What are you doing here?" Adele asked, standing.

"I wanted to see this for myself," she said, smiling. "You, working in an office." Then she looked Adele up and down. "My God! Look at you!" She kept her volume down but her enthusiasm was evident. "Oh my God, you said you lost a few pounds! I think you lost fifty! You look fabulous!"

"Thanks," she said. But then she took a closer look at Justine. Her sister was wasting away. "You've lost a little weight…"

"Not too much," she said, shaking her head. "You know. The famous divorce diet. I could spare it."

Really, she couldn't. Justine was thin as a whip before learning of Scott's affair. Learning of it because Adele told her.

"Let me tell my boss I'm breaking for lunch. This may take a few minutes. I have to find someone to man the desk."

"No worries, Addie. We don't have to have lunch. I just wanted to stop by and say hello. I'll just let you get back to work and—"

"No, we're going to take lunch. It's okay. I eat in every day so this is a good idea. One minute."

Rather than bothering Fran, she went to Ross. "My sister dropped by just to see me working, and I'd like to take her to lunch. She's going through a divorce, and she looks like she's wasting away. Can you cover me for an hour?"

Ross made a face, but not because she was put upon. "I gained thirty pounds with my divorce. See? I told you life is not fair."

"I promise to be back in an hour or less."

"You take your time, Adele. You've been putting in some long days, helping me."

When she went back to the reception area, Justine was gone. She grabbed her purse out of the desk drawer and stepped outside to find her sister waiting in the hall. With tears in her eyes. Addie had never witnessed that before. "There you are! I was half afraid you'd bolted! What on earth is the matter?"

"I'm sorry," Justine said. "I'm a little overwhelmed by how wonderful you look!" She dug around in her handbag for a nonexistent tissue. Addie finally gave her one. "That's the price I pay for not coming to see you in so long."

"We were both so busy," Addie said. "Come on. Let me feed you."

"I'm really not that hungry," Justine said.

"Are you going to let a divorce kill you? You have to eat!"

"It turns out you don't have to eat very much," she said. "But a quiet place to talk would be nice."

CHAPTER SEVEN

Addie directed them to a nearby pub. It was just off campus, so it was crowded.

"I think it's just stress," Justine said, referring to her weight loss. "I've been running myself ragged, getting everything in order for the divorce, taking the girls to counseling and just trying to be there for them, anticipating one or both having a crisis."

"And they're okay?" Addie asked.

"We've had a few emotional moments but they're largely stable. It's as if nothing is happening because to them it doesn't feel as if much has changed."

"How can that be?"

"Well, Scott and I have an oath not to say anything terrible about each other. They know Scott is in love with another woman, even though he won't admit it. All he will admit to is that they have a lot in common and they enjoy the same things, that they get along and have become very close."

"Come on! You don't walk away from a thirty-year marriage and two kids because you have a new friend! Do the girls think you accept this?" Adele asked.

"No," she said. "No, they know how much this hurts me. But I've told them they will always have two parents. We will both do our best to be good parents in spite of the fact that we're not going to be married."

"I can't imagine," Adele said. "What about *her*?"

"The woman?" Justine asked. "That's where I draw the line. I'm not welcoming her into my family. I might have no control, but... I don't want her around my kids if I can help it. I don't know how she landed Scott. I don't know if he's just an idiot or if she's amazingly manipulative. It doesn't matter, does it? He is throwing away everything we've built for a woman with a failing business, no assets and a bad track record in relationships. So, I made a term of divorce that we'll split the equity in the house if she never sets foot in it. Never, ever. If she does, he relinquishes his half of the equity. He didn't contest it. He signed off on our settlement."

"How will you know?" Addie asked.

Justine smiled. "Cameras. In the most unusual places. I don't trust him the smallest bit. He will lose the house."

Adele was quiet for a moment. "Let's order some lunch. Look at your menu."

Justine opened it and gave it a glance. "I'm not all that hungry..."

"But you have to eat something. You're just too thin right now. For the first time in my life, I'm worried about you."

"I'll be fine," she said. Justine found it impossible to say that food just didn't agree with her, that she was having trouble keeping it down. Admitting that made her feel weak. "Maybe a little soup or something," she said.

"Are you just not eating?" Addie asked. "I understand, you've been through a terrible shock, but you can't let yourself get sick. You have to eat. I have to see you eat."

"I'll eat," Justine said.

"Scott should have trouble eating," Adele said. "The bastard."

Justine studied the menu. "Scott is gone," Justine said. "I don't know the man who has taken his place. This one is emotionally vacant, except when he talks about just wanting to be happy. I thought he was happy. I supported his desire to indulge his outdoorsy pastimes, and he encouraged and praised my work. Then something happened, but it happened so slowly I didn't see it. I thought we'd merged into a new kind of love, one not pressured by constant need and desperate passion. And that was okay with me, as long as I had my best friend and confidant and partner. And some affection—I needed that. Some touching and holding. That Scott needed it a lot less than he used to never concerned me." She sighed deeply. "I've been going through our banking records. The cheating has been going on a while." The waitress came to the table. "I'll have a cup of chicken tortilla soup," Justine said.

"Would you like bread with that?" the waitress asked.

"No," Justine said. "Thank you."

"Bring her bread," Addie said. "For me, can you please bring me a lettuce, tomato and avocado salad with a scoop of tuna salad or grilled chicken strips? No bread. A little ranch dressing on the side. And a diet soda. Justine, do you want something to drink?"

"The same. Diet cola."

"Talk to me," Adele said once the waitress left. "Tell me where your head is."

"We've talked every few days for weeks," Justine said.

"Yeah, but I didn't see you. Clearly we've been skimming the surface in our talks. Is it completely over with Scott? Is there no hope?"

"Addie, I'm afraid to try again, and Scott doesn't want

to. I've asked him countless times. He thinks this might be for the best. He wants to divide the assets and part ways. We haven't actually separated because he claims to have nowhere to go and I don't know what I'm going to do next— I'm thinking about what I want. We're going to share the house and parenting duties for a few more weeks, at least. It will take some scheduling finesse. And a spine of steel..." Justine dabbed at her mouth, though she hadn't been eating. "At first I thought maybe I could save the marriage if he at least wanted to, but then I looked at the bank statements. He's been taking hundreds and hundreds of dollars out of a debit machine every month. For what? Cash at the hotel? Dinner in a nice restaurant? Her car payments or something else she needed? I'd ask him, but there's no chance I'll get a straight honest answer. Hundreds, Addie. Thousands! Small withdrawls every two or three days for a couple of years. He's been lying and cheating and creating a narrative in which it's my fault for putting in long hours. That's probably the most painful thing. I'm hearing from friends, you know. Friends who have talked to Scott. He's telling a story of a cold, overly busy, neglectful wife who put her career first, didn't participate in family activities, ignored him. I'm so angry with him I want to kill him. He's used me and played the field. I don't know what he sees in her." Their drinks came. Justine lifted hers. "But she has kayaks. You know how Scott loves toys."

"And activities," Addie said.

"He's telling everyone our split is my fault, but he knew exactly what he wanted. Cash. He didn't ask for half the pictures or books or special things we'd gotten as wedding gifts. Just money. Money and half the value of the house."

"What are you going to do?"

"What I said I would do from the start—give him what

he wants right up to half. He liked the zeroes. There are a few caveats—as long as we're joint tenants, he has to pay his half of the mortgage or lose his half of the house. He signed off. I'll be legally divorced in a matter of weeks. In fact, any minute. And then he's not getting another thing from me, not even a smile."

Their lunches arrived. Addie buttered some bread and slid it over to Justine. She cut up her tomato and avocado slices, dipped her fork in the dressing and then stabbed a bit of chicken.

Justine smiled. "You look amazing," she said. "Addie, I've neglected you. We were both raised as only children, but you hung in there with Mom through the dark years, when she barely communicated."

"I knew what she was communicating," Addie said. "Sort of. Most of the time."

"What are you doing this weekend?"

"Nothing special. I usually get my meals ready for the week, shop for food, exercise a lot, hit a meeting at my weight loss support group…"

"Let me take you shopping. I'll ask the girls if either of them wants to go along. We can have lunch, too."

"First you have to tell me something," Addie said. "I need to know how you're really feeling."

"I told you already," Justine said. "There isn't any more."

"But of course there's more because underneath you're not so much in control as it appears on the surface. I want to know. I want to hear. Maybe you need real counseling, not just that sham of a marriage counselor who Scott was so successful in lying to. I won't know how to help you unless you're completely honest with me. I see women all day long who have been abandoned or divorced or abused and have barely escaped, and I can't ask them. I look at them and know they're covering up an enormous mound of toxic, terrifying feelings, but I'm not a counselor and I can't ask. I know what you're doing. I want to know what you're feeling."

Justine took a slow sip of soup from her spoon. She thought for a moment, dabbed her lips and said, "I'm not withholding from you, Addie. Nor being untrusting of you. It's just that I'm so careful about what I let myself feel because I'm afraid I might crack. And if I crack, I'm might collapse and never get up again. I have to be strong for my girls, for my ability to support us. What I feel is terror. I don't think I've ever felt so alone. I can't let the girls see how afraid I am. All those years I asked Scott for his opinion on something or asked a favor, like would he mind stopping at the bank, or called him from work to ask him what he felt like for dinner, or just called him to ask if he heard some news item and talked to him for five or ten minutes. He draws me as job obsessed and cold, yet we texted, talked and emailed each other all day long." She pulled out her phone and scrolled through her texts.

Hey babe, I pulled out that pork loin to thaw. Does that sound good?

Sounds delicious.

I'll stick it in the crock pot if you'll bring home some deli potato salad.

Sure, and I'll find something green. Love you.

Love you!

Sweetheart, I'm running a little late and won't get home till about seven. Tell the girls we'll work on homework then if they need help.

Sounds like pizza night. Will that work for you?

Perfect. I'll pick it up on the way home if you'll order it.

Okay. And I have some pants at the cleaners if today is a good day to run by there.

I will. Anything else?

Just that I love you.

Love you back.

Addie read only a few. All were friendly, cooperative, affectionate.

"That's the man who said he hasn't really loved me in a long time," Justine said. "I never saw it coming. I might as well have been hit by a train. Can you see why I'm afraid to feel much? Afraid to let myself cry? I've never in my life been lied to so thoroughly. So successfully."

Addie handed back the phone. "I get it," she said. "We're going to get through this, together."

Adele found the dichotomy of Justine's strength plus her vulnerability completely disarming. Her sister, the epitome of power and grace, had been reduced to an extremely thin woman consumed by pain. It felt, at the moment, they had only each other, yet they really didn't know each other at all. They'd been raised in the same house in different eras.

The recent turn of events demonstrated they weren't really familiar with each other's private lives at all. Their relationship was like that of neighbors who were civil and polite while barely scratching the surface.

Adele was a little late getting back to the office. Nothing was said about the time. Ross actually smiled as Adele entered the office. The woman's resting expression was usually anything but cheerful. Ross asked her if she had a nice lunch, then went back to her office. For the duration of the afternoon, Adele was a little distracted.

At five o'clock, when Adele was locking the desk drawers and turning off her computer, Ross stuck her head out of the door that led to the offices and meeting rooms.

"Adele, can you come to my office for a minute?"

It was more request than question. She left her purse and followed her.

Ross sat behind her desk. "I'm sorry I overstayed my lunch," Adele said preemptively. "I promise I won't let it happen again. It was kind of a special circumstance. I—"

"No problem, Adele. You've barely taken a lunch since you started. But I saw your sister, briefly, and you've been a little off since you got back. Is everything all right?"

Adele was temporarily struck silent.

"You've been very quiet. I can usually hear your chatter with the clients…"

"I'm sorry! I can keep it down! I think I just feel so compelled to reach out to each one of them and—"

"Adele! Stop! I'm not complaining or scolding you! I want to know if you're all right!"

She was confused. "Me?"

Ross sighed heavily and folded her hands atop her desk. "You told me your sister was going through a hard time. The divorce. I saw her. She looked very thin and had dark circles under her eyes. You took an extra long lunch break, which is not like you at all. And you've been very quiet all afternoon. I'm not upset with you. I want to know if you're all right."

It wasn't the first time Adele had been asked if she was all right. Many people did after her mother passed. When she started losing weight, it was noticed and again, a few people asked after her health and well-being. But that Ross, who she'd known for such a short time, would ask, left her feeling humbled. Ross, who had to listen to the troubles of displaced women all day! Shouldn't she be low on energy and not have any to spare for her now?

Adele felt a tear run down her cheek. "No. I'm not really okay. My sister is having such a hard time and I'm useless!"

Ross frowned. "Now, of course you're not useless. Tell me what's going on, then I'll help you work up a plan."

"Well, she's lost weight. I always envied her figure, till now. Her husband of almost thirty years cheated, they're getting divorced, she's shattered and she won't let herself feel it. She said she's afraid she'll crack. My nieces are sixteen and seventeen, different as day and night, and they're having a hard time too. Justine is depressed, not eating, refusing to let herself cry, worried about the future. Her husband has never really worked and he wants alimony!"

Ross gave a helpless shrug. "Support payments are part of the law," she said.

"He could have worked. He just likes to have fun," Addie said. "I hate him so much! Justine has worked so hard and—" She sighed and wiped at her eyes. "My sister is twenty years older than me, and she's always been the most together, successful, strongest woman I know. Here she is, falling apart. And I can't help."

"You can probably help if you want to."

"I would if I had any idea how!"

"Of course you can help," Ross said. "First of all, one of the most important things you can do when someone is going through a traumatic life transition like this is listen. Let them vent and rant and just listen patiently. You can also suggest counseling…"

"They went to marriage counseling," Adele said. "She said Scott lied all the way through it until their last session, when he admitted he'd been having an affair—after she said she had proof of it. It sounds like it was going on for a year or two…"

"Not unusual," Ross said. "A person who has learned to lie to his spouse every day for years has no trouble coming up with a good story in counseling. And that year or two? It's never a surprise when it's double that."

"Double that? And he wants alimony!"

"Even though that causes rage and feels unfair, it is the law—no fault, community property. Right now what's important is that your sister protect her assets, the most important of which are her children and her self-esteem. Nothing can gut a woman's self-esteem like being rejected and abandoned."

"She's a lawyer," Adele said. "A friend of hers is drawing up the divorce. The paperwork. I think it's almost completely filed already and should be final quickly."

"Then other than urging her to get good professional advice, I'm assuming she's in the driver's seat. Well, except for the shock and pain of it. And the grief. None of us escapes that, and there's no way through it but through it. Adele, who do *you* have to talk to? Because this is obviously your pain and transition, too."

She gave a helpless shrug. "I have friends. I have my weight-loss support group, even if I don't tell them that much really personal stuff. I have Jake, my friend since we were kids. His mom was my mom's best friend, and Jake's always looked out for me. When he can."

"Not your sister?"

"It's hard to explain, but with Justine being twenty years older, we sort of relied on each other without ever being really close. She relied on me to help with things like babysitting after her children were born, and I relied on her financially when our mom was bedridden. Justine helped, since I couldn't work. We've always loved each other, but we weren't like friends. I was working on my graduate degree in English when my dad became an invalid and I—" She shrugged.

"You dropped out to help at home," Ross said.

"I wasn't sure I was on the right path anyway," Adele said. "My plan was kind of falling apart. It just didn't feel right anymore. Dropping out to help at home gave me a break to think about things. And then it just sort of stretched out."

"That must have been frightening for you," Ross said.

"You have no idea," Adele said.

"And was Justine supportive?"

"She was amazing. At that time, it was the closest we'd ever been. Of course, I was so needy. I felt like such a screwup and failure. But she reassured me that it was all right, that I should take all the time I needed, and it had nothing to do with my parents needing me. We could have gotten help from elsewhere. Except I was there and I wanted to be useful. So…"

"And you didn't want to go back to school?"

"Not until I was sure of things. My parents were disappointed. But Justine supported my decision and kept my parents cool."

"Eight years of taking care of invalid parents is a hard job, especially for such a long time…"

"Once you commit to something like that, it's impossible to change your mind," Adele said. "You don't wake up one day and say to your marginally conscious mother, 'I think I'll go back to school now. I'll try to find someone to come in and wash and feed you.' Imagine how terrifying that would be to someone who has lived on the fringes of understanding for years. I just knew I was in for the duration. I knew my mother's care was good."

"Did you ever turn her care over to others? To home health practitioners?"

"Sure, for an hour here and there. I observed, I was present the first few times, I monitored afterward like a detective. That's how we got by."

Ross opened her top drawer and pulled out a printed list of names. She slid it across the desk to Adele. "Here are the best counselors I know. They've helped people in all sorts of transitions, not just displaced or reentry clients. One of them was my counselor for a long time. I'm not telling you which one. You're free to give this list to your sister if you like. A little emotional support could really help. Professional emotional support."

"Thank you," Adele said. "I'll encourage that idea."

"Adele, I think you should consider that, as well."

"What?"

"Counseling."

"I don't have a lot of time, what with my job, my new exercise and diet program, trying to get the house in shape…"

"These counselors keep all kinds of hours."

"I'll think it over."

"Or, you can use one of our counselors," Ross said.

"For myself? Wouldn't that be a conflict of interest?" she asked.

"How so? We all have the same objective here. We rely on each other regularly—use each other as sounding boards, help each other clear out the cobwebs. I've been here a long time. My husband used to beat me, then left me with four kids under the age of ten. I got on my feet with a lot of support from this office, got my degree and my master's in counseling and have worked here since. Now if I have a problem, I talk to Fran or one of the other counselors. And sometimes they talk to me."

"And that's okay?" Adele asked.

"If you're comfortable," she said. "If you feel the chemistry is right. On this, you have to trust your instincts. Your gut. No judgment from anyone on that—you talk to the person you trust and feel safe with. That choice is all on you."

Adele felt like she could cry, she was so grateful. Instead, she composed herself and said, "That's very generous of you, Ross. Thank you."

"It's what we do," she said. "Getting people on their feet—it's a very rewarding mission."

The first week in June, Justine received an email. Her divorce was final. She had all the finalized and notarized documents saved to her cloud account and printed out and filed in her locked desk drawer. She gave copies to Scott. Her car was now registered in her name only; she had all new charge accounts. Their financial management team had immediately separated, divided and created new accounts and trusts for each of them. The custody situation was left as joint unless one or both of their daughters made a decision otherwise—they were entitled to their own choices since they were both over sixteen.

After receiving the notice of the divorce, she cried all day. She asked herself for the millionth time, *How did this happen to us?* She had trusted him, and not only had she been wrong to, she didn't think she'd ever trust a man again.

If there was anything more sad than realizing you no longer loved someone, it was realizing you had not one ounce of respect for the person you had trusted with your love for so many years.

At the end of the day, her face puffy and chafed, she had had it. She was done.

"I spent the day at home, alone, crying," she told Logan, her bedroom door closed.

"How are you feeling now?" he asked.

"Finished," she said. "Tired and weak and done. It's very hard to keep from showing my rage—I so hate him for the betrayal. I am going to do my best to completely avoid him. We will take turns staying at the house with the girls."

"And what will you do when you're not there?" he asked.

"I have a friend just a few blocks away who has generously offered her guest room until I reestablish myself. That puts me close to home, and if the girls need me, they have only to call."

"Sounds excellent. Except for still having to deal with him so much."

"When you have common children, that's how it is. But that won't last forever, I hope. Thank God the girls aren't six and seven!"

"In the meantime, what are you doing?"

"Polishing my résumé and visiting law practices from San Francisco to Monterrey. I've met with a half dozen small firms, even had a couple of offers."

"So, you're really going to do this," he said. "Can't you make a much better living if you stayed where you are?"

"Actually, no. Not as long as I'm committed to giving Scott half. I have no problem with the settlement, which gives him half of our retirement savings, and it's very generous. But…it's complicated…"

"I have time," Logan said.

She sat on her bed, sipped a late-night chardonnay, enjoying the conversation. They had started talking two or three times a week, and she found herself looking forward to each call.

"I've been kind of jealous of Scott, if you want to know. Of his fun lifestyle."

"So—you were jealous of his time off?"

"Not just that," she said. "I felt a lot of pressure to earn money and to earn as much as possible so we'd have a solid retirement, so we wouldn't have to worry like my parents did. I was burned out on the rat race of corporate law for a big company years ago, but I would never have said so. I stayed on that treadmill because the pay and benefits were good, but I was dying to slow down a little. Well, the kids' college accounts are good enough. There's nothing preventing them from getting good educations in good schools. What's left of my retirement fund is good enough for me. I'd like some flexibility. I'd like to take a morning or afternoon off sometimes. I'd like to take the girls on a trip, just the three of us. Most of all, I'd like to build a practice that's mine. Admittedly, when you do that, it takes a while. But that's okay. My half of the savings will help me get from month to month if I don't earn much." She cleared her throat. "I put in my notice. I'll be wrapping up my corporate duties in a month."

"Whoa! It's really happening?"

"It's now or never," she said.

"I've always heard you shouldn't make a major change for a year after a death or divorce," he said.

"I've heard that, too. But otherwise I have to keep working at that frantic pace and for what? For Scott? To make sure he's comfortable in his divorce? To make sure he has plenty of money to spend on *her*? I haven't been having fun for a long time now. And you know what? Scott has obviously been having fun!"

Logan laughed. "Is this you saying he's done having fun on your dime?"

"That's not how I mean it," she said. "It's really much simpler. He doesn't want me. After all my dedication, he's leaving me for another woman. And so he's getting what the law says he's entitled to—half the savings, half the retirement funds, half the house equity. But I'm claiming my future."

Logan laughed. "I smell revenge," he said.

"If I wanted revenge, there's probably a better way. I want to change my life. I want to feel valuable again. I want to feel some sense of self-worth. Probably the worst thing this divorce has done to me is bring on feelings of irrelevance. I worked so hard for us, so we could afford the things Scott wanted to do. It made me happy to know he was enjoying his life. I never wasted a second on resentment. Then he threw me out with the trash. Because he just wasn't happy *enough*. And on top of it, he complained that I was too focused on my work. I suggested that if he resented my long hours, perhaps he shouldn't take so much of the money I earned, and he said that was precisely why he should take the money. He said the money was the only thing I'd really given him."

Logan whistled.

"I have a lot of feelings I can't escape. I'm angry. I've never been so angry. I'm afraid of a million things—afraid I'll be alone for the rest of my life, afraid I won't make it on my own, afraid I'll always feel bitter, afraid my stomach will hurt every day, that I'll wake up and my first thought will be of Scott and that woman day after day, and yet... And yet the very worst thing of all, I have zero respect for a man I loved and admired for thirty years."

"People make mistakes, Justine," he said.

"It wasn't a mistake, it was an indulgence. It wasn't as if he was abused or unloved. Oh, he might be trying to convince himself now, after the fact, that his marriage wasn't perfect, but I'm here to tell you he was not neglected. If anyone was, it was me!"

"And you put up with that because...?"

"Because I wanted him to be happy," she said softly. "But Scott Somersby's happiness is no longer my concern. I'm going to work on some boundaries, some tender care of my heart and a little self-indulgence of my own."

"Good for you. For what it's worth, I think your husband is an idiot. Good women don't grow on trees, and he might learn that sooner than later. I bet he'll come crawling back."

"He's already too late," she said.

"I know this is tough, but I have a feeling in a year you're going to be in far better shape than he is. In fact, in better shape than you were."

"I hope you're right," she said. "I could sure use something to look forward to."

"When's your next night in the neighbor's guest room?" he asked.

"Thursday. Why?"

"Maybe we can meet at Chen's. And if you want a preliminary report on the law firms you're looking at, I'd be happy to help. Free of charge."

"That's very generous, Logan."

"That's what friends are for."

CHAPTER EIGHT

Adele told herself that she was doing Justine a favor by going shopping with her. Adele hated shopping.

"Maybe what you hated was not finding anything you loved, but today might be different," Justine said.

Justine insisted on driving all the way to Half Moon Bay on Saturday morning to pick Adele up. Justine knew the best places to shop, and if she was doing the driving, Adele was captive. And her sister had said she'd mention this excursion to the girls, but Adele hadn't been overly optimistic about that. Her nieces were always busy. And yet there they were with Justine.

"Oh my God," Adele said. "Witnesses!"

"Stop being so negative! You're a working woman now. And you have a whole new body. You need a few outfits to get you through the summer," Justine said.

"And I'm going to do your hair and makeup," Amber said.

"I'm going to stake out a bench and read," Olivia said.

Addie reached out and stroked the girl's pretty hair. "You should have been my child. I'd rather read, too."

Her nieces were both beautiful but were as different as

Justine and Adele. Amber was tall like her mom and had her eyes. She had trouble sitting still unless it was for a mani-pedi or facial. And she didn't read nearly as much as Olivia, but both girls did very well in school. Amber was gregarious and Olivia was a complete introvert.

"You and I, we'd be happy with a couch and a book all day long, wouldn't we?" Addie said.

"I don't even need a couch," Olivia replied.

"You want to stay here, at my house, until this shopping thing is over? Since your mom has to bring me home, she'd be back for you."

"Nah," Olivia said. "I hear there will be lunch."

"No complaining," Amber said. "The only person allowed to complain is Aunt Addie. Her shopping muscles are underdeveloped. Now come on, let's do hair and makeup."

"I'm not shopping for a wedding gown, you know," Addie said. But she followed as Amber led the way to the bathroom. She carried what looked like an overnight bag, stuffed with cosmetics. She sat Addie on the closed toilet seat and got to work. After pulling Addie's thick hair into a messy bun, she began on her face.

Addie could hear Olivia and Justine talking in the other room—Justine asking how far Olivia was into her book, then commenting on the story, which she had also read and loved. This was one of the things Addie admired about Justine's relationship with her girls—she could let them be individuals. She could discuss books with Olivia, who loved her reading, and discuss fashion with Amber, who had a real interest in haute couture.

Adele closed her eyes and listened to Justine and Olivia talking about Olivia's current read. Simultaneously, Amber was having a conversation with her about makeup. "A little more color here, I think. You should work on eye makeup, Auntie—you have the most beautiful, big eyes. I think we'll leave your hair like that in a messy bun—it's just the thing."

And soon they were on their way to a couple of malls. Justine steered them to a couple of good, women's discount clothing stores, and once Adele was trying on the piles of clothes Justine and Amber delivered to her, standing in a dressing room in her underwear most of the time, she started to enjoy the process. "I feel like a fairy princess," she said.

"A fairy princess with very bad underwear," Justine said. "We'll take care of that, as well."

"Lighten up, Justine. No one's going to see it."

"More's the pity," she said. "You're getting new underwear. And a couple of nightgowns. You might as well get a completely fresh start. You'll be amazed at how much better you'll feel when you're brand-new from the skin out. And, I brought a few things from my closet."

"What? What of yours could I possibly fit into?"

"I have a few things that I haven't worn in a while that might've been a little loose fitting. Of course, right now everything is loose on me. I wouldn't want to lose another ounce. I think I'm one of those people who has sharp features that only get sharper when I'm too skinny. I'll be damned if I'll have a mean expression because of Scott!"

"Speaking of getting thin, is it going to be lunchtime soon?" Addie asked.

"Absolutely!"

They left their second store with bags bulging with clothes—including new underwear and nightgowns. Justine insisted on paying for everything. Adele argued that this must be a particularly difficult time for Justine to be spending so much, but Justine just brushed her off. "Life has sucked for the past six months, for both of us, and I haven't had a chance to spoil you at all. We're going to get through this year, Addie, and next year is going to be so much better. For both of us."

"We've never done this before," Adele said, a little catch in her voice.

"Of course we have," Justine said. "Amber, go get Olivia. She's right on that bench over there." Then, turning back to Adele she said, "It's been a long time, I guess. But we've shopped for the girls together, for Mom and Dad, for special occasions."

"This is completely different," Addie said.

"Well, it's the first time you've needed new work clothes. You didn't need my help with clothes for school. In fact, you probably didn't need my help with this, but I wanted to."

"It's really completely different. We were always in a rush those other times. And it was so long ago." She sniffed. "I don't know what to say. Thank you isn't enough."

"You're just emotional. Let's go over to the Olive Garden. I'm craving a glass of wine."

"And you're going to have some pasta," Adele said. "I think you're going to blow away."

When they were seated in an out-of-the-way booth, they started talking about the purchases, making a fuss over how wonderful Adele looked in her new clothes, laughing over the ones they rejected. "That brown thing made you look like a bag lady," Amber said.

"I liked that one," Adele said.

"That's why I wanted to go with you!" Justine said.

"That's the thing about books," Olivia said. "They don't care what you wear."

"I think they closed the stores behind us," Amber said.

"We were way too much trouble. I consider shopping an aggressive sport."

"That dressing room looked like your room," Justine said.

"Looking good just isn't easy, Mom."

"It is for me," Olivia said.

They laughed and poked fun at each other until suddenly Adele had tears running down her cheeks.

"What is it, Addie?" Justine asked.

She shook her head. "I'm not sure," she said. "I hate shopping, but that was the best day I've had in forever. I don't know what happened, but you're different. I've never known you like this. Don't tell me divorce made you fun?"

Justine bit into a bread stick. "Divorce broke my heart. I think it's going to hurt for a long time. But it gave me permission to try a few things. First, I don't have to worry about getting home to make sure I've done my share around the house. I'm not stressed out about Monday morning meetings. Actually, I guess I should tell you all. I gave my notice at work. I need a new schedule where I'm not working excessive hours. I've already had a couple of offers from smaller practices, but I'm not accepting anything yet. I'm still looking around. I'm fifty-percent terrified and fifty-percent excited. I think once I get on my feet, I'm going to have fun again. Now that I look back on it, I wasn't having enough fun."

"Good for you, Mom," Amber said. "But I'm not fifty-percent excited. Dad wants to take us out to dinner to meet the girlfriend."

Justine went visibly pale. "Really?" she said.

"Do we have to?" Amber asked.

"It's entirely up to you," Justine said. "I'm certainly not going to insist."

"What if he insists?" Amber asked.

"I'm not," Olivia said. "I'm just not."

"I still love my dad, even if I think he's stupid and mean," Amber said. "If we say no, he'll be mad."

"Oh well," Olivia said. "Guess he'll have to be mad. I'm just not."

"Then I'm not, either," Amber replied.

"Have you suggested to your dad that you'd love to have dinner with him but you don't feel like meeting his girlfriend?" Justine asked.

"I haven't," Olivia said. "I see him at home a couple of nights a week, and he spends most of that time on the phone with *her*."

"I'm just saying, if there's a way to have a relationship with him..." Justine tried.

"And I guess I'm saying he could have made the decision to leave his girlfriend—you know, say something original like 'Hey, I'm married, so this can't happen.' But instead, he left us. Seeing him right now is not high on my priority list," Olivia said.

"I think I need wine," Adele said.

Justine had Adele home by six, and by then they'd spent as much money as had been reasonable and lunch had long since worn off. While Adele and Amber worked at putting away the new clothes and sorting through Justine's castoffs, Justine and Olivia walked to Bronski's Market.

Jake was putting out fresh vegetables. "Well, hello stranger," Justine said. "It's been a long time."

He turned and smiled when he took in mother and daughter. "Justine! It's been way too long. What brings you to the neighborhood?"

"We just finished a day of shopping with Adele," Justine

said. "She needed some new clothes for her new job and, in case you haven't noticed, new shape."

"Oh, I think everyone in town has noticed. She's been walking every day, sometimes twice a day, and eats like a rabbit. What can I help you find?"

"I know where everything is, Jake. We've decided that since we don't have any other plans, the girls and I will help fix dinner and hang out awhile. Adele is busy putting away her new things. Hasn't she gotten beautiful?"

"She's always been beautiful," he said.

"True," Justine said, momentarily sidelined. Because of course Adele had always been pretty, but she also had a tendency to let herself go, to dress in baggy clothes, eschew makeup, not fuss with her hair. And there was the weight— she'd packed on a good forty pounds since the pregnancy. "I think the new job has really charged up her self-image, and everything in her world looks good right now."

Jake leaned against the lettuce stand. He glanced to the left as Olivia wandered over to the fruits, bagging up a couple of apples. He turned back to Justine. "How's your new world, Justine? I'm so sorry about the divorce."

"Thanks, Jake, that's sweet. Today I felt good all day and hardly thought about the shithead." Then she smiled at him. "I'm a little angry."

"You're entitled," he said. "What a fool he is."

"Why don't I get another chicken breast, Jake? Come on by the house and join us for a casual dinner."

"You don't have to do that, Justine. I appreciate the offer—"

"Hey, hey, hey!" a voice boomed.

Justine jumped and met eyes with Marty, Jake's younger brother. Marty was grinning like a Cheshire cat. He appeared to be wearing Joe Biden's teeth. "Hi," she said.

"Aren't you looking fantastic! I hear you're on your own these days and as luck would have it, so am I. Tell you what I'm going to do. I'm going to give you a call and take you out to a nice dinner. It'll help you break into the new life you're trying out!"

"What is it you know about my new life?" she asked. "And *how* do you know?"

"Our mother," Jake interrupted. "Adele mentioned it. That's where you heard, right, Marty?"

He nodded. "What do you say? How about dinner?"

Justine just smiled. "Thank you for the nice offer, but I'm not quite ready to date yet, Marty."

"Let me put my number in your phone," he said, sticking out a hand.

"I'll get your number from your mom when it's time for my coming out," she said. "Awfully nice of you to ask. Excuse me, I have to go fetch another chicken breast." She turned to Jake. "I'll see you later. Thanks for the help."

"Ah, don't mention it," Jake said. Then he turned back to his crate of lettuce while she walked away.

Justine and Olivia bought the dinner supplies and walked back to Adele's house. "This is one of the things I've missed while living in San Jose," Justine said. "I like this little old town, like shopping at the small, neighborhood stores. The beach is handy. The people here just don't seem to be in a big hurry. Everyone in San Jose and the Bay Area are rushing to and from work all the time. I'm kind of tired of rushing around. I hope I find work in a little town similar to this."

Olivia bit into one of her apples. "You'll be bored."

"I don't think so. But if I am, I'll welcome it. I'm going to build a new kind of life as a single mother. Looking back, things didn't work out the way I thought they would. The way I hoped."

"Do you miss Daddy so much?"

She thought for a moment, her lower lip caught in her teeth. "I haven't had a chance to miss him yet, passing each other at the house as we do so often. I hope you'll forgive me for this, Livvie, but I don't miss him a bit. It's been three months since he decided he was done with our marriage," she said. "The thing is, when I look at the last thirty years, all those long hours and sometimes exhausting work, I thought I was banking hours for my future. For our future. I thought I was building something so I could have a lighter load and less worry. I had this idea that by the time you girls were done with college, things would slow down. I'm in no hurry, but I plan to be a very fun grandmother. Before we get to that, depending on how the next few years stack up work-wise, maybe we'll take a really great trip—just you, me and Amber."

"I bet Amber, who has always had a boyfriend since kindergarten, will find someone to marry her. But I'll go with you," she added, grinning.

When they got home, Adele was wearing one of Justine's hand-me-down outfits. It was black slacks with a camel-colored knit top. It made Justine smile and tilt her head, appreciative of the look. "I think that looks better on you than it did on me."

"I can't believe I'm actually wearing something of yours," Adele said.

"You're beautiful. Mind if I chop and stir in your kitchen?"

"That would be great."

"I invited Jake," Justine said. "He looked a little doubtful, but I told him to come. And then his brother put a move on me. Marty."

"Not to burst your bubble in case you were feeling special, but I think Marty has put the moves on every woman he's ever met."

"I think I'm at least a dozen years older than he is."

"And according to Jake, he's got a serious girlfriend. And two ex-wives. And kids."

Justine just laughed and headed for the kitchen. "Not my type, sorry." She put her groceries on the counter and located the cutting board. "Help me out here. I need olive oil, a large skillet or wok and your spice rack."

"I haven't done that much cooking," Adele said, rummaging around for things. She turned up garlic that was spoiled and black, but Justine had bought new. No soy sauce, but Justine had anticipated that as well, and bought some. There was olive oil, since it was important to Adele's new diet. The spices, kept in a drawer, were bleak and old.

"Okay, I've got this now," Justine said. Amber was on her phone in the other room, Olivia curled up on the couch with a book. "Pull up a stool and just talk to me. Tell me more about your new job."

"Well, the best part is that I'm in counseling, by accident. A couple of times a week I get about thirty minutes with one of our best social workers, and she's hearing my life story. Are you getting any counseling?"

"Not at the moment," Justine said. "That marriage counselor Scott had us seeing, to what purpose I can't imagine, was so useless, it turned me off counselors for the time being. I'm feeling pretty good at the moment. I might wake up tomorrow feeling horrible, but right now I feel good. But I think counseling is a good thing and I'm glad you're going."

"I had no idea how much I wanted someone to listen to me until Ross, the social worker, said, 'Tell me everything.' And I did."

"That's fantastic. Tell me more."

Adele explained that they talked about everything in her life from junior high on. There was still so much to talk about because in a couple of thirty-minute sessions, they'd barely scratched the surface.

There was a knock at the front door and Adele let Jake in. He'd brought a bottle of wine, flowers and some ice cream. "For the girls," he said.

The five of them sat around the table, enjoyed a light and delicious meal of teriyaki chicken, stir-fried veggies and rice, and conversation. Amber and Olivia both got phone calls, which they took care of quickly. Then as they were about to pick up the dishes, Justine's phone chimed. She looked at it and saw it was Scott. "I'll get back to him later," she said. But her phone chimed again and again. "Well, I guess he won't give up. Sorry, Adele."

Jake took that opportunity to carry dishes to the kitchen but Adele stayed where she was, nursing a glass of wine and listening.

Justine answered the call. "Scott, couldn't you leave a message?"

"No, I couldn't," he said. "Have you asked the girls to refuse to meet Cat? I want to take them to dinner. They're refusing to go."

"I have not told them anything. I have said more than once that it's up to them, but it's entirely possible they know how much I disapprove of that idea. I find it very painful. She is the woman you left us for. You can't expect us to be happy with either of you, but the fact that you do means you're more oblivious to the damage you've done than I thought."

"We're divorced," he said angrily. "I expected you'd get over it by now!"

She laughed. "In a few weeks?" she asked incredulously.

"Check back with me in a few years." She disconnected. She looked at Adele. "Sometimes this divorce seems like it exists on another plane. In another solar system. He just said he thought I'd be over it by now. We've been apart three months and divorced three weeks." She laughed again. "I don't even know him anymore."

"He really said that?" Adele asked.

Justine rolled her eyes. "He's taking this all so well..." she said facetiously.

"If you think about it, Scott has never been overly concerned about anyone but himself. I mean, he seemed a nice enough guy and I suppose he was a good dad, but he had one primary concern. Himself."

"I think you're right. But I did think he loved me," Justine said. "Now I wonder if he's had many girlfriends over the years. God knows he had the time. I've decided not to burden myself with that question."

"You're different now, Justine," Adele said.

"So are you," Justine tossed back with a smile.

"How am I different?"

"Well, you've taken the world by storm. You have new confidence. Do you even realize how beautiful you are? You've always been, but you never seemed to wear it so well. I think it's the combination of the new job and your new weight loss. I noticed it first with the job. Even when we talk on the phone you're stronger and more self-assured. I'm very proud of you."

"It started with you," she said. "Or, more accurately, Scott. I know it must have hit you hard, but it had a wallop effect on me. I remember thinking we can't count on anything. Or anyone. If Scott could leave a brilliant, beautiful woman like you, there is no point in counting on anyone but ourselves. It motivated me. The first thing I did that very morning after leaving your house was find a weight loss program and began an earnest research of jobs."

Jake brought the bottle of wine to the table. "You girls just visit while I clean up."

"Leave it, Jake," Adele said. "I'll get it later."

"I'm having a good time watching you two visit. I'm happy to pitch in. Then I'll join you."

When he left them, Justine said, "I should have been so much more supportive of you and all you did, Addie. I regret that now. I can't remember the last time we had a nice dinner together. I gave all that energy to a man who didn't deserve it."

"It makes sense that the divorce, especially after so many years, would have a huge impact on you but I didn't expect this change. I have never seen you this relaxed."

"I am, at the moment. But it comes and goes. When I wake up in the morning without that stomach cramp, when I realize the feeling of abandonment and betrayal wasn't my first feeling when I woke, I just pray it lasts all day. Or that I have a few mornings in a row like that. It's getting better. I'm learning to enjoy a day without feeling lost. And afraid."

"I never once thought of you as lost or afraid," Adele said.

"Law school tends to train you in the appearance of confidence even when you don't feel it. There is something I noticed, however. Once I realized that no matter what, I would never take Scott back, I started to get a new feeling. It was the sudden realization that I don't ever have to care if Scott is happy again. I felt like I lost a ton of deadweight."

"Did it just happen?" Addie asked.

"Kind of," she said. "I did get a piece of good advice. A friend encouraged me to start focusing on what I have rather than what I lost. I'm finding that very helpful. I think in a year or so I'll be very happy. When I'm done being so pissed I could bludgeon him."

"I'll be happy to wipe your fingerprints off the club," Addie said, smiling.

Then they melted into laughter.

It was nearly ten by the time Justine and her daughters left, their sides aching from laughter. Adele, Jake and Justine had told stories from the days before the girls were born, back when their parents were friends and played cards every week. They told of neighbors like Mr. Swank who fed stray cats and when he passed away it was discovered he had over forty living in his house. And Mrs. Hall who spent twenty-five years as a crossing guard and no one knew she had never been hired by the school district. There was the librarian who had a years-long hot romance with a studly lifeguard, and the pair of brothers who ran a local farm who it turned out were never brothers at all. Jake had a hundred funny stories related to running the neighborhood market.

Adele promised to leave a key under the flowerpot in case her nieces wanted to drive down from San Jose to go to the beach, since school was out and both girls had part-time summer jobs. Olivia was babysitting and Amber was working at the food court in the local mall.

When they said goodbye, they all hugged as though they'd just wrapped up a holiday dinner.

"I'll call you," Justine promised Adele.

"And I'll call you. We'll have to do this again."

Then they were gone, and Adele and Jake stood on the front porch, waving goodbye until the car was out of sight.

"I guess I'll shove off," Jake said. He draped an arm across her shoulders. "This was a nice surprise, Addie. Thanks."

"I guess you should thank Justine. I need to see more of my sister. I can count on one hand the number of times I've had that much fun with her. I should find a way to put a few pounds on her without putting pounds on myself."

"I'm going to tell you what I told Justine—you look great, but you were always beautiful. You just never seemed to know it."

"I think I did it to myself," she said. "I became a shut-in. I called myself a caregiver and I did help. I did take care of my mother the last few years. But I had a broken heart and I was hiding away."

He gave her shoulders a light massage. "There was a lot you didn't tell me."

"Do you want to come in for a while?" she asked him.

"Sure, but you don't have to tell me."

"Thanks. Let's see what comes naturally."

"Can you handle it if I have a bowl of ice cream?"

"Sure. Of course."

So they went inside. Jake had ice cream and Adele talked. She told him about some of the problems she had come to know in her new job, no names or descriptions, of course. She explained how she was starting to relate to them. She'd shut herself away for years because it was easier than facing the world and risking her poor heart again. Even though Jake knew all about her pregnancy and the stillborn baby, they had never talked beyond the surface of it.

"I guess I was traumatized," Adele said. "Well, my dad's injury was bad. He was in and out of the hospital so many times, having surgeries on his back, stuck in a wheelchair, and here I was, my belly growing bigger by the day. I hardly even cared that he was angry with me for getting pregnant and having no husband. I made a nursery for the baby, did you know that?"

"I've never been upstairs," Jake said. "My mother was the one who told me the baby didn't live."

Jake had sent flowers at the time. Adele hadn't had a proper funeral for her baby. She had her mother, father and sister and they buried him in a lone plot, not a family plot. He had died before he was even born. She didn't talk about it, she didn't tell Hadley, who she assumed couldn't care less anyway, and she didn't get any kind of help for her grief. Her parents, not in the best shape anyway, seemed relieved that she didn't want to talk about it.

"This counselor I've been talking to, she wonders if maybe I need a little closure on that. On a lot of things."

"Hmm," he answered. "What do you think?"

"I don't know. My whole life has started to change, and I almost feel like a normal person. For the first time in years."

"Addie, I don't know all that much about counseling and stuff, but here's what I think. I think you do whatever makes you feel like you're growing into your best self. You seem happier these days because you're active and you're with people, and correct me if I'm wrong, but I think you're needed at that new job."

"I am feeling that way, slowly but surely. You've been just about my only friend the past few years."

"Nah. Everyone in town knows you, Addie. Everyone waves, honks, yells hello. You know a lot of people. You just haven't been too social."

"Yeah, but I'm talking friend, Jake. I want you to know that I'm really grateful."

CHAPTER NINE

"Is it too late?" Justine whispered into the phone.

"No," Logan said. "I'm watching a movie. I'll pause it. Everything okay?"

"Yes, better than okay, and I just wanted to tell you. I had a beautiful day with my girls and my sister, a day like I haven't had in a million years. We went shopping with Addie. She's lost a lot of weight and needed new clothes..."

"But you said you and your girls go shopping all the time," he said. She could hear him sitting up in bed, getting a little less comfortable.

"Not like this," she said. "We always need something, so we have to hurry, can't waste any time, rush, rush, rush. Today we were all about getting good deals and nice clothes and laughed a lot. Then we went to Addie's house, the house I grew up in, and I made dinner. We kicked back, took our time, laughed our heads off, and didn't worry about when we got home. I'm at home tonight. Tomorrow night I'll be in Jean's guest room. But Monday I'm back on the prowl, checking out law practices. After spending the evening in Half Moon Bay, I remember why I liked it so much. I like the speed."

He chuckled. "Maybe I should give it a look."

"Well, it's out of the question for me," she said. "The other woman lives there. And I assume Scott will be spending a lot of time there. I'd be happier if he'd move to Florida."

"Scott and the other woman could just as easily be in San Jose, so just get over it."

"What are you saying?" she demanded. "I don't want to see them. Especially together!"

"I understand, but if you let that be your criteria, you might miss out on the best experience for yourself. You could reject a job or location because you're avoiding them and settle somewhere you like far less. Then what if they do up and move to Florida? Justine, you are now free to serve your own needs first."

"Huh," she said.

He laughed. "This is all still so new, isn't it? The idea that it's just you."

"Well, me and my girls. But what if I run into them and I throat punch her?"

"First offense," he said. "You won't have to serve too much time."

She laughed at him. "There is a law practice in my old town, a one-man firm. He's been there forever and I found, during my search, he's been looking for an associate. He might be thinking of retiring, but he's been looking for a long time. I had pretty much written it off. Not only is it in the town where Scott had his affair, my girls go to school in San Jose. There's a potential opportunity I'm going to visit in Monterrey."

"All these small coastal towns... You're going to have to just think of where you want to be without regard to

Scott and his girlfriend. Thinking of them will only slow you down."

"Can't you relate?" she asked. "Were you willing to see your ex?"

"I wasn't happy about anything for a year or more, but you forget. I know I told you. My ex and my sister are best friends. I ran into her all the time. I had to sit across from her one Easter dinner. It was excruciating. And then I ran into my ex and her new partner, a woman who hated me on sight."

"How long did you wait before you started dating?" she asked.

"I don't know," he said. "Maybe a few months, but I didn't get involved. Just a little companionship. A couple of years after my divorce I dated a woman who was fairly serious—we were a couple for about three years. Then a few years later, another woman I was semiserious with. Till she took back her ex."

"Hmm. Well, I was hit on today," Justine said. "A man at least a dozen years younger than me asked me out. He was so gross about it. He said he heard I was on my own now and so was he, so…?"

"Did you like him?"

"I've known him forever. I think I might've babysat him, but I don't recall. I told him I wasn't ready for my coming out just yet."

"Justine, there are going to be men. Lots of men. You're beautiful, successful, fun, smart and there will be men. I know you think that isn't going to happen right now, but there will be—"

"I don't want a man," she said resolutely. "I want good people in my life. I want trustworthy friends. I am not looking for a man."

"And I'm not looking for a woman," he said. "But I have an open mind. There's a street fair in Carmel tomorrow," he said. "Hell, Carmel by itself is a street fair. Why don't we go together? You can practice running into people. You can learn how to say things like, 'Didn't you hear? Scott and I are divorced.' And 'This is my friend Logan. We've worked together on a couple of cases.' We might even hold hands so you can get used to the idea that a date doesn't automatically lead to marriage and divorce. I'll buy you something to eat, we'll have a glass of wine at one of the outdoor bars with a view of the bay and maybe you'll see a painting or macramé you just have to have."

She was quiet for a moment, thinking. If she was going to have a date with anyone, she'd like it to be Logan. But she was barely divorced, and she was seriously afraid of letting a man into her life. If she was honest, she hadn't had a man in her life in years. She had Scott who, she was beginning to realize, wasn't that much fun. And he was a liar. So she finally said, "What time?"

"I have a couple of things to do—chores. Let's meet at noon. Parking will be annoying, so let's meet on the edge of town at Blueberry Hill restaurant. It's a little breakfast place with a big parking lot. Wear comfortable shoes and we can walk into town."

When she was falling asleep after her phone call, she was thinking about so many different things; it was like a mosaic. There was a lifetime of Scott in many different incarnations, from the loving father who cried when his daughters were born to the self-centered oaf who said, without much regret, "Don't you want me to be happy?" She thought of Addie, changing her life after losing so much and giving so much; Addie who was every bit the butterfly coming out of the cocoon. About her girls, taking on the next phase of their lives without the father they had known and trusted. And Logan, the last thing she had expected—handsome, sexy and smart Logan, who would hold her hand so she could practice saying, "Yes, this is my friend Logan, whom I'm *seeing*."

She started to ask herself, would she *see* him? She hadn't dated anyone since she met Scott in college. Was she ready for that?

The house was pretty quiet in the morning, the girls still tucked away in their rooms. Justine rushed through a few chores, tidying up, cleaning her bathroom and changing her sheets. Scott didn't use the master bedroom when he spent time at the house, and she wondered how long it had been since the sheets and towels in the guest room and bath had been laundered. Since laundry had always been her job, she suspected not at all.

She had a third cup of coffee, browsed the news, dressed for the day. By the time she came out to the family room, Amber was up.

"Wow, you look cute," Amber said.

"I'm going to Carmel for the afternoon. I'm meeting a friend. A guy I worked with a while back."

Amber's mouth hung open. "Is this like a...*date*?"

"Just friends, actually. I don't have much interest in dating."

"Who is he?"

"His name is Logan. He's a private investigator I've used. My office uses them routinely. And he's also divorced, though much longer than me."

"But I guess you *will* date," Amber said tentatively.

"I haven't given it any thought till this minute. You know what I've given a lot of thought to? You and Olivia going to college. I think your college funds are enough to cover everything, but I'm prepared to have to add or use some of my retirement fund or borrow. And I hope when you guys graduate we can celebrate with a trip or something. And you know what else? I want to spend more time with your aunt Addie. It's like we're finally getting close enough in age to have a real friendship."

"Addie is brand-new," Amber said.

"I know. And I want to be brand-new, too."

Justine parked at the edge of the restaurant lot and found Logan standing near the entrance. He wore jeans, a collared shirt and topsiders, no socks. He was in amazing shape, and she assumed it had to do with his years of being a police officer; by his physique, he probably worked out regularly. At forty-eight with a full head of hair and tanned arms and face, he would be drawing looks from the women all afternoon.

When she approached him, he surprised her by pulling her close for a friendly hug. "Good to see you, Justine. How are you doing?"

"I'm doing great," she said. "In fact, I can't believe how well I'm doing. Six weeks ago I didn't think there was any hope I'd feel this good about my life. I mean, it creeps up on me sometimes, but I'm okay."

"Good," he said. And he took her hand. "Let's take on this town."

The street was closed off, with people crowding the sidewalks. In addition to the stores and shops, there were several booths erected in the middle of the street that led to the ocean. They passed a wood art booth, a couple of large booths filled with paintings and sculptures, a booth selling hummus in a wide variety of flavors, one featuring wraps and shawls and even a leather goods display. Several food booths sold corn dogs, slushies, taffy, cotton candy, ice cream, flavored popcorn and chocolates. They poked around, checking out the wares, and made their way all the way down the hill to the beach. It was such a beautiful June day, the beach was crowded with people from kids to grandparents as well as lots of dogs.

With the time they spent looking at art and crafts and other offerings, it took them two hours to get to the beach. From there, Logan pointed out a restaurant with a large patio and suggested a glass of wine and maybe a snack. They settled into chairs with a view of the Pacific and ordered.

"What's on your agenda this week?" he asked.

"Well, I don't have any appointments yet, so first thing in the morning I'm going to get on the computer, see if I can locate any more small practices in the area that I can visit. I'm staying in my friend's guest room tonight, but I'll check in with the girls and find out what they have going on and then plot my day. You?"

"I'm working on a couple of cases. Both involve surveillance. A couple of us are tag teaming. One young woman's wealthy parents are trying to determine if their daughter is involved in some nefarious behavior with bad people and drugs. Another we're investigating is a businessman who no longer trusts his partner. The first is almost a wrap. Nefarious behavior never takes a holiday. She is in a mess. The second will take longer but is more interesting."

"Wow," she said. "Every day must be a fun day!"

He laughed. "Depends on your idea of fun. I admit, I like solving puzzles. And we're busy all the time."

"As I will be, if I am fortunate enough to begin to build a new practice."

"I know this isn't exactly what you planned," he said. "But this must be an exciting time."

"It's more terrifying than exciting. I have to admit, I'm struggling with the added responsibility. I've taken on the bills, my own savings and retirement, the girls' expenses..."

"Aren't you getting child support?"

"Sort of. I'm deducting a small support payment for the girls from what I've agreed to pay Scott. And I'm keeping careful track of the bills—if he wants alimony and half the house, he has to pay half the household bills."

"He's getting support?"

She nodded. "For five years. But it's not a fixed amount. Child support is a fixed amount, but the support I have to pay Scott is half of what I earn. I left my job last week. There will probably be nothing for a while."

Logan sat forward in his chair. "Will that come as a surprise?"

"To him? Undoubtedly. Though I did tell him I meant to make a change and that I didn't want to work for a large company anymore." She stared at the ocean. "I've been with the same company since I passed the bar. I've always had a decent paycheck. I think Scott just assumes it will always be that way. This is the first time I've been out of work since college."

The waitress brought them drinks and a plate of artichoke dip and bread. Logan lifted his glass to her. "Here's to your new life."

"Thank you," she said. "Talking to you has helped, Logan. Thank you for making yourself available."

"I've enjoyed it, too. Tell me more about your girls and what they'll be doing this summer."

"Well, they both have part-time jobs. Amber will go to cheerleading camp in August—fortunately it was half paid for before school was out. I've suggested she look for a part-time job she can manage during the school year, and she said she'll look around. I told her I won't have as much spending money for her during her senior year, so she'd better. Olivia has some steady babysitting lined up and is going with the family of her young wards for their vacation in July. She's a miser. She'll be okay. Amber thinks she wants to be a fashion designer or an actress or a home decor designer—we'll see. Olivia wants to be a librarian. That goal hasn't changed since she was a little tot and sat on the librarian's lap during story time."

They talked through a second glass of wine and some stuffed mushrooms. The sun was just starting to descend over the ocean, and Justine realized her phone hadn't chimed with an incoming call or text the entire afternoon. She pulled it out of her purse and looked at it just to be sure.

"Someone looking for you?" Logan asked.

"Nah. I have no curfew tonight. I'll check in with the girls on my way to my friend's house."

"This has to be getting old," he said. "Staying at someone else's house on Scott's nights."

"It won't last forever," she said. "For now, I'm making sure Scott has every chance to be an involved—" She went silent before finishing her sentence and was looking down the hill toward the beach. Then she flat-out stared.

Scott was right there with his mistress, strolling across the beach. She was small of stature, much shorter than Justine. She wore tight white capris, a short T-shirt that showed her belly and she had tattoos down one arm. Her hair was streaked or colored white-blond, and spiky. Justine longed for binoculars. She couldn't really make out the details of her face, except that she had a long, pointy nose. They held hands and strolled like lovers.

"Oh-oh," Logan said.

"This is my first time seeing her," Justine said.

"There's not much to see," Logan said.

"There are some amazing tattoos to see," Justine pointed out. "I have to admit she's not what I expected. But she does have a good figure. At least from here she looks like a solid little thing."

"Justine, you're beautiful," he said. "And brilliant."

"And somehow, not enough..."

"That's grief talking," he said. "And at the end of the day, you'll be better off than he will be."

"But will I be better off than *her*?" she asked.

"Now that I can't tell you," Logan said. "But what I do know after all I've been able to learn about them, is your ex-husband is very stupid."

"Seeing them, like that... It's a little shocking. But it doesn't make me want him back. Shouldn't I want him? I gave him everything I had for thirty years!"

"I don't know," Logan said. "Maybe you're happy you aren't going to give him thirty more?"

"I'm still a little afraid of being alone..."

"Justine, you're not alone," he said. "I just bought you wine and artichoke dip! Man, you really work a guy hard!" And then he grinned at her.

She laughed and decided she liked him enough to kiss him later. If he asked.

They walked slowly up the hill to the parking lot and, good to his word, he held her hand. It was odd how that gave her so much confidence. The old Justine wouldn't have so much as touched the hand of another man, and would probably be looking over her shoulder to see if her husband was in the vicinity. She was thoroughly comfortable, liked the touch; her ex-husband's feelings never once crossing her mind.

Then he was there, right in front of her.

"Justine," Scott said. "What are you doing here?"

She jumped in surprise when she was face-to-face with him. She looked left and saw the woman at his side, then swiveled her eyes back to Scott. "I'm taking in the art walk." She looked at him closely. "That's a nasty bruise." A big purple bruise on his cheek had blackened his eye, and there was a small cut on his lip.

"I was helping out at the kayak shack and whacked myself right in the head," he said. He cleared his throat. "Aren't you going to introduce us? This is Cat."

She thought about saying a hundred mean things. She noticed the woman did not smile. In fact, she wore a very superior expression, almost a sneer. But why wouldn't she. She won. And Scott was the prize?

"No," she said. "There's no need. We're not going to be friendly. Next time you see me, just keep walking."

"Rude," Cat said.

"Want me to tell you what's rude?" Justine said. "I'll tell you what's rude! Sleeping with another woman's—"

Logan pulled her away. He slid an arm around her waist to hold her close against his side and walked with her toward her car. "Not that I can't appreciate a good fight, but I'm going to save you from jail time," he said.

"Did you see how smug she was? I should've punched her."

"I think she's had practice," Logan said.

"I shouldn't have spoken," Justine said. "I should have just walked away. If I ever run into her again, I'll just turn my back."

"Good idea," he said. "Because she enjoyed that little temper you had."

"How do you know that?"

"Her expression. I've been reading expressions for a long time. She's got a mean streak."

"Do you think she'd do something bad? To me or my girls?"

"Not directly," he said. "That expression, that one uttered word? I think she likes the upper hand. She didn't flinch at meeting you, even after she's done her part to destroy your marriage. Possibly she has no conscience. Best to stay away from her."

"Scott wants her to meet the girls."

He stopped walking. He looked down at her. "If you have any influence, I'd give it a year before you do something like that. Can you convince your girls to put that off?"

"They don't want to meet her."

"Better still."

"Whew, I'm very glad you were there to drag me away. I was going to throw her down."

He laughed softly. "I felt that energy coming off you." He arrived at her car. He turned her around, pressed her up against the car. "Don't look for him," he said. "Just remember, he's gone and you're a single woman. Just don't look. Look here," he said, giving his head a nod, focusing on her eyes. "Tell me if you had a good time."

"All but two minutes," she said. "Yes, I had a very good time. Good conversation, nice walk through town, delightful and relaxing view with wine…"

"I had a good time, too," he said. "If fact, I think there are going to be more good times." He leaned toward her and put a brief and soft kiss on her lips. "No, don't look around to see if he's there. We're fine. We're not cheating on anyone."

"That's a strange feeling, right there," she said.

"It might take some getting used to," he said. "You're not one of a pair anymore."

"I'm not," she said, leaning toward him for another kiss. Just a short but meaningful kiss. "Is it all right if I call you later?"

"You call anytime you feel like it," he said. "If you don't call me, I'll probably call you. I love talking to you."

"It was kind of an awkward day, after all," she said. "I'm sorry about that."

"Nah, it had to happen. I'm glad I was with you. Now that's one more thing you don't have to worry about. You're going to run into them. You're up to the challenge. You can do it without violence."

"It was close, though."

Justine's friend was out for the evening and had left her a note on the kitchen counter. Justine phoned the girls, made sure they were settled in for the night. Amber said that Scott had called and said he'd be there by ten; Justine didn't mention having seen him in Carmel. She simply said, "I'll call you in the morning. Then I'm going to go job hunting again."

If there was anything good about running into Scott and Cat, it was learning that she would not perish from seeing them together. And while it had been tempting to punch her in the throat, she hadn't. She had perfected see-ing Scott in passing and never lost her cool because they were co-parenting. She didn't scream at him that he was nothing more than betraying scum, a liar, a cheat, a waste of air. Tears no longer rose in her eyes. She didn't long for him. In fact, she began to see his flaws more clearly. His hair was not just touched with gray, it must be graying rapidly and thinning fast because he was using some kind of cheap coloring that stained his scalp. He had a weak chin, his nose was crooked and his teeth should be whitened.

He was very fit, she'd give him that. How else should he be since all he did was play? But being fit couldn't keep your face and neck from sagging. In fact, all that time in the sun was not helping the aging process. But all that was just the rigors of aging, and she would have looked on his flaws with affection, willing to grow old with him. She would have gone to the end, of that she was sure. She never questioned whether or not she was deeply in love. She never asked herself if she was in love enough. She only asked herself how much longer they had if they stayed relatively healthy.

That was no longer possible. There was no more for them now.

But if she was going to run into him and his mistress in Carmel on a sunny Sunday afternoon, she could run into them anywhere, anytime. Avoiding Half Moon Bay was no longer an issue.

Spending the day with Adele had put her in a nostalgic frame of mind. She longed for the comfort of a small beach town. She'd love to get up early and walk to the beach with her sister, exercising before work. She wanted work that was satisfying and a lifestyle that was healthy. When she stopped for groceries after work, she'd rather walk to Bronski's than fight for a parking space at Super Foods. In fact, wouldn't it be great to walk to work?

With that in mind, she went to the law offices of Sam Gillespie, Esquire. He was located in what passed for the business district of Half Moon Bay, nestled between a photographer's studio and a bookstore. Down the block was a beauty shop and day spa. On the other side was a sandwich shop and bank. Also on the block were a secondhand clothing store, a hemp goods store, a UPS store. There was a bakery, a fast food restaurant, a barber shop and a place called The Beach Club, displaying board shorts and flipflops in the window.

Just looking up and down the street, feeling the desire to browse, to look into the shops, chat with the owners or sales people, confirmed what she was looking for—a quieter, less rushed lifestyle. Room to breathe. A life where all she had to worry about was food, shelter and the ability to take care of and educate her girls. Could she do that, knowing Scott and his mistress were just down the street?

She went into the office; a buzzer sounded, bringing a man from the back.

"Can I help you?"

"I wonder if Mr. Gillespie is in?"

"I'm Sam Gillespie," he said.

She stretched out her hand. "Justine Somersby, attorney. It's come to my attention you're looking for an associate, and I'd love to hear more about the position and your practice when you have the time. I can make an appointment, if you like."

"I have a few minutes to talk," he said. "What brings you to Half Moon Bay?"

She smiled. "I grew up here. My sister still lives in the house we grew up in. I've been gone about twenty years."

He leaned a hip on one of two desks in the front of the office. "Almost exactly as long as I've been here. Where have you been working?"

She opened her briefcase and pulled out a copy of her résumé. "Over twenty years with the same software manufacturer in San Jose, corporate law, some of that time as general counsel. Given the size of the company and number of employees, I handled some human resources issues. I'm recently divorced, and now that I don't have to concern myself with supporting a nonworking spouse, I'm looking for a slower pace. I have two daughters, sixteen and seventeen. They both drive. I resigned from Sharper Dynamic."

His eyes lit up. "There's been talk of a takeover," he said.

"Actually, there's a merger," she said. "There will be some reshuffling internally. It was an ideal time to move on."

"I have a lot of questions for you," he said. "You will undoubtedly have some for me. Why don't we meet tomorrow, if you're free. My afternoon looks good. Two o'clock?"

"Excellent. I can't wait."

CHAPTER TEN

The month of June became a month of huge changes for both Adele and Justine. Justine took an associate's position in the law office of Sam Gillespie just a few blocks from Adele's house. Justine explained to Addie that Sam wanted to wind down his hours a bit. He'd gotten three kids through college, he was in his late fifties and his wife, Maddy, was a professor at Berkeley. He had no plans to retire, but he and Maddy wanted to travel a little more, spend some time with their kids and two grandchildren and spend less time in the office.

"Sam said he'd begun to despair of ever finding a mature, experienced attorney interested in such a small storefront legal firm. The term *experienced* should be used loosely. I don't have much by way of small town lawyering, but Sam said he looks forward to showing me the ropes."

Justine was commuting from San Jose because the girls were there. She was spending her days in Half Moon Bay while Adele was at the college working. Sometimes they'd have an early dinner together. Justine was getting settled into the neighborhood law office. and she was still staying at her friend Jean's house in San Jose when it was Scott's night with the girls.

After working in Half Moon Bay for two weeks, she texted Scott.

Sharper Dynamic downsized again and I left the company. I've accepted a position at the law office of Sam Gillespie in Half Moon Bay. I will be commuting to work from San Jose and keeping close tabs on the girls as usual. There's no need to change our schedule.

Amber and Olivia shared a car, and there were times they drove down to Half Moon Bay to have dinner with Adele and Justine. In all the years they'd all lived in this close proximity, they'd never had so much togetherness or such fun.

Adele couldn't help but notice that Justine was changing; she had always been confident but now she was also calm and self-assured. It was just a slight change. She was a friendlier, happier person.

"Is it possible you weren't entirely happy with Scott?" Adele asked her while they were preparing dinner one night. "Because you're more fun now. You seem better than ever."

"I was happy," Justine said. "I loved Scott. But there was a lot of pressure. I had a serious job and a husband and two busy girls to think about. I was keeping a lot of balls in the air, constantly afraid to drop the glass ball, never knowing which one it was. Scott wasn't under any pressure. I think the girls have experienced real stress and pressure for the first time with our divorce. They've had a few meltdowns but they're doing so well. Don't you think?"

"You're all doing well," Addie said. "There's one thing.

The girls don't seem that interested in their dad these days. They hardly talk about him."

"He comes with baggage now," Justine said. "He's been pressuring them to meet the girlfriend. He asks them every week. And since they won't do it, he's spending more time away from home, away from the girls. I can't believe I'm saying this but mark my words—he's going to give up his daughters. I've noticed that he doesn't get home to the girls as he should. He misses dinner with them most nights, gets home late, leaves early. That's why I'm staying close. I check in with them constantly. If Scott isn't going to be home for dinner, I bring them something or take them out. I've stocked the freezer with easy microwavable meals."

"Isn't he hanging out with them on the weekends?" Adele asked.

"They took a long bike ride together three weeks ago or so, but I haven't heard of anything else. He says he's working. You'll never guess where…"

"I know where," Addie said. "The kayak shack. I see his car there almost every day. I walk a little out of my way to check because I just can't stand it. I can't believe he can abandon his family like he has." She snapped her fingers. "So fast, so easy."

"It hasn't been easy in my heart," Justine said. "But the last couple of weeks have been great. Sam Gillespie's practice is like the fantasy I've been having for about ten years. In fact, the whole town is like a fantasy. Of course I didn't appreciate it when I was young, but after twenty years in Silicon Valley, this is paradise. Have you noticed that no one honks at a stoplight? The only people I see rushing are young mothers trying to get their kids to school on time. It took one week for everyone in the market and on most of Main Street to know me by name. When I start living in the area, after the girls are gone and the house can be sold, I'm going to spend a lot more time walking that beach."

"You know there's a guest room here. No bed or dresser yet, but we could take care of that," Addie said.

"For now I like being either with the girls or only a couple of blocks away," Justine said.

"I can understand that," Addie said. "And...we've never lived together."

"Maybe we never will," Justine said.

"I hope we do," Adele said. "I hope we at least have sleepovers."

It had been a long time since all the bedrooms in Adele's house had been used. When Justine went to college, she commuted at first. When she left home, she took her bedroom furniture with her mother's blessing—it was pretty old, after all. Adele's mother's furniture, by the end, had been functional hospital furniture. It was gone within days of her passing.

Adele started looking online for bedroom furniture and within two weeks had found a bed and dresser at a very reasonable price. She went and looked at it, bought it and had it delivered. Two days after showing it to her sister, Justine decided to spend the night. "Just this one night," she said. "I don't want to get in your way."

"You're not in the way, Justine. You help a lot."

It was true. Justine was a neat freak and tidied up constantly. She loved to go to the market and get fresh food— much fresher and better quality than the chain supermarket she'd been using for years. And Justine's new job was so close. By July Justine had settled into one of the upstairs bedrooms with the used bedroom furniture and new mattress that Adele had purchased.

Half Moon Bay had a fantastic beach, and Scott had

proven himself to be very inadequate about spending time with his daughters. He was *working*! Thank God they weren't young and could take pretty good care of themselves. The combination of Scott's delinquency and the draw of the beach saw Adele's nieces coming to Half Moon Bay when their summer job schedules allowed. At first they came for the day and stayed for dinner, then they brought blow-up mattresses with sheets and blankets from home and duffels holding their clothes and stayed overnight. July saw the three of them, Justine, Amber and Olivia, at Adele's more often than in San Jose. Instead of Justine going to San Jose to spend nights with her daughters, they were coming to her. They tried to arrange their work schedules for the same days and would drive back to San Jose together, returning to Half Moon Bay at the end of the day.

Scott was relieved of his parenting duties by his daughters who would rather be with their mother and aunt.

Finally in August, Olivia ran into Scott at a beach bar. She was getting herself a drink while he was ordering a couple of sandwiches. She looked around carefully before she said, "Hey, Dad."

He started. "Olivia! What are you doing here?"

"I've been reading on the beach the last couple of hours and now I'm walking back to Aunt Addie's house."

"Why didn't you tell me you'd be in town?" he asked.

She shrugged. "Because you said you were busy working at your girlfriend's business."

"You can come by! See the place! Meet her!"

"We talked about this," she said. "I don't really feel like meeting her."

"Why the hell are you girls being like this? It's wrong! The divorce has been final at least a couple of months! She's a part of my life now. That's how it is!"

"Fine," Olivia said. "See you in San Jose, maybe. Be sure to let us know when you'll be visiting."

She turned and walked away.

"Olivia!"

She turned back.

"You have to treat me and Cat with respect!" he said.

"I'm respectful," Olivia said. "She might be part of your life, but she isn't going to be part of mine." She turned to go again.

"Look, there are changes," he said. "We're all going to have to get used to the changes!"

"Maybe we will," she said. "Two months isn't enough time for me. Let's talk about it in a year or two."

"Did your mother tell you to say that?"

"Oh heck no," she said. "My counselor asked me how I felt about meeting your girlfriend. I told her how I feel and she said I should be honest with you. Maybe I'll be willing to meet the woman you left our family for in a couple of years. Maybe in ten years. Maybe never. Didn't you ever think that in leaving your family, there might be consequences? Like—we might not be happy about it?"

"But don't you want *me* to be happy?"

"Is that just a guy thing? That your happiness is more important than anyone else's happiness? Because you being happy seems to have caused a whole bunch of people to be unhappy. Doesn't that bother you?"

"Of course!" he said. "What I want is for us all to be happy! If you would just make an effort—"

Again she shrugged. "And if you had made an effort…"

"But I wasn't happy! I've been unhappy for *years*!"

"Really? What was that Christmas Eve toast you made? I am the luckiest man alive with the three most wonderful, beautiful women… Oh gee, did you mean four? Listen,

Daddy, we're onto you. You're telling yourself a story that makes it seem like you had nothing to do with this mess, but the truth is, you created it. Any time you want to be my dad, let me know. But I'm not interested in your girlfriend."

"I shouldn't have to choose between you!"

"Sounds like you already did." Tears sparkled in Olivia's eyes. "When you're telling your story about how unhappy you've been, though no one knew it, you should remember you left us. You're making a new life. You're making all new rules and changing what family means. We're just trying to cope. And understand."

She walked away from the beach bar and charged up the hill from the beach, her bag slung over one shoulder and her smoothie in her hand, tears running down her cheeks. She loved her daddy so much; there had been so many beautiful memories. He had been a constant in her life, always there, always on duty. And her mom, so beautiful and strong, picking up where Daddy left off. She had grown up thinking she had the most awesome parents in the world. She had her fun and playful dad; her dedicated and completely committed mom.

And then one day, with no warning at all, he was done. He had his eye on a better life. A new life. With a new woman, leaving their mother so broken and thin, dark circles under her eyes. Olivia just wanted her family back.

"Oh-oh," a voice said. "You could use someone to walk you home."

Olivia looked up, way up, into the warm brown eyes of a young man. She'd seen him around, on the beach playing volleyball with friends, hanging out near the beach bar. "I…we… I don't know you."

"Yet. But we've seen each other. At least I've seen you.

And I think you saw me see you. I'm Jared. Jared Morrison. And you're...?"

"Olivia. Livvie for short. Livvie Somersby. I actually live in San Jose but my mom and aunt are here, so I'm spending a lot of the summer in Half Moon Bay."

"San Jose isn't that far. On a good day I can get there in twenty minutes."

She laughed in spite of herself. "Is that a day when your car can go a hundred miles an hour?"

"See, I made you happy already. Why don't you come down to the beach after dinner, like around seven, and play some volleyball?"

"I should see what my sister is doing. I should see if my mom and aunt need any help with anything."

"You can bring your sister. Is she the one I usually see you with? Brown hair?"

Olivia nodded. "She's a senior."

"Most everyone around here works a lot so we're not on the beach that much in the daytime, but there are a lot of us at night. Come down. I'll introduce you to a few of my friends. If you're gonna hang around Half Moon Bay, you might as well know people. Right?"

"That would be nice."

"We've got at least another month of late sunsets."

"Are you a senior?" she asked.

"I graduated last spring. Now I'm working at the lodge on the bay, and I'll be taking some classes at the community college."

"Which one? My aunt works at Banyon."

"I'll be at San Mateo, starting in about three weeks." He laughed. "We don't have much time, Livvie. Will you come down tonight?"

"I think so," she said, smiling in spite of herself.

* * *

Justine had emailed Scott a copy of her pay stub and no check for the month of June. Her itemized statement had been prepared by Sam's accountant; it showed her billable hours, her deductions and her pay for the part of the month she had worked. It was practically nothing. Scott called and asked her what was up with that. "I've barely started here," she said. "It will take a while to build a clientele."

"Didn't you at least get a severance package from Sharper Dynamic?"

"No, I'm afraid not. I resigned rather than accept a big salary cut."

"Great," he said, disgruntled. And he hung up.

July hadn't been much better, but then not only did she not have a large number of clients, it also took a while to complete legal work and do the billing.

"A lawyer can usually expect it to be at least ninety days between legal work and payment. The billing alone takes a good month, and that's after the work is done," she explained to Scott.

Toward the end of August, Justine was in her office when the office manager, Charlene, asked her if she had time to see a Mr. Scott Somersby. Charlene was frowning.

"Sure," Justine said.

Scott stood in her office door. This place suited her fine, but it was nothing like the office she'd left behind in Silicon Valley. Her office at Sharper Dynamic was intimidating and designed to be. This office was quaint and more welcoming.

"Hi, Scott. What are you doing here? You can just email or text me if you have a question."

"The question is what the hell is up with your pay?"

"Well, as I've explained, my tenure is brand-new. I serve

as an associate and need a lot of consultation with Mr. Gillespie to be sure I'm operating according to his established practices, and I don't have many clients. But I'm sure it will grow. Given time."

"I don't have that much time," he said. "I'm short of funds."

"I gave you a very generous settlement," she said. "You're usually very good with money."

"I still am, but I invested it and my cash flow is limited. I was counting on the monthly income. My money is not liquid."

"Ah. I'm afraid I can't help you there." She squinted at him. "What's that mark on your eyebrow? Looks like you're imitating Jason Momoa."

"Work injury. I was whacked by a kayak I was trying to hang up. We're going to have to do something about the money."

"Aren't you making money at your new job? You are getting paid, aren't you?"

"Of course! Look, we're going to have to do something—refinance the house or get an equity line of credit or something. Either that or cut the child support."

"Hmm. You should have a healthy bank account, Scott. Do you mind if I ask what you decided to invest in?"

"Yes, I mind!" he barked. "That's not your concern! It's enough that you realize I'm a little tight and having trouble with expenses and half the mortgage. Unless you start paying support, I'm not going to be able to pay the bills!"

"You're going to have to leave now, Scott," she said calmly. "I'll call you after work to discuss this, but we can't do it now. This is a law office, and the only people allowed outbursts in here are disgruntled clients. I'll call you this evening."

"Fine," he said, clearly rattled.

Justine watched him go. She walked out into the reception area to note that he had driven from the kayak shack to her office.

"The ex?" Charlene asked.

"The one and only. I'll speak to him tonight and make sure he understands he can't bring our divorce business to this office."

Apparently it had only just occurred to Scott that Justine might not always bring home that fat check he'd always enjoyed. And what would he do? He must not have a plan. And he didn't know what it felt like to have the pressure of earning fall to his shoulders.

Adele loved her job every day, even on the days that a client's story made her want to cry. In fact, sometimes on those days she loved it even more because she watched in fascination as the team of social workers somehow closed ranks against a challenge and found a solution. Sometimes it seemed they just kept paddling along until they ran into a solution.

Something similar seemed to have happened in Adele's home.

"Over summer the most surprising dynamic shifted," Adele told Ross. "Of course you knew about Justine staying with me so she can work in Half Moon Bay, but then her girls started sleeping over and for the first time ever, we were a family. It was like Scott's leaving was almost a good thing. Well, probably not for Justine, but it worked out pretty well for me having more time with my sister and nieces. Then as summer progressed, the girls started spending more time on the beach with local kids. Now they don't like going home so much. They only live in the San

Jose house when they have to because it's Scott's custody night, and that's not going so well, which means they're at my house more often than not."

"What's not going well?" Ross asked.

"He makes a lot of excuses to get home late and leave early, so the girls end up sitting home alone rather than having fun or spending time with their father. He claims it's work, but they already know the kayak shack isn't open late. They know it's more about the woman in his life, and it's not something they take quietly. Justine doesn't go back to San Jose as often as she did last spring." Addie sighed. "More and more of their stuff is taking residence in my house." Then she smiled. "Our house. It's still half Justine's, of course."

"I take it you're feeling pretty good about these changes?" Ross asked.

"I've been feeling better about a lot of things, and it started with getting this job. I wanted to tell you something. I'm going up to Berkeley to talk with a career adviser. I was over a year into my graduate program, and now I want to change direction. Depending on how many of my credits are transferable and whether I can change grad programs, I think I'd like a degree in counseling."

"Is that right?" Ross asked with a smile.

"You smile so much more often these days," Adele said. "When I first met you…" She couldn't finish. She was afraid she'd already said too much.

"I know," Ross said. "I'm not cranky. I'm serious, that's all. There is a difference, but not many people bother to look at the differences."

"It's true," Addie said. "You've never been what I'd call angry."

"Oh, I used to be pretty angry," she admitted. "Life was

hard. I had a terrible husband, a bunch of kids, trouble making money, no one to help, nowhere to turn."

"And you turned here?" Addie asked.

Ross shook her head. "Not exactly. There were other people along the way who served a similar purpose. My church, my neighborhood, a couple of women in the same boat who I went to school with. But I eventually ended up here, a brand-new social worker when this program was just starting. It didn't pay well but it got me by. Then I became invested in the program and the people."

"I think I'm already invested in the program even though I don't do anything to help."

"Now don't you be saying that. You're the first face most of them see. You're the first person they talk to. It's your expression and your encouragement that gets them going, gives them hope. Your position is a very important one. It's not an easy one to fill. I want you to make the most of your opportunities, but I sure hope we don't have to replace you too soon. You'd be tough to replace."

"I hope I can continue my advance degree while working," Adele said. "It's all a matter of whether I have to pick up undergrad credits before resuming my graduate studies in a new program. There are lots of possibilities. But there's something that wasn't available before—there are tons of online classes."

Ross's face grew very soft as she gazed at Adele. She looked as sweet and lovely as Adele had ever seen her.

"I'm going to give you some advice. Advice that was given to me that I struggled with. You've had many changes this year, starting with your mama's death after years of being at home, caring for her. Then you began to grow in so many ways, remarkable ways. I'm so proud of you. We're all so proud of you. I'm on your side, I promise you. And

I want you to achieve your dreams. But while you're making the decisions that will lead you there, be very careful to take care of yourself. Don't spread yourself too thin. Don't make yourself sick or too tired or get frustrated and angry, because what you want to do sounds rewarding and wonderful. Getting there will be hard but worth it. Please don't overdo yourself. Remember to try to enjoy the process as well as the destination."

"You're right," Addie said. "That's very good advice."

But Adele was thinking, *It's this job and these people who made me want to finally find a life that matters to me.*

"And I want you to be able to enjoy this new sense of family you have."

"I'm so surprised by this, and it's my sister's broken heart that began to bring us together. We were never really sisters before. I always loved Justine and admired her, but we never really bonded until now."

"Life happens that way sometimes. Out of the ashes comes the beauty."

Justine's conversation with Scott went badly. She was frankly surprised it had not happened sooner.

"You should have told me you were planning to quit your job," he said.

"I wasn't planning to," she said. "I was planning to stay at Sharper Dynamic for as long as possible, but the company is going through a merger, the positions were rapidly shifting and I was going to be moved to another department and it involved a significant pay cut. Plus my marriage was suddenly over, our assets divided as was our future. We would no longer have a team future. If I wanted to make a change, I could. And I've wanted to make a change for a long time. I was always honest about that. I told you I was getting burned out on corporate law years ago."

"But you didn't say you were going to quit! When you said you were happy to give me half your earnings for five years, you didn't say your earnings would be down by a hundred percent! If you were so burned out, why didn't you quit years ago?"

"Because we were playing as a team, and we had to make decisions like that together! You're on another team now. Besides, what's the panic? Didn't you walk away with over two million dollars?"

"I invested in a business!"

She shouldn't have been surprised, yet she was shocked. "Oh, Scott, you didn't! Did you invest in that kayak shack? With the girlfriend?"

"I do have a degree in business. I managed our investments, income and retirement funds very successfully for many years," he said.

"Except we had the advice of a professional financial planner and accountant. Did you enter into a partnership with that woman? She's had two bankruptcies, you know. And the business is failing!"

"How do you know that?" he demanded angrily.

"Scott, it's a matter of public record," she said.

"You lied to me! You cheated me! You offered me support, knowing you wouldn't have to pay it!"

"And you offered me a lifetime of marriage, telling me you loved me while you were having an affair! How long have you known we wouldn't stay married? Because I decided to work for myself rather than for us after you left me for another woman!"

"It's not the same thing and you know it!"

"How is it different? Admit it, it was easy to end the marriage knowing you'd have a plush income, a healthy war chest and another woman to keep you company!"

"And you're deliberately pulling the rug out from under me as revenge!"

"You couldn't be more wrong," she said. "I've decided on a different and more satisfying life, just as you have. The only real difference is, you decided before you were divorced. At least I waited until after."

"How am I supposed to get by?" he asked. "Come on, Justine, I've spent the last twenty years as a stay-at-home dad! Supporting your career! Raising our kids! You owe me support."

"Are we really going down that path again? You could easily have taken on a full-time job—you do have a business degree, after all," she added, mocking him.

"You were bored and you found a woman—a woman with a kayak shack in trouble. Was she about to lose it?"

"That's none of your business, but in the spirit of cooperation I'll just say that if anyone can turn that business around, it's me."

"That's what I thought," she said. "You've committed your nest egg to Cat Brooks and her floundering business. I wonder how long ago you decided."

"You're doing it again, making up some narrative that leaves you blameless in the divorce. You want everything to be my fault when you ignored me in favor of your prestigious job for years. And you made sure everyone knew you were the breadwinner, didn't you?"

"You made a deal with a woman you're having an affair with to give her money and help her get her business on its feet, though you have no way of knowing if you can. And now you need money. I think we are finished. Except for our kids, you and I have nothing more to say."

"We have to find a solution to this together," he said.

"We're not a team anymore, Scott. You wanted to be free. You wanted your half of everything we'd accrued. I asked you several times if you were sure."

"Yeah, but you tricked me!"

"No, I didn't. I just got on with my life. It's a different kind of life for me now. I wouldn't have chosen it, at least not at this time. Later. I had hoped it would come later, after the kids were through college, when it was you and me. I had no idea you were planning something else."

"And just what am I supposed to do now?"

"Gee, Scott. Do whatever you want. And good luck."

And then she ended the call.

CHAPTER ELEVEN

Adele's first appointment at Berkeley was with Dr. Hennessey, a young female PhD in the department of social sciences. They had a pleasant conversation about Adele's change in direction and a new graduate program, and it gave her a chance to sing the praises of the reentry program where she worked.

There would be a boatload of work to do to complete an application—a mission statement, all her transcripts, including her original GRE test for graduate study. There would be a series of interviews and if all went well, she could be admitted as early as spring. Dr. Hennessy looked over course programs and saw that while there were a few courses she would have to attend, she could fill in with a few online courses and required papers. At first glance it looked as though it would be no harder than her original graduate program, and ironically, that psychology class she took from Hadley. Hutchinson would count toward her counseling degree.

Adele was able to forward copies of all her paperwork to Dr. Hennessey, and she followed up with another meeting a few weeks later. It was the first of October, back to school season was in full swing, the leaves on the California hillsides were changing color. It was a time of year that always filled Adele with a sense of freshness and energy. Her nieces were going to football games and a couple of high school dances, but what was interesting was that they continued to balance their time between Half Moon Bay and San Jose, spending more and more time in Half Moon Bay.

As Adele was walking across campus carrying a cup of coffee after her second meeting with Dr. Hennessey, she heard someone call her name. She turned to see Hadley taking long strides toward her.

"Adele!" he said. "Addie!"

Curse him. Now in his forties, he was devilishly handsome. Just the slightest touch of gray graced his temples. His face was tanned, his eyes as blue as the sky and his long lean body lithe and hard. She remembered that body, all of it.

Suddenly, she thought about Scott and how he'd spent so much money on hotels and spas for his affair while Hadley had seduced her in his campus office, the front of his car or on a blanket on a hideaway beach.

"Professor," she said, looking up at him.

His face was bright with happiness, his eyes twinkling. When she addressed him as professor, a smile broke across his lips. Oh those teeth—big and straight and super white.

"Adele, what a sight you are," he said. "You look wonderful! It's been years! And look at you. You've grown even more beautiful! What are you doing here?"

"I…ah… I was visiting an acquaintance who has an office here. And I guess this means you're still teaching here?" She was scrambling to sound casual even though Dr. Hennessey was not actually an acquaintance and she knew perfectly well he was still teaching at the university. She checked the website regularly.

"I think about you all the time, hoping we'd see each other again. I assume you finished your degree at another university?"

"Not exactly," she said. "It's a long story, but I was needed at home. Listen, I've got to get—"

"Please," he said. "Don't run off. I don't want to lose touch with you again. Do you have time for a cup of coffee? Oh, I see you have a cup. Lunch then, or something. Please, I've thought about you for years. Can we at least sit somewhere and catch up? For just a little while?"

"Do you think that's a good idea?" she asked. "We didn't part on the best of terms."

"My fault," he said. "You can't imagine the regrets I've had about that. Or the number of times I wanted to track you down and insist we at least talk it through!"

"But you didn't," she said. "I never heard from you."

"You told me you'd never speak to me again! You were so angry. And so hurt. I couldn't…"

That was at least partially true. Yes, there had been a fierce argument after she told him she'd seen him with his wife. She'd told him to stay away from her.

"You lied to me about everything!" she said.

"You don't even know what you saw! Did it ever occur to you that she was emotional because I'd told her I wanted a divorce?"

"She was pregnant!"

"I know. I felt terrible about that. It happened before… us. I found out about it after us. I planned to take care of them, of course. And I have."

"What do you mean, you have?" she asked.

"We're not together. It's only been a few years now, but

the problems started a long time ago. I have two daughters. We work out the custody arrangements. It's been complicated and at times difficult. But what's done is done. Obviously my marriage was in trouble or there couldn't have been...us."

Adele felt her heart plummet in her chest. No, that wasn't how it was. It wasn't that way. He begged for more time to do what had to be done, but meanwhile, while she waited for him, she was to get an abortion. That was how it was.

"I remember it a little differently," she said, and to her horror a tear slid down her cheek.

"Oh darling, I know how traumatic it was for you," he said. "And you were so young. I must've been a monster to let myself fall in love with you."

Yes, he had said all those words—that he was being selfish, that many men would want her and he would probably be her worst choice, but still, he couldn't help what he felt.

"I just wish you'd have let me be with you during that difficult time. The baby lost, your grief..."

"It wasn't lost the way you think," she blurted. "I didn't go through with it, the abortion. I couldn't. But I lost him anyway. It felt like I was being punished..."

The look on his face could have stopped a speeding train. Shock and dread etched lines in his face. "What?"

"I didn't have an abortion."

"But we planned..."

"I just couldn't. I went home. And my father had an accident so I stayed on to help take care of him. I didn't go back to school."

He shook his head as if to deny what she was saying. "I knew you dropped out. Of course I knew that. But I thought... I guess I thought you'd come back or finish somewhere else. I thought about looking for you but then

I told myself I'd already done enough damage." He looked around as if to see who might've overheard them. "Addie, we must talk. For just a little while. Come with me to Mac's," he said, speaking of a small, dark little off-campus pub. They'd logged many a romantic hour there, whispering and holding hands in a corner booth.

"No, I really can't…"

"Please. I want to know everything that happened to you, and I want to tell you what happened with me. Please."

She hesitated, but ultimately she said, "Fine. I'll meet you over there."

She hadn't seen the inside of that old bar in years, but the only thing that seemed different was that it had somehow become shabbier. She remembered it as quaint and charming, but now it seemed shopworn. There were just a dozen or so people in the place, but it was midafternoon.

She saw him sitting in the back corner booth and a wave of nostalgia washed over her. She went to him and slid into the booth. He ordered them each a glass of wine.

"Tell me everything, Addie."

So she did. She told him how deeply hurt she'd been by the picture of love and tenderness displayed by him and his wife, their angelic little girl between them. She had confronted him that day, accused him of lying to her, told him to go to hell and never bother her again. And she remembered she was crying the whole time.

And even then, in her rage, she protected him by going to his campus office where no one would witness the confrontation.

She told him about having the baby, a stillborn boy.

"A son," he said wistfully.

Then she told him about the years that followed and how she'd completely lost interest in her education until recently.

She heard a melodramatic story from him about being brokenhearted by her anger and pronouncement that she'd been a fool to ever trust him. "I wanted to look for you—you wouldn't have been very hard to find. I really just wanted to be sure you were all right. But then I thought about it and told myself you were better off without the complication of me in your life. My wife wasn't going to let me go easily. It was going to be a long, drawn-out ordeal. I told myself to just stick to my part of the agreement that I'd get a divorce and when that was done, I'd look for you. It was not an easy time, baby on the way, my wife wanting our marriage and yet so angry with me that she could barely look at me across the table. She threatened to complain to the department head that I'd fraternized with a student, but I guess alimony was more important to her than revenge.

"When the divorce was finally done, I was stripped bare of worldly goods and emotion. It was a very dark time."

He thought about searching for her, but then realized that after all the pain he'd caused, it was a selfish thing to do. He made the decision to let go of the past and hope she'd found happiness.

"But now we've found each other," he said. "It has to be fate. God has given us a fresh start."

"God?" she said. "I doubt God had anything to do with us bumping into each other. But I am glad we cleared the air."

"We'll see each other again, won't we?" he asked.

"Something tells me that would be a mistake."

"Why? We had something wonderful!" he said. "I thought about you for years! Our passion! Our love was like poetry."

She might've laughed except he was so damned beautiful. And there had been a time her love for him was so overwhelming, she could barely breathe.

"The campus rumor is that you've had many passionate loves."

"Not true. After my divorce, I dated a few women but none were serious. And the campus is a fungus of gossip. It grows like weeds, and only a tenth of it is actually true."

After two hours of talking, Adele said she had to get home. The place was filling up with college kids and others. Hadley wanted to know when they could meet again.

"I'd like to think about all the things we talked about. I'm not sure we're a good idea." He would never know how hard it had been for her to say that.

"Give me your number," he said. "I'll call you."

"No," she said. "Just give me yours. If I think it's a good idea, I'll call you. But really, as much as I once loved you, our history is not great."

So he had relented and given her his number. On the sidewalk outside Mac's, he put his hands on her cheeks and boldly kissed her mouth. Memories of hot, steamy kisses filled her and she nearly swooned.

But she pulled away and went to her car. She thought about Ross and her bad husband and passel of kids. She thought of Felicity and her lost husband and child. She thought about the many clients who came into the office, their options few and their hope dwindling.

Then she thought about falling for this handsome, poetic guy and having the whole scenario repeat itself, and she took a deep breath. *No way.*

But she cried all the way back to Half Moon Bay. Because back then, before it all fell apart, she had been so in love.

Livvie and Jared quickly became an item at the Half Moon Bay beach, spending most evenings holding hands and having deep talks. Jared's parents had divorced a few years ago, and he empathized with Livvie's feelings. Amber made friends as well, but there wasn't one special boy. Rather, everyone liked her and she became popular at both Half Moon Bay and maintained her popularity at her high school in San Jose. Because of that, she was happy commuting from her aunt Addie's house. It seemed that after the trauma between their parents early in the year the sisters were finding solace in their family life later in the year. Addie jokingly, or not so jokingly, referred to their house as The Dormitory.

The girls saw their father regularly but briefly. He frequently walked from the kayak shack to the beach where he'd run into either Livvie or Amber. The first time he brought Cat along, Livvie just walked away. Amber followed.

"So rude," the mistress said, which made Livvie and Amber seethe.

Later, when they ran into Scott and he was alone, he said, "You're just trying to drive me further away."

Livvie wasn't having it. Amber held her tongue, but Livvie said, "Hey, you're the one who left! What you did was not okay."

"So now you don't have any affection for your father? No respect for me and the choices I had to make?"

She straightened her spine and said, "I love you, Daddy. I will always love you. I miss the old days when we spent a lot of time together. I miss the dad who loved and cared for me. And I'm sad that you thought it would be better for you to be with someone else. That's your choice, I guess. You should have said, 'No, I'm a married man and I have a promise to my wife and kids.'"

He shook his head sadly. "Maybe someday you'll understand."

"Someday maybe you will," she said.

Livvie was proud of the fact that she could do as her counselor suggested and express her honest feelings, but it always left her in a funk, made her depressed and sad. There was a part of her that wanted to make uncomfortable compromises just to have her father back in her life.

She talked with her mother about that a lot. She wanted to know if Justine missed him, too.

"I miss the man I loved," Justine said. "The man who could lie to me so easily—I don't really know that man. Whoever he is, I couldn't share a home with him. He's just too selfish."

"Daddy wasn't selfish before," Livvie said.

"I didn't think so, either," Justine said.

"Do you think you'll ever get back together?" Livvie asked.

"That would be very hard," she said. "I would never say never, but it would be very hard. He's just not the man I loved anymore."

"What happened to him?" Livvie asked.

"I don't know, sweetie. I hope it's worth it to him."

It was Saturday, the second week in October when Livvie was going to meet Jared at the beach and saw Cat's red BMW SUV driving away from the kayak shack. She had a sudden urge to see her dad, to say hello to him, manage a civil conversation not about the affair. She hadn't been in that shop even once since her parents divorced. She decided to brave it.

She heard the running water of a hose in the back and walked around the shop. It was unseasonably warm for

October, and she found her father shirtless, hosing down a couple of kayaks. "Hi, Dad," she said.

He jumped in surprise and turned toward her. Then he grabbed his shirt off the rail that supported several kayaks. "Livvie!" he said.

"I saw your girlfriend leaving and I thought… Dad, what happened to you?" she asked.

"What?" he said, quickly shrugging into his shirt.

"You're all bruised. You're hurt."

"Huh? Oh, I took a fall and got a couple of bruises. Nothing, really."

He was covered with bruises on one side of his chest and upper abdomen. "It looks like you were in a car accident! It looks really bad!"

"Damn wooden beach stairs," he said. "Why'd you stop by?"

"Just to say hello," she said. But the image of his bruises had distracted her. "I've never even seen this shop and when I saw that she wasn't here…"

"Come on in and look at the place. It's really a great little store. I'm glad you stopped by."

He led the way through the back door into the shop.

"We have forty-two kayaks, a dozen paddleboards, snorkel equipment—that's new since I came on. We're going to increase inventory for next summer and add clothing, shoes, beach gear. I'm even thinking of adding a patio and getting a food handler's license so we can sell drinks and sandwiches and snacks."

"We?" she asked.

"Cat needs a little help turning this place around. I have a lot of retail experience, you know. Not to mention a degree in business."

"So are you planning to work here for long?" Livvie asked.

He grinned. "Can't beat the view or the working conditions," he said. "We might be able to take on a little part-time labor next summer, if you're interested."

She was about to say not on your life, but instead she just said, "Thanks."

He was clearly proud of the little shop, as though he'd built it or something. There wasn't much to it—a counter, paddles and netting tacked to the walls, one room with kayaks and boards stacked on racks on either side, not a lot of moving around room. The floors and walls were weathered wood with a thin coat of sand covering the floors. She'd been around Half Moon Bay for months now, and she'd never seen many cars here, nor had she seen many kayakers or paddleboarders in the ocean just off this beach. There were many more just north of here where the water was calmer.

"We might expand and carry some scuba gear, but first we need a top-notch ad and coupon program, see if we can uptick the rentals. Maybe get into some sales by undercutting the local surf shop by a few bucks. We'll see. Things are going to slow down over winter, and that'll be a good time to concentrate on a new business plan."

"I thought Aunt Addie said the woman owned it with her brother," Livvie said.

"That was temporary. Her brother has another business in San Luis Obispo. Since I'm on board, he's moved home."

"Ah," she said. "Well, I'm glad I stopped by to see it."

"You're not leaving already, are you?"

"I have to meet Jared. He has a little time off today and works tonight at the lodge."

"I see," he said. "You're not getting serious, I hope."

"No, Dad. Not serious," she said. But yes, she was kind of serious about Jared. They seemed to have a lot in common, spent hours talking, got together whenever they could and had had some very wonderful times making out. Right now one of the best things about Jared was that he let her talk about her confusing and painful feelings toward her father.

"How old is your girlfriend?" she asked suddenly.

"Forty. Why do you ask?"

"Just curious," she said with a shrug. "Gotta go. I hope your bruises are all right."

He grabbed her upper arms and gave her a kiss on the cheek. "Great seeing you, honey. You'll have to come back and check out the improvements as they happen."

"Sure," she said.

For some reason she didn't talk to Jared about the bruises, but it troubled her. Instead, she spent her time with him talking about his classes and his job, both of which kept him busy nearly all the time. It was a real challenge for them to find time together. While Olivia wouldn't even consider working in the kayak shack, she was beginning to see the merits of finding part-time work in Half Moon Bay.

Jared was working on Saturday night. He walked Livvie home, kissed her good-night, promised her they'd have a real date soon and left her to go to work. When she entered the house, she found only her mother in the kitchen, chopping veggies.

"Where's Amber and Addie?"

"Amber's going to stay with her girlfriends in San Jose," Justine said. "Addie is shopping and should be home before long. I'm making us dinner—shrimp lo mein. How does that sound?"

"Good," she said, though at the moment she wasn't feeling hungry. "I stopped by that kayak shack today. I saw the woman leaving, and I thought maybe I could see Dad without her. I don't know why I wanted to."

"Maybe in time you and your dad will work out the kinks in your relationship," Justine said, chopping away. "I know he loves you. He must be all messed up."

"That woman," Olivia said. "I think she screwed him up."

"Could be," Justine said. "On the other hand, he's an adult and is making his own choices."

"But he never made these kind of choices before," Livvie said. "Leaving his family? Moving in with another woman?"

Justine put down the knife. "Let's be clear about something, Livvie. When I found out how involved he was, I knew it would be a long time before I could trust him again. Maybe never. The divorce was my idea. He agreed pretty quickly, but I was the one who—"

"Mom, he's really bruised," Livvie said. "He was hosing down kayaks with his shirt off, and I saw bruises all over him. On his chest, his side, even his arm. He put his shirt on real fast, but he's banged up. He said he fell down some stairs on the beach."

"Huh?"

"I asked him how that happened and he said he took a fall. He looks like he's been beat up."

Justine was speechless for a moment. "You know how active he is," she said. "Remember when he took that fall off his mountain bike. That was ugly."

"Yeah, but then he looked like he'd fallen off a bike— road rash and cuts and stuff. I don't know, something about this is really screwed up. The way he insists on trying to get us to meet her, the way he's thrown himself into her business, the way the second you found out about her, he went for a divorce? It's like he's not the same man. This just isn't the Dad I knew."

Justine sighed. "I've thought that a thousand times," she said. "The hardest part about all this is we might never know the real reasons why. We might never know what happened to him to make him change all his values. I remember when his buddy John got himself mixed up with a younger woman and went off the deep end. Said he'd never *really* been in love before—after twenty-five years of marriage. He was leaving his wife to move in with her, and your dad begged him to get his head examined. There hadn't been any real evidence of marital problems. Oh, after the fact, John said he hadn't been *really* happy in a long time, but I suspect a revision of history. You know, making an excuse for cheating. Your dad tried to get John to go to counseling or something, but John left his wife. Then a year later, after the younger woman dumped him, he went back to his wife, saying he'd made the biggest mistake of his life."

"And maybe Daddy will do that."

Justine smiled sadly. She put her hand against Livvie's cheek. "I don't think that will happen, honey. And if it did, I don't think I'd take him back. See, he wanted to move on. Fantasies of a new woman, a new life, a chance to start over, maybe. But I did move on. I'm starting a whole new life. I wouldn't have chosen it, but I'm growing to like it. Maybe *like* isn't the word… Let's just say, there are pluses and minuses."

CHAPTER TWELVE

In the days that followed Adele's chance meeting with Hadley, she thought about little else. She was distracted, moody and unsure of herself. She found herself remembering the days and weeks of romance they had had. He was twelve years older; she was young and tender. He was something of a poet and managed to say all the right things. *I want to give you everything; I want to hold you closely forever. Just your scent makes my head swim and I forget where I am and what I'm doing.*

The entire time they were a couple was three months; they professed their love for each other in two weeks. Of course she believed he had an unhappy marriage since they spent so much time together. It could be nothing else.

The landline in the house rang early one evening. None of them used it much, and the line probably should have been disconnected. Adele had it only because of her mother's ill health—911 on the landline brought instant medical help as the address and name popped up for the dispatcher. Since her mother's death it seemed to only ring with surveys and robo calls. They rarely answered it and invariably hung up. Justine answered and said, "Sure, hold on." Then she held the cordless phone toward Adele.

"Hello?" she said tentatively.

"There you are! It's Hadley. It's taken forever to find you. But you didn't change your number after all!"

"Um, can I call you back?" she asked.

"Sure, but when?"

"In just a few minutes. I'd prefer to call you from my cell."

"Absolutely," he said. "I'll be waiting."

Justine didn't ask who it was and her nieces were off in their own space, one in the guest room and one curled up in the corner of the sofa. "Let me return this call and then I'll be back to help clean up."

"I've got it, Addie," Justine said.

Addie sat cross-legged on her bed and stared at her phone. This was either wonderfully good or horribly awkward; she wasn't sure which. But she wanted to know—was this what true love felt like or was this just an extension of an earlier mistake. The loving had been so fantastic, the breaking up so painful.

She clicked on his number, stored in her phone.

"Hi," he said. "How are you?"

"I thought you were going to let me call you?"

"I grew impatient," he said. "I haven't thought of anything but you since seeing you."

"It's only been a few days," she said.

"It feels like a hundred days. Listen, jump in the car. I'll meet you in Half Moon Bay. There's a nice little sushi bar near the lodge. It's called…"

"I know what it's called, but really, I have things to do tonight."

"Won't they keep? Can't we steal an hour? Just to talk about things?"

"You're in the car now, aren't you?"

"Yes. Coming to beg, if necessary. Come on, Addie. I've missed you so much."

"I was going to think about this for a while before I got in over my head."

"I won't let anything happen to you, Addie. I think we both learned a lot from the last time. And you're in charge. Just talking to you will help me get through the night."

"But why? Why me? You're a handsome and popular teacher. You're divorced now. You can have any girl you want."

"It should be abundantly clear there isn't anyone I want. At least not the way I've always wanted you."

Damn it, she thought. She had needed someone to say something like that. For about eight years, as a matter of fact. She had been so happy, then so devastated, then for a long time, so empty.

"I can tell you're unsure, Addie. Time to dive in and be sure. This thing we had—it moved mountains. We made some mistakes, but we're older and wiser now. Let's not walk away from it until we're sure. It's possible we're those star-crossed lovers who just can't live without each other. Maybe we've always been meant to be. Just had some complications the first time around."

This once, she thought. Because she'd like to be sure, too. "All right. I'll meet you. But I'm not promising anything."

"Just come," he said in that deep breathy way that had once made her want to take off all her clothes.

She changed, putting on something she considered special but casual. She fluffed up her hair, freshened her makeup and dabbed on a little cologne. When she got back to the kitchen, Justine had nearly finished cleaning up. Addie said she was running out for a glass of wine and would be back in an hour or less.

"You look nice," Justine said.

"Thanks. Do you need anything, since I'll be out?"

"Nothing at all. Have fun."

But fun wasn't even on the agenda. Even though they'd already cleared the air at their old hangout, it felt like there was so much baggage. She was nervous as a cat, her insides kind of squeezing, her heart feeling a bit larger than usual. If only she felt she could be cool.

When she got to the sushi bar, he was parked in front. He was leaning against his car, waiting. His appearance had the same impact on her. He was relaxed; he was suave. He looked intelligent. His hair was neatly trimmed, and he wore a sport coat over a knit shirt and pair of jeans.

She parked just two spaces away and got out. And he opened his arms.

It was as before—she seemed to do as he commanded. She walked right into his arms, and he immediately covered her lips in a scorching kiss. Her arms wrapped around him, his arms encircled her and they were locked like that in front of anyone who should drive or walk by.

"Addie. Addie," he said softly in her ear. "I don't think we want sushi after all."

"I've eaten already. I was just going to have a glass of wine and watch you eat."

"Good. Then let's drive up to the lookout where we can talk in private. Jump in."

He opened the door for her, and the first thing she noticed was a soccer ball, a helmet and knee pads, child-size, in the backseat. "What's that?"

"My eight-year-old is on a soccer team. I take her to practice and games whenever I can. My twelve-year-old is into music. They're very different."

"Oh. Is your wife remarried?"

"Sarah? Ah, let's just say she's having trouble finding herself. Since she's never been much of a housekeeper, I suggested she look under the bed. How's work going, Addie? You mentioned it, but only briefly."

"The lookout is kind of isolated. I'd rather talk inside. Or right here."

"There's more to do than talk." He took her elbow and tried to urge her into the passenger seat.

"Talking is really all there is for me. In fact, I don't know what more there is to say."

He reluctantly closed the passenger door. "I've been thinking about us," he said. "I think our relationship was good, then we got derailed. Ran amok. I admit, I made a lot of mistakes."

"Mistake number one—you shouldn't have gotten involved with a student. You were married. It was a disaster just waiting to happen."

"You got pregnant," he said. "I just assumed..." He shrugged.

"I don't know what I was thinking, taking a chance like that. I was in love. You said you were getting divorced. You said your marriage had been bad for a long time, but it wasn't all that bad if you managed to make a baby with your wife."

"So many misunderstandings," he said. "Marriage is complicated. There are good days and bad days. You can be talking about divorce but then your wife is pleasant and you don't just refuse to— I can't explain it easily. We had talked about divorce, but we hadn't taken any action. And you're right, I shouldn't have gotten involved with you, but then you shouldn't have gotten involved with me, either. You were old enough to make good decisions."

"I should make one now," she said, her voice low.

"Don't be hasty, darling. We both made mistakes, but what we had was powerful. Brief, but amazing."

"Do you plan to pressure me?"

"Not intentionally. But having you back in my life has taken over all my thoughts. And here we are, different people. Older, smarter. And you're more beautiful than ever. I don't know how that's possible, but—"

"I lost a little weight," she said.

"I don't remember you as overweight," he said.

"Most of that happened after," she said, meaning the pregnancy.

He turned toward her, pulling her in for another kiss. "See what I mean?" he whispered. "When we are together, it's like fireworks. I know we had our misunderstandings, but don't they seem small now?"

They did not seem small, she thought.

I don't know why I kept letting him come back.

That thought came out of nowhere and she recognized the voice—one of their clients who had been in a dead-end relationship said it had been her own fault. Every time her deadbeat boyfriend came back, full of apologies and promises, she let him. He rarely worked, didn't help out with the kids, she hadn't done anything with her life and she was thinking of taking him back yet again just to make the rent.

Why did I always feel like I needed a man, that man, in my life when he never did anything to make my life better?

How many similar stories had Addie listened to in the months she'd worked at the office? She was thirty-two, for God's sake! Hadn't she learned by now not to listen to empty-headed sweet talk that had no real substance to show for it?

Adele pushed Hadley away. "No, this is not going to work. Not like this."

"Like what?" he asked, reaching for her.

She pushed him away again. "It's not going to be like this. We stumbled into each other, had a talk about our failed relationship, cleared the air and now you seem to think we're just going to get back together. We're not."

"I just think we should try it out. Act on our feelings, see where we stand..."

"I'm going home now, Hadley," she said.

"Addie, don't be angry just because I'm in love with you!"

"And don't say that," she admonished. "You couldn't possibly be in love with me. You know what? In eight years you never called me, but it turned out you only needed a few days to find my phone number. You didn't call me because there was no reason to. I'm done. Let go of me."

"But Adele, I—"

"Now!" she said firmly.

With a grunt and a heavy sigh, he dropped his arms. He muttered that she was being unnecessarily difficult, that she should know by now he was sincere.

She nearly laughed, but inside she was a little too sad. And in desperate need of some hard-core counseling to find out what it was about Hadley Hutchinson that made her insides melt. What had he ever shown her that was deep enough to ponder? Anyone could tell you you're beautiful; anyone could say holding you was like coming home.

"Goodbye, Hadley," she said. "Good luck with everything." She walked briskly to her car.

"And that's it? After all we've been through?"

She turned to face him. "Would you like to talk about the fact that we fought about an abortion you wanted me to have, yet you never once called me to see if I was all right? Or the fact that you had my number all these years and yet you act as if some great detective work was required to find it?"

"I didn't have it," he said. "I lost a lot of numbers, and you said you didn't want to hear from me ever again."

"And yet even knowing I was pregnant, you didn't try to find me sooner? Oh Hadley, you're not very convincing. If you really had loved me, you'd have been concerned."

"I was con—"

"I'm going home. I'm not ready to rehash all this with you. Besides, you don't want to talk. You're looking for something else."

"You misjudge me," he said. "There were a lot of unfortunate circumstances, a lot of harsh things said back then, and—"

"Good night, Hadley."

She got into her car, locked the doors before starting the ignition and began what was a short drive home. And she cried. Not because her heart was broken, not because of the disappointment, but mostly because she felt stupid. It wasn't as though she had longed for him for eight dreary years. At first she ached for want of him. Then she hated him for what he'd put her through without ever looking back. Then she chalked him up to a devastating mistake and, more recently, let herself wonder if it had all been a misunderstanding of giant proportions.

As she drove by the market, she caught sight of Jake pulling in the awnings. The sun had set some time ago; it was now nearly nine. The market closed at ten. She pulled into the space in front and got out.

"Getting ready to call it a night?" she asked.

"Pretty soon," he said. "What are you up to?"

"I'm thinking about some pistachio ice cream."

"Are you celebrating or consoling yourself?"

"I'm not entirely sure, I guess."

"Wait for me on that bench," he said, pointing to the secondhand store across the street. They closed at six and the shop was dark. As she sat there, she couldn't help but think of the many times she'd leaned on Jake when she was upset or unhappy or even a little lonely. He never once complained.

In just five minutes, he came out of the store with a quart of ice cream balanced in one hand. He crossed the street and pulled two spoons out of his pocket. He sat down and put the ice cream between them, then handed her a spoon. He lifted the lid, put it aside, loaded up his spoon and aimed it at her mouth.

She took the bite.

"Better?" he asked.

"Yes," she said with a laugh. "You are a master at knowing my needs."

"Actually, no. I get no credit. You asked for pistachio ice cream. What's eating at you?"

She filled the spoon and aimed it toward his mouth. "I ran into the professor," she said.

"*The* professor?" he asked, his countenance darkening.

"That one, yes. I actually ran into him a few days ago on the Berkeley campus, and tonight he wanted to know if we could meet and I went. That might've been a mistake. I'm still thinking about it."

"You were at the campus?"

"Yes. I'm planning to start my master's program in counseling, so I went to see the career adviser. You know, to see what credits transfer, that sort of thing. And there he was, walking from the parking lot. He asked if we could have a glass of wine and talk about things, so I did."

Jake scowled and fed himself a scoop of ice cream. "You did," he repeated.

"It's been eight years. You know the details. You and Justine are the only two people who actually know. When I told him I'd had the baby and he died, he seemed genuinely sad. Remorseful. He's divorced now, he says. It stirred up some old feelings, I guess you could say. It brought to mind how hopelessly and stupidly in love I was at the time. I had no control of my feelings. None."

"Back then or now?" he asked.

"I was thrown back into the past for a little while—he played me like a fiddle, I think. Then he called me tonight and asked me to meet him. To talk. I assumed there was more he had to say or maybe to ask me. So of course I went. He wanted to drive up to the lookout so we could be alone, but he spoiled it all by kissing me. It was a fantastic, memorable kiss, but it tipped me off that maybe talking wasn't a priority. And his dialogue was much more interesting. He was hoping this reunion would lead to a second chance."

"Since the first one went so well," Jake grumbled.

"I'm so dense sometimes," she said, scooping another spoonful out of the container. "But then I haven't had that much experience. There were a couple of pretty unexciting boyfriends in high school and college. Then after Hadley and the baby, the only guy I dated was you."

"Addie, what we did wasn't exactly dating…"

"Pizza, the occasional movie, wine and dessert from the deli…"

"Those things were the things friends do," he said.

"And we've always been good friends," she reminded

him. "Besides Justine, you're the only person I confide in. And when Justine lived in San Jose, I talked to you a lot more than her. I'm glad I ran into Hadley. I figured something out that I should have known a long time ago. He is a clever man. If he had wanted to call me, just to see how I was holding up, he would have. All that business he gave me about our painful breakup and how I told him I didn't want to hear from him—that never would have stopped him. He's just a player."

"I could've told you that," Jake said.

"So is your ex, Mary Ellen—just a player."

"Definitely. Now she's with some old guy who looks like he's gonna croak any second, but I hear he has money."

"We've spent a lot of time over the years bad-mouthing the exes."

"A time-honored sport," he said. "I have to admit, I'm well over Mary Ellen. I can't even remember what fantasy I was engaged in that made me think we'd have a life together. A great life. It wasn't great for fifteen minutes."

"I was thinking the same thing. Hadley said he loved me in no time. Two weeks, I think. How do you know if you love someone in two weeks?"

"Infatuation, Addie. That's what it was." Then he grinned. "Pretty cool at the time, wasn't it? Fills you up inside till you think you might explode."

"Yeah, boy," she said with a deep sigh. "He said I was old enough to know what I was doing. I was twenty-four. And now I'm asking myself what I thought was so great about him. The man has no depth. No substance. He's all talk and manipulation. I let him cost me years of loneliness."

"That's not a fair assessment," Jake said. "He might have been the original cause, but then things snowballed. Your dad, your mom, and before you know it, you've put your life on hold to help others. I think what you did was very brave."

"For all those years I was stuck at home, I spent a lot of time online—I had a large group of friends around the country in similar situations, and we communicated online. We talked books and politics and traded recipes. There was also social media—I spent a lot of time at that. Since I took my job at the center, I haven't paid any attention to those people. I have people sending me messages asking if I'm all right, if I'm sick or something."

"Is he going to be back?" Jake asked. "The professor?"

"You won't say his name," she said, smiling and dipping her spoon in the container again.

"I hate him," Jake said.

"Because he hurt me?"

"Not that simple," he said. "You can get over a broken heart. It's harder to get over self-doubt."

"It's kind of amazing what losing forty pounds and getting a job where you actually feel necessary can do for your self-esteem. But then, that's the whole mission of our re-entry program—giving people purpose, raising their self-awareness and making them feel a part of society again. A functional, productive part."

"Yeah, well, if it makes you happy then it makes me happy, but Addie, you've always been beautiful and you've always had a hard job where you helped people."

"You help people every day, Jake. Most of this neighborhood would be lost without you."

"I don't think of it that way. It's my business. If I'm a good neighbor, I do a better business."

"Jake, I think I've taken you for granted all these years. You've been my best friend. I counted on you, and you never let me down."

"I never felt taken for granted," he said. "And you never let me down either."

He lifted her chin with a finger and looked into her eyes. "You weren't ready to even think about anything more complicated than friendship, for obvious reasons."

She dipped her spoon into the ice cream container and aimed it at his mouth. "One of these days, we might revisit that issue." Then she laughed. "Now that I have a house bursting at the seams with people."

"Addie, I have my own house. And you've never been inside."

"Well now," she said. "There's a thought."

Scott called Justine and asked if it would be convenient to stop by Addie's house to have a talk with her and the girls. "A talk about what, Scott?"

"About the house in San Jose. A house that no one seems to be using at the moment."

"We could probably have this conversation, again, over the phone."

"No, I'd like the girls to be a part of it. If it's okay with you."

"It's okay with me," she said. "Don't bring her. That's nonnegotiable."

"She's out of town, visiting some friends. This is between us. Our family."

Poor Scott, she thought sadly. He just can't digest the fact that we are no longer the family we were. He thought he'd just step out, form new liaisons, step back in when it suited him and everyone would adapt to his needs. How could he not understand that they were a torn apart family glued back together in an awkward, lumpy, uncomfortable fabric that chafes and scratches.

"Your dad wants to come over and talk with us about the San Jose house," Justine said to Amber. "He'll be here in about ten minutes."

"Isn't that between you and Dad?" she asked.

"Well, it's your home, too. I guess he wants to include you."

"Great," she said, putting in her earbuds, escaping back into music.

"Livvie, your dad is coming over in a few minutes. He wants to talk with us about the house in San Jose."

"What about it?" she asked.

"I don't know. I'd be guessing. Since he'll be here in a few minutes, let's just get it from him."

"I hate this stuff," Livvie said.

"Me, too," Justine agreed.

She was so done with him. She hated that this Band-Aid was being pulled off so damn slowly, that the negotiations seemed never ending, that there was always one more piece of business. Since he'd made his choice, since he didn't love her anymore, she wanted him to just go away. She wanted to rebuild her life in peace and tranquility.

She loved her little law office. She was fond of Sam and his wife. She wanted to get to know Logan better. She was sure she would never remarry and she wasn't sure she could even entertain the idea of a serious boyfriend, but it would be nice to hold hands while walking on the beach, to talk politics without arguing, even to compare exes and learn about singlehood, something she never expected to experience. Having been with Scott so long, she felt as if she'd been born married. The ringing doorbell interrupted her thoughts.

"Hi," Scott said. "Thanks for letting me come over."

"Sure. I hope we can get to the end of these constant negotiations, Scott. I'd like to concentrate on other things."

"Sure. Me, too."

The girls sat in the living room, stiff and waiting. He kissed each one; hugged them. Justine noticed he got a little emotional and seemed to swallow it down.

"So, it appears you're hardly ever at the house," he said.

"Well, you're hardly ever at the house," Amber said. "We're not spending any time with you. But here, we have dinner with Mom every night."

"And you don't mind driving so far to school?" he asked.

"Yeah, I mind it," Olivia said. "But I also mind living alone at the big house."

"This place," he said, looking around. "It's a lot smaller and older..."

"They like the beach," Justine said. "They also enjoy the time they get to spend with Addie. And it's very rare for me to have to work evenings. Very rare. My schedule is much more relaxed now."

He leaned back in the chair. "You look more relaxed."

And yet he didn't, Justine thought. He looked stressed and a little too thin. "Have you been working out more?" she asked.

He laughed uncomfortably. "No, I've been busy at the shop. See, I took a look at that kayak shack, ran some numbers and I'm sure, given time, I can turn it around. I have a lot of experience, you know."

So he kept saying, she thought.

"Let me get to the point. No one is using the house. There's a lot of equity tied up in that house, and I could use the capital. I'm investing in the kayak shack. It's my plan to own it. I'm investing over time to keep some of my assets available. It's a helluva deal, really. Even if the shop doesn't do as well as I hope, the land it sits on is valuable. But we don't have any plans to sell it. Not without giving the business an overhaul and letting it make money. The thing is, winter is coming and with the fog and chill, we'll experience a temporary lull..."

"We?" Amber said.

God bless her, Justine thought. She hadn't wanted to ask, though in her gut she knew. He wasn't just sleeping with her. He was partnering with her—possibly even supporting her. Marrying her would probably be cheaper.

"Cat owns the place. It has a little debt on it, not too much. Very affordable mortgage. And a small business loan. But here's what I propose. I think we should let the house and some of the sporting equipment and vehicles go. I'll see the girls more often if they live here in town anyway. As long as Amber and Olivia are happy here, it's more convenient for me. It seems like you're bringing more and more stuff from home—"

"Just clothes and some bedding," Livvie said. "But I'm ready to make this permanent."

"She has a boyfriend," Amber said.

"A boyfriend!" Scott said. "I thought you said you weren't getting serious?"

"Jared and I met at the beach and we have a lot in common. He's in college."

Scott frowned.

"His first year," she said, clarifying.

"The girls spent so much time here over summer, they met a few local kids," Justine said.

"But are you ready to give up a house near your school? Because it's important to me that you be happy," Scott asked them.

Amber laughed. "I wouldn't exactly call it a silver lining, Dad. I mean, you and Mom are divorced. You have a girlfriend."

"Look, I realize it's a very difficult transition. Change always is hard. But it's not like it's a rare thing, people growing apart, getting divorced, starting new lives. I think once we get used to the new normal, things will fall into place. I mean, your uncle Ben and aunt Judy are managing their new family dynamic very well, don't you think?" he asked, speaking of his brother and sister-in-law.

"They've been divorced for ten years, Scott. And it was by mutual choice," Justine said. "It's not up to the girls to create a new normal. All they have to do is create their own lives, which right now is school and friends."

"Okay, I get that. I do. So, the question is, can you adjust and be happy if we don't hang on to that house in San Jose? Because it's sitting almost vacant. How much time do you girls actually spend there?"

"If they need to be in San Jose for a school event or project, I go and stay with them," Justine said.

"Okay, then let me ask you—now that you work here, are you about ready to think about putting the house on the market?"

She was, but not for the reasons he voiced. She found that more and more she resented the place. It was like living in the scene of the crime. Everything in that house, that lovely house, was carefully chosen for their family to enjoy. She'd lived in that house for a dozen years. She had loved it. But after everything that had happened, she was not in love with it anymore.

"I'll go with what the girls are comfortable with," Justine said. "If they need to have that house available to make them feel more secure, I side with them."

"Girls? What do you say? The market is really good right now," Scott said.

"It's a couple of months until Christmas," Justine said. "Spring is the ideal time to sell if that's what we want to do."

"Usually, but real estate is doing great right now. And," he added, looking around, "you might like some of your furniture in this place. This stuff is pretty old and beat up."

"Don't you want some of the furniture?" she asked.

"I figured we'd split it up somehow, maybe sell some stuff…"

"Oh, that's going to be a giant pain…"

"It makes a lot more sense than having a house full of stuff we don't use just sitting there. Well? Girls?"

"I'm going to stay wherever Mom stays. I have friends in San Jose if I need to overnight for some reason," Olivia said.

"Me, too," Amber said. "I'm graduating in June anyway. I have a lot of friends, some I could stay with the whole school week if I wanted to."

"I can't believe my little girl is graduating," Scott said.

Olivia rolled her eyes.

Justine knew they would probably get more money for the house if they waited until spring to sell it, but if it meant one less connection to Scott it couldn't happen too soon. "Fine, right, let's sell the house. Let's go through and divide the property, but let's leave it in the house. It'll sell much better furnished. And I have to talk to Addie about this, as well."

"Perfect," he said. Then he stood. "Thanks, Justine. Thanks, girls."

"Dad, you shouldn't put your money into that kayak shack. It's losing money," Olivia said.

"How do you know that?" he asked, a bit of anger in his tone.

"Everyone in Half Moon Bay knows it," she said, shrugging. "Your girlfriend is like the third or fourth owner, and no one has made money there."

"Which is exactly why I'm needed. Believe me, I'm up to the challenge."

CHAPTER THIRTEEN

Scott had planned very carefully. He knew the exact ways to make the kayak shack into a thriving business. He and Cat had actually discussed it for years. It wasn't long after she bought the place a few years ago that they started talking; he was one of a few regular customers. It never really picked up speed. Cat thought the previous owner—and the one before that and before that—didn't have much business sense or a decent business plan. But she was struggling, as well.

He told her he'd come up with a plan. Cat had been so grateful.

That's what really started everything. His ideas, his plan. From there they became closer, and he realized that's what had been missing in his marriage. Cat was a woman who really admired his intelligence. He hadn't even realized how lonely he was until he began talking with Cat. Just talking. They had so much in common. The obvious was their view of exercise and athletics; naturally a woman who would buy a kayak business was into sports and the outdoors.

Scott used to engage in these outdoor events with guys he knew. Of course in these groups of weekend athletes there were some women. But now there was one woman, and he was in love with her. She excited him, and he hadn't been excited in a long time. Before he even began discussions of divorce, he signed a lease on a sexy little beachfront bungalow. Cat had been having issues with living with her brother and his friend, so it made sense. Besides, they needed a place they could be alone. Nights in hotels became expensive. And Cat needed a place she could call home. A beautiful place.

"Not quite as nice as your house, but better than my brother's pad."

"But what a great view we have," he pointed out to her.

"If you like taking in the view alone most of the time," she said. "It's such a waste, you living in San Jose with her where you get no moral support."

"Soon we'll be together, but we have to be patient."

It was much sooner than he thought it would be. He hadn't expected Justine to find out about his affair and demand they split. The truth was, he wasn't entirely ready to divorce; Justine had a good job so their income was steady, their equity was growing, their investments were stable...

"If I don't get some help with that kayak shack, I'm going to lose it and lose my investment. Honestly, I can't sleep at night," Cat said, crying.

"I'm helping," he said. "I've given you the new business plan and I'm working around the shop for free..."

"What am I going to do when my loan is called and I can't afford to pay it off?"

"Maybe I'll help you get another loan? Let's worry about that later. You know I'm in this with you."

"But not really," she said. "Because you're married. At least I'm separated."

They had talked about the state of his marriage. Cat made

him realize that he wasn't happy, he had to admit. Not that much had changed in his marriage; he was just sensing this mood of discontent. Fighting it, but still it was there. But he had two daughters, and it was only going to be a couple of years and they'd be out of the house. He was kicking around the idea of asking for a divorce when the girls were gone. He'd planned to spend those last couple of years putting away money so that when he left, there'd be a healthy pot.

Then Justine discovered Cat. They separated, worked out a settlement that gave him plenty of money, with support payments to follow, and it was over so quickly.

But Justine screwed him over by changing jobs.

"You should take her back to court," Cat said. "She misled you into thinking she'd have a regular high income!"

"There's no going *back* to court because we didn't go to court. We both signed the paperwork, turned it in and it was uncontested."

"She tricked you!" Cat said. "She's a lawyer and you're not! She manipulated the whole thing. You didn't know what she was planning."

"I don't think she planned for her company to cut jobs," he said. "I've known for years she was burned out on corporate law and would have liked to make a change, but she couldn't while the kids were still in school."

"What about your child support?"

"I'm not taking care of my daughters! They're with their mother. They won't come to my house because they're not willing to be friendly with you. They're not happy about us."

"You should demand that they meet me and that they treat me with respect," she said.

"I'm not going to demand anything of them," he shot back.

"You said we're in this together," she yelled. "How can

I let you and your lies drive me so crazy?" She ran to their bedroom.

Scott could hear Cat crying. He took a deep breath and followed her. He lay down beside her. He put an arm around her. "We are in this together," he said.

She sniffed back her tears. "You hurt me, you know."

"Look, we talked about this. We knew there would be adjustments. A transition. I'm hoping the girls will come around in time, but I can't force it."

"It's like you're ashamed of me or something," she said.

"Don't be ridiculous. I introduced you to my wife!"

"And was that her boyfriend with her?"

"I don't know him," Scott said. "She said it was someone she worked with. It's irrelevant. We're divorced. We can be with anyone we want. But the girls are young, idealistic, haven't experienced a situation like this before, and we are going to give them time. If you push it, it'll take longer."

"I don't think you really care," she said. "I'm starting to wonder if you really love me as much as you said."

He kissed her and asked, "Need some reassurance?"

"That might put me in a better mood," she said, smiling.

Scott obliged, making love to her. Then they went back to the kitchen and worked together on making a lovely dinner. He opened a bottle of pinot noir, and they sat out on their deck to watch the sun go down.

They talked about how he could make things better, and he bought her a new car to prove his commitment.

There had been a couple more big blowups since then.

While Scott went to see Justine and the girls about selling the house, Cat had been off with a couple of girlfriends for three days in Vegas that he'd paid for. He hadn't talked to her much, a minute here, a minute there. She just asked him, "Have you talked to her yet?"

He was saving the good news for when she got home.

He had already signed the paperwork to take over the title on the store and assume the loan payments. When they closed, he'd be giving up most of the settlement from his marriage. He thought he might even have to take another job to make ends meet, unless the house sold fast and for a good price.

Despite the fact that Cat was expensive, very high-main-tenance and at times very difficult, he did not question his love for her. Their love for each other. He told himself that the best love did not always come easy. He would never be bored, and for that he was grateful. He missed her. He couldn't wait for her to get home so he could tell her he was putting the house on the market.

That would make her so happy.

Justine asked Adele to go with her and the girls to their San Jose house to take inventory of the furnishings. Of course the girls could take all their possessions immedi-ately—Scott would have no claim to those things. The girls also had a chance to look through some of their family pos-sessions and choose some personal items they wanted— pictures, accessories, family heirlooms.

And Addie was expected to have a say as she helped Justine choose furniture, kitchenware, linens and miscel-laneous items that would be moved into the house in Half Moon Bay. They would mark and list the items Justine wanted but leave all the furniture, paintings and decora-tor items where they were so the house looked well staged for showings.

"I feel terrible about this," Addie said when they en-tered the house.

"Well, it was going to happen at some point. Scott is

right—an empty house isn't doing anything for anyone. The girls have decided they'd rather be with us in Half Moon Bay than here, usually alone."

"What I feel terrible about is that this is a beautiful, tasteful home, so carefully decorated, the furniture so thoughtfully selected, and my house, *our* house, is old and falling apart."

"Well, maybe we can do something about that," Justine said. "We can make some improvements. Not a huge remodel. It's a fine old house, after all. But it needs some repair and I have some savings. Plus this house will sell and I'll make the mortgage payments until it does, deducting Scott's share from the equity. He hasn't made his payment in almost six months."

"I feel bad putting your beautiful furnishings in our old house with the uneven floors and peeling paint."

Justine smiled at her and pinched her chin. "We'll fix that."

Amber held up a multicolored glass vase and matching plate. "Mom, I found these for you at the market. Can we take them?"

"I think so," she said. "Write them down. We can take your bedroom furniture and the kitchenware now, but everything else should stay until the house sells. But we need to get rid of some things. There's stuff here we never use."

"What about all the stuff in the garage?" Addie asked.

"Hello?" came the sound of Scott's voice.

"In here," Justine called. "We were just talking about you. What are we doing with all the sports gear in the garage?"

"I hooked up the trailer. I'll take that stuff out to clean up and will sell anything we don't keep. I assume you want your bikes."

"Yes, I think so, but not all that dune racing or water sport stuff. I assumed you would take all that."

"Yes, I'll take it. And you can have the books. But I want the couch."

"What? You hated the couch. You complained about that couch for years."

"You did, Dad," Amber said.

"I like it now," he said.

"No, he doesn't like it," Livvie said. "Someone else likes it. Right?"

"Don't be ridiculous," he said.

"Red flag," Justine said. "Whenever he says don't be ridiculous, it's because he just got caught in a lie. Has she been here, Scott?"

"Don't be—" He cleared his throat. "I really like the living room furniture. You can take the master bedroom, dining room, kitchen furniture and the bar stools."

"She wants the living room, doesn't she?" Justine asked.

"*I* want the living room furniture, Justine."

"Wait a minute," she said. "This has to be equitable. The sports toys are worth thousands. And you have no use for books. How about I take the toys and you take the books."

"This is going to be a very long day," Addie said.

There was a little more arguing and give-and-take until Justine told the girls to go pack up their rooms since there was no dispute there. Addie went to help them. Justine and Scott sat at the breakfast bar and worked things out on paper. Fortunately, there was not a lot of extra room in Addie's old house so, from a practical point of view, Justine was able to let a lot of things go. She tagged a few books she wanted to keep and claimed the dining room table and chairs but not the breakfront. She didn't want or need the master bedroom furniture. "I have a feeling there could be unknown DNA on that," she muttered.

Scott admitted he was planning to sell all the toys from the garage, minus the girls' bikes.

"We can have an estate sale after the house has sold," Justine said. "But I am taking the living room furniture and the decorator pieces that I chose and bought. Buy your girlfriend a new living room set."

"It's not for my girlfriend," he insisted. But he blushed slightly and didn't argue.

Later, Addie helped Justine box up some dishes, pots and serving platters from the kitchen. Scott did the same with glasses, a few countertop appliances and some flatware. He had his trailer, but Justine had a truck coming at two to transport the girls' bedroom furniture and her boxes to Half Moon Bay. The main rooms of the house remained furnished, that furniture tagged either red for Justine or blue for Scott. The house looked almost model perfect. After the cleaning ladies made a run-through, it would be show-ready.

"How are you holding up?" Addie asked her sister.

"It's very strange," she said. "This doesn't feel like home to me anymore. I don't know that man anymore. The Scott I loved and trusted is gone. If his lips are moving, he's lying. I don't actually want that living room furniture, so I'll sell it and we'll get something new for the living room, but it was so obvious that his girlfriend wants it, I wasn't going to allow that to happen. But I'm anxious for a clean slate. A new beginning."

Addie put an arm around Livvie when she came to join them. "You doing okay?" she asked her niece.

Livvie nodded. "This place just makes me want to cry," she said. "The last few months with Daddy hardly here for us were just terrible. I felt like an orphan. I don't want to live here anymore."

I hate him for what he did to my nieces, Addie thought. *What a selfish, cruel bastard.*

The men on the rented truck quickly loaded, drove and unloaded in Half Moon Bay. They set up the beds for the girls and left everyone to unpack. As there was no room in Addie's kitchen for boxes full of dishes and platters, those boxes went to the enclosed back porch until they could make some choices, keeping the best and discarding the worst. There were boxes everywhere—against a living room wall, at the top of the stairs, in the kitchen and bedrooms. There was a freestanding garage, but it was already full of stuff that had belonged to their parents. Another project for another weekend. "I promise to help with the kitchen after I get the bedroom settled," Justine said.

Addie looked around at the crunch of boxes and furniture and felt claustrophobic. Sleepovers were one thing. Even spending almost the whole summer together it had never felt too crowded. But this—giving her house over to three more people and their possessions... She suddenly felt as if she was disappearing.

"I'm getting some ideas," Justine said. "We should resurface the beautiful hardwood floors, get some new area rugs, forget reupholstering and shop for some good furniture deals. How do you like peach for the kitchen and beige accented by navy blue walls in the living room—that would be stunning, I think. The bathrooms should be redone from the tile up. And I'd love to texture the walls in the entry and hang a large silver framed mirror and maybe an understated chandelier. We can talk about all this later... For the dining room—"

"I can't concentrate right now," Addie said, feeling as if she might suffocate.

"I'll get this confusion cleared up and things put away quickly, Addie," Justine said.

"No worries," she said. "I think I'll go out for a while, maybe meet up with Jake. Can I bring you back something to eat?"

"You go out and get away from this mess. I know it's stressful, and I'll make something simple—grilled cheese maybe for me and the girls."

Addie stepped out onto the porch and called Jake.

"Well, hey! You okay?" he asked.

"I'm fine," she said with surprise in her voice, just realizing she almost never called him, only when she needed something. "Are you working tonight?"

"If I have nothing better to do," he said. "Do I have something better to do?"

"I wonder if I could see your house?" she asked.

Adele hadn't truly been that interested in Jake's house when she called him. She really wanted to talk about the conflict she was feeling. She wanted Justine and the girls to live with her; she didn't want Justine redecorating her house so that it reflected Justine and not Adele. Not that Adele had come up with any good renovation ideas in the eight years she'd had to think about it.

When all the boxes started stacking up, it felt like the walls closed in on her. When Justine started picking out colors for the walls, she began to feel as though Justine was the parent and she was the child, and she had to get out. Now she was standing on Jake's porch waiting because he wasn't home from the market yet.

She remembered when Jake bought this old house six

or seven years ago. He said he bought it because he liked the look of the stone porch and the slanted roof with dormer windows. He had said it was a bloody awful mess that he looked forward to renovating. When she questioned the wisdom of buying a run-down house when his mother lived in a perfectly nice house, a paid-for house where Jake could live for free, he'd said, "An investment is a good idea, and one that I can take all the credit for is an even better idea. The trees around the yard are mature, the frame is solid, the wiring and plumbing are still sound and very little has to be done on the outside. Besides, how long should a single man live with this mother?"

Another complication of living with his mother was every time Marty had a marriage or romance fall apart, which seemed to happen with regularity, he moved home to their mother's house, and he was the kind of force of nature that sucked all the air out of a room. Jake and his mother had lived quietly. There was not a quiet bone in Marty's body.

Jake pulled up and got out of his truck. He had a grocery sack in one arm and a bunch of cellophane-wrapped flowers in the other.

"Oh, you shouldn't have…"

"I didn't," he said. "They were going to be thrown out so I grabbed them. I do that all the time. Most of my diet is made up of expired food. I might not spend a lot of time here, but when I do I like it to be nice."

He unlocked the door and motioned for her to step inside. When he came into the entry behind her, he flipped on a light. The foyer was small so the light shone into the living room. As the house wasn't big, she could see the living room and dining room in an L-shape, and she assumed the kitchen was behind the wall on her right. She walked into the living room and looked around. The kitchen was separated from the dining room by a breakfast bar that could seat three. On the living room wall to her left was a large stone fireplace, the stone matching that on the front of the house and porch.

It was beautiful. Masculine with the dark velour sectional and recliner, heavy side tables and coffee table, chunky wood dining room table with six chairs. He had a buffet over which hung a painting of an antiquated lean-to surrounded by wildflowers with a mountain in the background.

The thing that impressed her the most was how clean it was. It wasn't just tidy. There wasn't a thing sitting out, not even a stack of mail. Not a speck of dust or a streak on the windows.

"Wow," she said.

Addie was, admittedly, a little on the messy side. She tended to leave dishes in the sink and let the laundry pile up until it became an emergency. She wasn't good about putting away her shoes, and she had far too many jackets or sweaters draped on chair backs—and that was before Justine and the girls added to the clutter.

While she was looking around, Jake went to the kitchen. He pulled some aging and tired looking flowers out of a vase, dropped them in the trash and rinsed out the vase. He snipped off the ends of the new flower stems right into the trash and created an instant centerpiece.

"How about a glass of wine," he said, unpacking his groceries.

She watched as he put away a half dozen eggs, two oranges, two apples, two bananas, some bacon and a loaf of bread, suspecting they were past their sell-by date.

"That sounds great," she said. "I had a tiring day. I went

with Justine and the girls to their San Jose house to help them with dividing the furniture. Scott was there, too. I'm not sure, but it seemed like it was more taxing for me than for Justine."

"How'd the girls do?"

"They were fine. Livvie said it made her very sad. They're saying goodbye to a way of life. But I think my sister is glad to let it go right about now. She thinks her ex-husband is an idiot."

Jake laughed. "Everyone thinks he's an idiot."

Addie burst into tears.

"Hey now," he said, pulling her close, stroking her hair. "What's got you upset? Was it the ordeal of dividing the property?"

She shook her head and wiped impatiently at her eyes. "Jake, Justine is going to take over my life. She's going to pick the paint colors for my house, choose the furniture, probably select our meals. To her I'm no different than one of her daughters."

"You might be worried about that, but it doesn't have to happen," he said. "I'm going to pour some wine and light a fire. Sit down and relax and tell me about your day."

She watched from the sofa while he puttered in the kitchen and brought two glasses to the coffee table. Then he got to the task of lighting a fire, a real fire. He pulled logs from the caddy on the hearth and stacked them neatly on the grate. He added some starter pine cones.

She was reminded of something she'd always taken for granted—Jake was an attractive man. He was tall, fit, had a full head of dark hair and his dark eyes glittered when he smiled. His butt in those jeans was a perfect fit, and they were neither tight nor loose. He always wore a greengrocer's shirt, and there was no belly spilling over the belt. He had big hands, and she imagined those hands on her and realized that he was patient and kind and quite sexy.

"I take you for granted," she said to his back.

He glanced over his shoulder. "I don't feel that you do." The fire began to take life from the starter cones, and he sat on the couch beside her.

"Why do you suppose you never remarried?" she asked him.

"And exactly who would I marry, Adele?"

"Oh come on, you know half the women in town would leave their husbands for you."

"And regret it, I'm sure. I think after a bad marriage and worse divorce, you get real picky about who you hang around with. I'd probably try it again if the right person came along. What's your excuse?"

A huff of laughter escaped her. "I was a shut-in for eight years."

"Not really. When you were helping with your dad, before your mom's stroke, you didn't get out a lot but you got out. I remember you worked at the Ridgemont Hotel for a couple of years."

"Part-time," she said. "But the last four years before Mom died I didn't get out much at all."

"You're sure on the go now."

"I'm almost too busy. And I'm going to add school to the schedule." She sipped her wine. "I'm pretty excited about that. Except that I suppose I'll be running into Hadley regularly."

"The professor," Jake said.

"But I'm thoroughly over him," she said. "At last."

"How do you know?" Jake asked.

"He was coming on strong, suggesting we give it another go. The nerve of that ass, after leaving me alone, pregnant, never once even calling to see if I was all right, after never offering to help in any way. If I see him walking across the campus, I might run him over with my car."

"This is a change," he said. "For a long time you were brokenhearted and grief-stricken, wishing things had worked out differently, that you'd met before he was married or after he was divorced."

"I know. I should have gotten out more. It might have been lack of fresh air, all my common sense dried up. Brain atrophy. In fact, I'll be honest. When I first ran into him and we sat down for a glass of wine and clearing the air, I had a slight relapse. He made good excuses for never reaching out. And he even seemed to be remorseful. The second time I saw him, he was all about getting busy. He used all the same lines that won me over the first time!"

"Ouch," Jake said.

"Nah, no ouch. I was angry. I don't know if I was angrier with him or myself. But I'm glad that's out of the way. He's no longer tempting. There's a lot of freedom in that."

"I remember the feeling," he said.

"Mary Ellen?"

"Sure. At first I was shocked, which I shouldn't have been. Then I was hurt. Then I was depressed. And finally I was pissed off."

"But were you tempted for a while? Even a little while?"

"No. Because she tried to get my business. Half of it, anyway. That just crushed me. And then it really pissed me off."

"We're a pair," Adele said, sipping her wine.

"Tomorrow's Sunday, not a workday for you. I go in for a while in the afternoon. I have an idea. Why don't I meet you for your beach walk then take you to brunch? How's that sound?"

"That sounds very nice, thanks."

"Now tell me about Justine. Tell me why you were crying. I haven't seen you cry in so long, I don't know when. There were times I wished you would just cry. I cry easier than you do."

"The Descaro women came without tear ducts," she said.

Adele talked for a while about how fun and yet overwhelming her house was. She loved not being alone all the time, felt she was developing a real relationship with Justine, but at the same time she was crowded, things were always put away where she couldn't find them, there was never complete quiet and they were four women in a two-bathroom house. Sometimes she thought she would explode. And other times she felt she was finally a part of a family. It was very frustrating and confusing.

She had a second glass of wine and Jake pulled a deli prepared chicken parmigiana dish from the refrigerator to warm it up.

"Is it expired?" she asked.

"Only by a day. Or so. Don't worry, I have good insurance."

By the time she was ready to leave, it was getting late. She had walked over so Jake drove her the few blocks home. He jumped out of his truck and went around to open the door for her.

"I had a really nice time. I can't believe it took me so long to see the inside of your house."

"Well, you were pretty occupied..."

"Now that I know the way, I may need to escape to your house regularly."

"I'd like that." Then he cupped her jaw gently with one of his big hands and brought his lips down on hers. This was not his usual chaste kiss on the forehead or peck on the cheek. This was the real deal. His kiss was powerful and delicious. All of him was. Had it been at any other time in her life, surely she'd have fallen in love with him.

But for a long time she'd been stripped of emotion. She didn't know if she was ready for this. Before she could truly respond, he pulled away.

"I'll see you on the beach at sunrise," he said.

CHAPTER FOURTEEN

There was a place just up the coast from Half Moon Bay with an outstanding restaurant. Justine had made reservations for two for dinner. Adele was spending at least part of the evening with Jake, Amber was spending the night in San Jose at a girlfriend's house where they were double dating to a school football game and then out for pizza or something. Livvie's boyfriend was coming over to the house, and they planned to watch a movie.

Justine was having her own date, yet another date she didn't tell anyone about. Having arrived at the restaurant a little early, she went to the patio to take in the nice ocean view. She chose a bench facing the ocean, and the moon cast a lovely glow on the water. The waitress asked her if she'd like anything, and she ordered a glass of pinot noir.

Logan came up from behind and put his hands on her shoulders. He leaned down and gave her a brief kiss on the head. "What are your roommates doing tonight?" he asked.

She gave him a quick rundown as he took the seat beside her.

"You still haven't told anyone about us, have you?"

"I haven't been specific," she said. "I will soon."

"I don't think we're doing anything we should be secretive about, do you? I've been single for years. You're divorced now, and it's been final for months. We've known each other over six months. We've actually been talking almost daily for that long. Doesn't anyone in that house ask you who you're talking to at night?"

"They might think it's the TV. But I'm surprised none of them have asked any questions. I think they're all too busy figuring out their own lives. Does it bother you that I haven't announced that we're dating?"

"I just don't like the idea of being kept a secret," he said.

"I'm not exactly doing that. It's just… Well, this is my first rodeo."

"You're doing very well," he said. "I look forward to each conversation, each date. Tell me about your day. Or your daughters. Or anything you feel like talking about."

"I have an interesting case—estate work for a family with a complicated will and a charitable foundation. The patriarch changes the will about every six months, and the matriarch just trundles along without argument. They spend a lot of time in the office. It appears they're a little uncomfortable about giving up control and keep coming up with ideas to manage their estate from the grave. Or maybe they just like to talk about it a lot."

"Clients like that must be like having an annuity," he said.

"Do you have any frequent flyers?"

"Oh yeah. Mostly jealous spouses. That's pretty depressing work."

"So, is everybody cheating?"

"That's not the depressing part. People are usually jealous for a reason. That's depressing. If you have a strong instinct telling you something is wrong, usually something is wrong. Or maybe you're in the wrong relationship."

"I guess I was too busy to be jealous," Justine said. "How's your new place?"

"I like it," he said. "It's smaller than I'm used to, but it has a partial ocean view from the back patio. The neighbors are nice, and the town is busy every weekend. I can't wait to show you. It's kind of a typical bachelor pad—small kitchen, big TV, leather furniture that can be wiped down easily. Carmel is pricey. I don't buy my groceries there."

The waitress brought Justine her wine and told them their table was ready when they were. They entered a casual but well-appointed dining room, nearly every table taken, and settled in to study menus. They ordered then talked about their families, their childhoods, their college years. He told her a lot of cop stories, but she didn't tell a lot of lawyer stories because corporate law wasn't a fun topic of conversation. But they agreed on a lot of things, especially the big ones—religion (none) and politics (they had many views in common) and finally books and movies. They enjoyed a delicious steak dinner, shared a couple of sides and nearly finished a bottle of wine.

"It's kind of amazing to me that we don't run out of things to talk about," she said. "We've spent hours on the phone and still haven't covered everything."

"Now that I'm in Carmel, hopefully we'll spend more time face-to-face. If your daughters will let you."

"I don't think they'd be upset at the idea of me dating. They knew about it when I went to Carmel with you in the summer."

"But then I was someone you had worked with," he said.

"I don't think it would be wise to ever tell them I hired you to investigate their father," she said.

"It's irrelevant, if you think about it. I didn't find out much you didn't already know. And I'm not pressing to meet them or get their blessing or anything like that. I just think it's a good idea that your family know where you are and who you're with. It's safe."

"You're right," she said. "I'll bring it up. I'll tell them I met you through a friend at the Silicon Valley office, which is true. I'll mention that we've been talking and have gone out a few times."

"Eleven times," he said. "And I'm starting to wonder what I'd do if I didn't have more of you to look forward to. I'm also thinking about all the fun things we can do together once your family signs off on me."

She leaned toward him, her arms resting on the table. "I'm sure they'll like you, but it doesn't matter whether they do or not. I get to pick my own boyfriend. I can't wait to hear what fun things."

"We might try concerts in the city—the Bay Area books some great musicians. I have a few friends who work security for special events, and I can let them know I'm interested in tickets. We could hit a hockey game in San Jose. They have a great team. Lake Tahoe isn't far. We might spend a day or two there. And just on the off chance you're ready…" He reached into his pants pocket and pulled out a key card. "No pressure. But I'm crazy about you. I won't elaborate because I don't want to scare you."

"I don't know how I would have gotten through this madness without our long talks, our eleven dates," she said. "But it's not that I'm just grateful, Logan. It's like I was dragged kicking and screaming into a new life, and largely because of you, I'm growing to love my new life. I never thought I was unhappy, but I recognize I really am happy now. It's a new state of being."

"I'm proud of you, Justine," he said. "I've been there. The betrayal and rejection is a terrible ordeal, and you've been brave. And strong."

"I've complained a lot," she said. "I've had some dark days. But my new home and new job are just right for me."

"I wasn't calling you to help you," he said. "I'm glad if it did. But I was on those calls and dates because I'm attracted to you. Because I wanted to talk to you, get to know you, spend time with you."

"I know," she said. "This can't be real, can it? That I would fall for the detective I hired to get the dirt on my cheating husband?"

"Stranger things have happened. What should we do now?"

"Maybe it's time to ask for the check," she said.

They stood just inside the door of the hotel room and kissed, wrapped around each other. His lips slid over hers smoothly, deliciously, and their tongues played. There was no awkwardness as this wasn't their first kiss. It was the first time they both knew they would end up in bed. Justine had fantasized about this for at least a few weeks, and so far, it was living up to her fantasy. His hands slid down her back to her butt, pulling her against him, letting her know there was much more in store for her.

She hummed approvingly against his lips.

"You taste so good," he whispered. "Being alone with you is just what I've been needing."

She was needing him, too. She'd thought about it for longer than she even dared to admit. The first time one of their late night chats veered away from her ex and her divorce into ordinary topics from the traffic in the Bay Area to what they were each reading, she had that lilting, tingling feeling inside that came when you found someone entirely and completely right. The feeling grew by the day; she couldn't wait for that text or call each day. And they had since invaded each other's day as well with good-morning texts and midday calls. They kept each other up to date on the news, weather, amusing current events and miscellany. There was a marathon in San Francisco that held Logan up in traffic for a couple of hours; he described every detail. There was a huge beach party that crowded Half Moon Bay with tourists. The commotion had lured Justine out of her office, and she described every interesting person to Logan.

Now, in his arms, all she could think about was his tall, firm body against hers. She abstractly recognized the difference between when she had been young and fragile and now, when she was mature and a bit weathered by life. She wasn't worried about words of love, she was only interested in the way he treated her. She didn't think about promises, she thought about character and integrity. She had little concern about the future because the future belonged to her. Her and her family. If Logan was the man she thought he was, the future would assert itself. In fact, she wasn't even looking for forever. She was looking for kindness, honesty, pleasure and a man she could trust. She was only interested in now.

"Take me to bed," she whispered.

He backed up toward the bed, pulling her hand. He untucked his shirt and unbuttoned his pants, then slowly helped her out of her blouse. One piece at a time, their clothes were tossed on the nearby chair. Justine pulled back the sheets. She slipped into bed first and he joined her there, taking her into his arms. He kissed her and held her close.

He kissed her palm. Then he slid her hand downward so she could touch him. She sighed and he moaned. His hands were moving across her body from her breasts to her butt and finally to that tender place between her legs. With his lips on hers and his fingers massaging her in exactly the right place, pleasure shot through her and she trembled. She kissed him harder and deeper, and her hips began to move against his hand.

"Oh Logan, this is so nice..."

"Better than nice..."

Their fondling became intense and before long Logan gently turned her onto her back, nudged her legs farther apart and found his way home. Their joining brought a gasp from her that turned into heavier breathing from both of them.

Justine closed her eyes, tilted her head back and rocked with him in a slow and steady motion. She felt the passion rise inside, and she found herself thoroughly caught in the storm of it, grabbing for his butt and pulling him harder and deeper. And then there was an explosion of pleasure that consumed her. Her body had taken her there with a will of its own and she was a clenching, quivering mass of woman, caught in his arms.

"Justine," he whispered.

"Oh my God!" she exclaimed.

A moment later he rode her hard and fast, and she felt his release. It was heaven and nearly caused her a second orgasm.

It was in the quiet of the aftermath that Justine really noticed how good it was. She felt safe and secure in his arms; he was a wonderful lover and for that she was so grateful. Fully satisfied, she let out a slow breath and snuggled closer. He ran his fingers through the short hair at her temples, combing it back. "Okay?" he asked gently.

She let out a little laugh. "Way better than okay."

He ran a finger over her lips. "Your lips are bright pink. Your cheeks are flushed. I like that look on you."

She opened her eyes to smile at him. "Thank you," she said. "I wondered what it would be like. I hoped we wouldn't disappoint each other and I could tell—we didn't."

"We didn't. Justine, you know I care about you. It's gone beyond that. I'm in love with you."

Her eyes grew round. "Logan, I don't think I'm in a good place to get serious about a man."

"I'm not asking you for anything. As far as serious feelings, we can be serious without committing to the future. I understand you just came out of a long marriage. One that ended badly. You would be crazy to get yourself into another committed relationship so soon—you're not completely over the last one. There's still a lot to settle in your head. That's okay. In fact, that's good. But even so, I want you to know that I love you. And you can trust that."

"That's just it. It'll probably be a long time before I can trust again."

"That's fine. We have nothing but time, and I'm up to the job of earning your trust. As long as we can spend time together…"

"I count on that," she said. "I look forward to every phone call. I love being with you. You make me feel…" She hesitated. "New," she finally said. "You make me feel brand-new. Thank you for that."

He kissed her cheek. "The pleasure is all mine."

"Not all of it is yours," she said with a laugh. "It's been so long, I was afraid I'd be awkward or embarrassed."

"It's quite obvious you weren't."

"Now comes the bad news. I have to get home at a civilized hour."

"I can't wait to hear what civilized is," he said.

Right on cue, her phone rang. It was in her purse. "Would you mind," she asked, pointing to her purse on the chair.

He slid out of bed, naked as the day he was born, and she admired his fine form. He was quite a good-looking man. He handed her the purse, and she pulled out her phone. She looked at the screen and answered, "Hi, honey. Everything all right?"

"Sure," Amber said. "Just checking in. We brought pizzas back to Melanie's so I guess we're in for the night."

"And Melanie's parents are home?"

"Yes. Janet said to tell you hi. What are you doing?"

"I'm actually out to dinner in town. Well, I had dinner and now I'm having dessert. I'm with a friend I worked with in San Jose."

"A date?" Amber asked.

"I guess it technically is a date. Now I don't want to be rude and be on my cell phone. Call me when you're headed home in the morning."

"Okay, sure. Have fun!" Then she signed off.

Justine laughed and dropped her phone in her purse. "When you have teenage girls, you do a lot of checking in with each other."

"Good idea. Now, can I get you a little more dessert?" And Logan crawled into the bed and took her in his arms again.

Logan walked Justine to her car. It was in a dimly lit parking lot outside the restaurant, which was on the other side of the building. They were talking about when they might be able to get together again. Just as they turned the corner around the building, Logan stopped short, a concerned look on his face.

Justine stood still and could hear voices. Angry voices.

It was mostly a woman, though she couldn't make out everything she was saying. She caught a few words. *Not what you said would happen. What about me? She's a greedy bitch. You could fix this. You're just a chicken.* If there was another person in the argument, that person had little more than mumbles to contribute.

Then there was the sound of a slap and a cry of pain. Then a man found his voice. "Get ahold of yourself! Ugh!" Followed by a lot of unintelligible sounds.

"Stay right here, by the door," Logan said. "Sounds like someone's having a domestic. I'll check it out and be right back."

"Don't get involved, Logan!" she said.

"Don't worry, Justine. I know what to do."

He walked into the darkness, between cars. She could hear the arguing continue though Logan was out of sight. Then she heard a voice she recognized. "Goddamn it, Cat! Stop that! You're out of control!"

That was Scott. And she knew only too well who Cat was. She got her phone out of her purse, turned on the flashlight, pointed it in the direction Logan had gone and attempted to follow.

It wasn't far. She heard Logan's voice clear as a bell. She saw he was using his flashlight, as well. "Hands off each other, right now. I'm calling the police."

Then Cat shouted, "Go away! This is none of your business!"

When she came through the cars, approaching Logan's back, she could see Scott and Cat, and Scott had a trickle of blood running down his lip and over his chin, staining his shirt. He wiped at it impatiently. Then he saw her.

"Justine! What are you doing here?" Scott asked.

"I was having dinner. And you are apparently having a fistfight."

"I was defending myself," Cat said.

"That's not what I saw," Logan said. "He was trying to hold your arms down to keep you from hitting him and you were kicking him. By the look of his face, you connected at least a couple of times. That's assault." He turned to Scott. "You should call the police."

"He's not going to call the police," Cat said. "We're getting out of here. You just mind your own business." And with that, she got into the car they were standing beside. She got in the passenger side.

"Scott, you should listen to Logan," Justine said. "He's a former police officer. He knows what he's talking about."

"It isn't safe to go home with her," Logan said. "Get over the idea that just because she's a female, you shouldn't fear her. She's violent. She has a temper. If you want a ride somewhere, I'd be happy to give you a lift."

Scott laughed uncomfortably. "I can work this out. You're right, she has a bit of a temper but she burns out fast. I should know better than to irritate her, get her riled up. She's really not like this. She's really a sweet, kind girl."

"No, she's not," Logan said. "She's an abuser. You're at risk. The police department can assist you. All you have to do is—"

"I appreciate your concern but it isn't how it looks. This sort of thing never happens. I mean she can get mad and yell, but she gets over it and—"

"And apologizes," Logan said. "And makes up. And promises to never do it again. Man, you're a statistic waiting to happen."

"You see the size of her?" Scott said with a laugh, absently rubbing his biceps. "She's no bigger than a ladybug.

I'm going to take her home. We'll have a conversation, and it'll never happen again. Thanks for your concern but we're fine."

Scott moved quickly to the car, got in and started it. Justine was frozen. She could see Cat sitting in the passenger seat, her arms crossed over her chest, a scowl on her face. She looked out the passenger window and didn't make eye contact with either of them. Scott pulled out of his parking spot and off they went.

Justine looked up at Logan. "Well now, that's very bad," she said.

"She was slugging him with all her might. Don't let the fact that she's small fool you. There's nothing preventing her from picking up a bat or a boulder. Or a gun."

"Oh Logan, surely Scott wouldn't let it get that out of control!"

"I don't know Scott. But I do know that some of these abusers have an amazing power over their victims. It boggles the mind."

"He left me for this?" she asked. "For a woman who would hit him hard enough to leave a bruise, make him bleed?"

"Here's something I took for granted. There were a couple of domestic calls that police answered in her last relationship. Maybe there were similar problems before that. I assumed it was the man in the relationship beating on the woman. I didn't go in and read the reports. I'll do that now. Maybe she's been the violent one all along."

"Would that be in the report?"

"No telling," Logan said. "Male victims are often reluctant to admit they are having trouble defending themselves. They hate admitting they're being physically abused by a woman. Most of them won't hit back. They're captives. Prisoners. The situation is just as bad as any typical domestic violence where the man is the aggressor. Just as dangerous."

"Will you check, please?"

"Sure," he said. "Of course. But Justine, don't get involved in this. You're too close to the situation."

"Maybe I'm too close to stay uninvolved," she said.

Logan called Justine first thing in the morning. "It was probably her, creating the domestic disturbance in the earlier relationship."

"Probably?" she asked.

"When the police arrived, they blamed each other. They were both charged with misdemeanor assault. I ask myself, how often has this happened with her other relationships?"

Justine was quiet for a moment. "What has he gotten himself into?"

"It's also not unusual for someone, man or woman, to leave a satisfactory relationship for one that seems more thrilling only to find it's loaded with problems. Only time will tell."

It wasn't as though this was the first issue of domestic violence Justine had ever heard of, but it was the closest she'd ever come to an actual case. And never in a million years did she think Scott could be caught up in something like that. Scott was too smart and sure of himself for that!

But then she hadn't expected him to have an affair, either.

It was a quiet morning at the house. Amber wasn't home from her overnight in San Jose, Olivia was on her laptop with her earbuds in, Addie had gone out for a long walk and had plans to do some shopping later. Justine spent an hour on her own laptop, sitting at the dining table. She read about male victims of spousal abuse and found lots of reading material. Then she applied herself to some laundry and cleaning, perfect activities when she wanted to think.

When she'd taken the job in this little town, she thought the hardest part would probably be seeing her husband and his mistress in blissful happiness living like college kids on the beach, nary a worry in their lives. She never in a million years thought she'd be seeing what she was seeing.

There was a certain amount of cynicism that came with her profession. She had to consider the worst-case scenario to be prepared to represent her company, or, in her new role, her client.

The household was full of activity. Addie came home, showered and changed and went off to San Jose for shopping. Olivia went with her. Amber came home and went straight to her bed for a badly needed nap after her night out.

Justine put on her tennis shoes and went out for a walk. She was wearing tight-fitting jeans with rips in the knees—high fashion these days, she mused. She pulled on an oversize poncho with a cowl neck over her dark long-sleeved shirt. She hadn't paid any attention to Scott's habits or schedule since they'd split up. In fact, she made it a point not to know too much about his current life. She didn't know exactly where he lived, though she knew she could easily find out. But he was done with her; she wanted to be done with him even if that was a difficult emotional space to occupy. Was she curious about him and his new life? Absolutely. It was hard not to be.

She walked to the kayak shack and, as she expected, it was closed. The October weather was cold and the few ocean goers were now often in wet suits. There were no cars there. She knew Cat drove a red BMW SUV, one flashy, pricy vehicle. She knew because Olivia had mentioned it, along with her observation that maybe that meant the kayak shack was doing better than people thought. It was not there.

She braced herself for the possibility of running smack into Cat Brooks, but she was relieved that she didn't. When she looked inside the shack, she saw Scott working on his laptop at the counter. He quickly closed the computer and looked at her.

"Wow," she said before even considering stopping herself. He was sporting a nice shiner. "Looks like you didn't work things out as quickly as you thought you would."

"It's none of your business, Justine," he said angrily.

"Hey, no need to shoot the messenger. I came to see you, for the first time, I might add, because I'm concerned about you. I mean, I hate you, but it looks like maybe you're in trouble."

"I'm not in trouble. Everything is fine now."

"I'm so disappointed in you, Scott. I thought by now you had perfected lying and here you go, bungling it. Clearly everything is not all right. You hooked yourself up with an abusive woman, and she's beating the tar out of you."

"It must make you so happy to think I'm in trouble," he said. "I'm not. We have a very good relationship. One little flare-up doesn't mean a thing."

"One?" she asked, raising an eyebrow.

"One!" he insisted loudly.

"Listen, indulge me for a second. Exactly what is it about her that would entice you to sacrifice your family?"

"I haven't done that," he said. "I had to end my marriage, but I had hoped that once you got used to the idea that we weren't married anymore, we'd still be friends. And I never intended to give up my children. I think you turned the girls against Cat and now I hope that in time they come around. I'm still their father. I still love them."

She shook her head. "I didn't have to turn them against her, Scott. They are very suspicious—naturally—of the woman who could make you betray all your commitments. You not only left us, you took half the money we earned together. Now it will take twice as long to reach that retirement goal…"

"But you said it—we earned it together. I only took what was mine."

There were so many responses she wanted to throw back at him, but what was the point?

"Well, that's what the law says. But will I ever know why?"

"I'm not sure I know why it happened. I wasn't expecting a woman like Cat to come into my life. She believes in me. She thinks I'm amazing and smart. She trusts me to save her business. I've never felt like this before. I've never felt so alive."

"Did you invest everything you have in her business?" she asked outright.

He paused for a moment, looking around as if seeking the right answer. "Yes," he finally said. "I can make this work. I know business. I've studied the market, the local and tourist economy."

"Where do you live, Scott?" she asked, taking a step closer.

"What does that matter?"

"I was just wondering. Do you live with her now? In her house or apartment?"

"No, I found a small house. Ocean Heights, just up the road. I'm renting. For now. She gave up her house. She lives with me."

"I bet it's a nice house," Justine said.

He merely nodded, clearly not seeing where this could be going.

"And you bought her a car?"

"Hers was limping along and I— Wait a minute. How do you know that?"

She shrugged. "I just guessed. Our divorce has been final about five months. You got a good settlement and you've already complained that you need money."

He stiffened, and his expression was angry though not, Justine believed, because she was questioning him. Rather he was angry that she seemed to already know the answers.

"I think you're in trouble," she said. "I think she's already gotten a generous share of the money you brought to your new life, and on top of that, she beats you up. I bet she's already asking for more, isn't she?"

"She doesn't beat me up!" he shouted, looking particularly ominous with his black eye, split lip and scarred eyebrow.

"She hits you, Scott. And she wants your money. You need to know something. I think you've been used. She went after you, caught you, got some fast money out of you and will only be with you as long as you continue to feed her habit. You're probably going to get beat up again and again, and really, you need help. Men don't like to admit a woman is abusing them, and sometimes they stay in it too long and end up in the hospital. Or worse. I can't help you."

"I don't want your help," he said bitterly. "You don't understand. You never needed me. You never admired me. You can't know how that feels."

"And so now you're going to somehow make this my fault? That I didn't show my appreciation quite enough? I gave you everything I had, you son of a bitch! I loved you! And I was faithful to you!"

"But it didn't take you long to find a new man," he chided.

She couldn't believe he was really jealous or that shallow. "I don't know you anymore, Scott. I think you've really gone around the bend. Please, be very careful. It seems you're in a bad place. I have nothing more to say."

"Maybe you're in a bad place," he taunted. "Maybe there's an argument that you used your advantage as a lawyer to talk me out of fair representation. Maybe we should go to court."

She sighed. Really, she had not expected this. "She wants more money, does she? You signed off, you got what the law says you were owed. If anyone was treated unfairly, it was me and the girls. We're done here."

She turned to leave and he said, "I can sue you."

She looked back at him. "Good luck with that! You can sue anyone for anything, Scott. Don't forget, I'm a lawyer. Throw away more money if you want, but I can assure you, you won't win. I don't owe you anything."

And she walked away, vowing never to return to that kayak shack.

CHAPTER FIFTEEN

Adele and Jake had been spending more time together at Jake's house since Justine and the girls moved into her space. This night they sautéed chicken breasts and vegetables with some Chinese noodles for dinner. They chose to watch Addie's favorite holiday movie, *Love Actually*, even though Thanksgiving was still weeks away. She watched it every year, but Jake had never seen it. Both the dinner and the movie were a roaring success—she already knew she loved it and was pleased Jake did, as well. After they finished eating in front of the TV and retired their trays to the kitchen, Adele snuggled a little closer to Jake.

And he pulled her yet closer.

"We should have a talk," Jake said.

"A talk?" she repeated. "Sounds serious."

"I think it is," he said. "I'd like to know what your plan is."

She sat up a bit straighter. "You already know everything, Jake. I'm going to keep my current job, go to school, emerge as a counselor who can actually do some good..."

"Live in your house with your sister and nieces, have

dinner with me twice a week, graduate from platonic kisses to hot kisses to weekly sex?"

She smiled at him. "I'm not opposed to that idea."

"That's why we have to talk. Addie, you take your sweet old time making up your mind about things. I think I've been on the back burner just about long enough."

"How can you say that? I have a great job, the first one I applied for, and I've committed to finishing my master's. In a new program yet!"

"You're going to think I'm being mean, but it took you eight years."

"Not really! I mean, in the first place I had a real serious trauma. A terrible relationship that led to a trauma. It was devastating and I admit, it took a while to recover. Then my mom…. But I always meant to get to this place!"

"So, here's my question, Addie. What place do I have in your life?"

"Jake," she said, shocked. "You're my best friend! I've told you a million times—I don't know what I'd do without you!"

"I like being your best friend. But I'd like a little something more."

"Like what? Like sex?" Then she smiled at him, trying to tease him out of this mood.

"This is my fault," he said. "I always wanted to explain myself better, to tell you how I really feel. It's hard for me. I think it's hard for most men, but I'm off the charts. The truth is, I want more. Maybe we don't want any of the same things, and if that's the case, we need to face it. I want a family. A wife and a couple of kids, but I'd be happy to have one kid."

"Jake, you've never told me that before!" she said.

"There's plenty of time but I don't want to play games. What about you? What do you want?"

"I used to think I wanted a child. I sure wanted one once. Losing him almost killed me. Now I'm focused on having a career. I want to be able to take care of myself. That's the one thing about Justine that I admire the most—she's completely capable of taking care of herself."

"You can take care of yourself, Addie. You've been taking care of yourself and your mom. I could promise to always take care of you, but those kinds of promises are no good. My father died young and my mom, she manages pretty well. If I wasn't around to do the heavy lifting, she could find someone to help. What I should have said a long time ago is I love you, Addie."

She put a hand on his arm. "I know, Jake. And that means a lot to me."

"I don't think you get it. I'm *in* love with you. I have been for years. I think it first occurred to me when you came home from Berkeley. But you were in love with someone else, and you were having a baby. Then you were so fragile and hurt. And then there was your mom. I vowed when you weren't grieving any longer I would be more honest with you, but I guess it took me a while."

She stared at him in shock. Through all the hours they'd shared, through the affection, the kisses and hugs, she had herself convinced it was little more than convenience. They were genuinely close friends. There was no one else for either of them, and they were, after all, adults. Buddies. Confidants.

"I thought this was the part where you cried for joy, threw your arms around me and—"

"But Jake, we've been friends for so long!"

"Yeah, and we can talk to each other, make each other laugh, have each other's back. Listen, I already had the experience of loving someone I didn't like very much, someone I wanted to trust. But I knew I was kidding myself. I've learned a lot since then. I want to be with someone I know deep down I trust, someone whose character I'm sure of. Someone I've loved for years."

"Wow," she said.

"Can you please do better than that?"

"I'm sorry, but something about this seems a little clinical. Like an arranged marriage. She's got a good dowry, strong teeth and decent birthing hips."

He grabbed her by the upper arms and pulled her toward him. Then he devoured her with his best, most powerful kiss. She'd had a few of these before and there was no question about it, he had a serious skill. She sighed when he let her go.

"Adele, you don't fall in love with teeth or hips. You fall in love with a heart, a spirit."

"Oh Jake," she said, nearly swooning.

"It's time for us to make a transition," he said. "Well, time for me. I understood all the complications of your life and never wanted to push you. You had so much to deal with. But you're sailing along now, and I want you to think about us."

"I counted on us being the same forever."

"That's the thing. That's not going to be enough for me. I want the real deal. I don't want to draw a line in the sand here, but I want you to know—I want more."

"How much more?" she asked.

"I thought that was obvious," he said. "Here's the thing. If you're also in love with me, we can make plans. They don't have to be traditional plans. But there has to be a future in this for me. If we're just going to be friends, I'm going to do myself a favor and get on with my life. That's not to say we won't be friends, but I can't be kissing you and holding you and spending all my time with you and hope to ever have a real relationship, one filled with hope and commitment. Or that family. Or the future with someone who wants a future with me. If we go on like this, someday you're going to just say, 'Jake, I met someone I really love.'"

"As you know, that can happen even to people with commitments," she said. "Even to people who have been married a long time."

"Not to everyone," he argued. "Some people of great courage and integrity say, 'No thank you, I have a commitment.' And you know what happens then? They pay attention to the relationship they have with their partner and make it good if they can. Maybe that temptation goes away if they don't feed it. That's my bet. And if they can't hold true, if they have to part ways, they haven't done so because of another person."

"I don't even know what to say," she said. She was acutely aware that she hadn't said, "I love you, too."

"Ever since you first came over here to see my house, ever since you started feeling a little crowded in your house, things between us have been heating up. I like it. I like it more than you realize. But I suggest we take a little break while you think about where you want to go with me. Because I don't want to be your Friday night guy forever."

"You act like you think I'm using you!"

"Nah, I know you're not that kind of person, Addie. But you take a long time to make a decision, y'know. And I've been hanging around a long time now. We gotta shit or get off the pot. Don't you think?"

"I don't know what to think," she said. "I have to process this."

He smiled indulgently. "That's my girl. You process. I'll walk you home."

* * *

During the rest of October, the leaves turned and the hill-sides east of the Pacific were aflame with colorful beauty. Justine's house sold, and some of her furniture appeared in Addie's house. Their house. The large yellow sectional replaced the old sofa and love seat that had been there for too many years to count, and while the piece was beautiful, it felt very awkward to Addie.

Every few days Justine brought home paint color samples, tile samples, flooring blocks or strips of wallpaper. Adele found it all overwhelming and was noncommittal.

"Really, Addie, if you don't give me your opinion..." Justine said.

"You're moving a little fast for me, that's all," she said.

"But you wanted to fix up the house. You talked about it for years. And I have some money from the sale of the San Jose house to apply to a little restoration. The big jobs will be the kitchen and bathrooms, so we might leave those for after the holidays. There's a guy in town that Sam swears by who can do a kitchen in ten days. He promises it! Once the kitchen is remodeled, it'll be easier to do new flooring. Will you at least look at some of these pictures I printed off the internet?"

"What if I'm not in the mood?" Addie asked.

Justine sat down at the table—her beautiful dining room table from San Jose—and said, "What's really wrong? Don't you like my ideas? Am I crowding you and making you uncomfortable? Are we too much for you here—the three of us?"

"No, I love having you here," she said. "I think I'm having trouble with change."

"Well, that's not good since you're making a lot of changes. Work, school, living arrangements..."

She doesn't know the half, Adele thought. There was that little skirmish with Hadley. He hadn't called or turned up since, so that was finally really over. She thought so, anyway. Then there was the ultimatum from Jake. He had stopped by the house a couple of times, bearing gifts of wine, fruit and cheese. He was his friendly old self, as sweet and lovable as ever. But they hadn't had any further discussions about the status of their relationship.

"Of course I love him," Adele told Ross. "I always have. But I never thought of him romantically, except to wonder could we be…you know…"

"Friends with benefits?" Ross said.

"Well, that's the only way I can put it. I mean, lately we've been getting much closer and I thought it might lead to something physical, but that's as far as I thought about it. But he wanted me to know that that kind of arrangement wasn't enough for him."

"And you interpreted that to mean?" Ross asked.

"Well, shit. He said he'd been in love with me for years. And here I always thought he loved me like a friend. Like a brother."

"Hmm," Ross said. "Do brothers usually act like that in your neighborhood?"

"I guess I just wasn't thinking," Adele said.

"Or listening," Ross said.

"I don't know what to make of this," Addie said.

"Then tell me something," Ross said. "Describe love to me."

She had to think about it for a moment. "Well, being in love with Hadley didn't really feel great, but I remember thinking it was great at the time. My heart seemed uncomfortably large in my chest, I was all aflutter, I couldn't think straight and my very existence seemed to balance on whether or not the phone would ring. I could barely express myself, and I didn't know what to do or say. It was kind of like a delicious torture. He said all the things I wanted to hear, like that I'd taken over his mind and he couldn't think of anyone else. That he wanted us to be together."

"Together how?" Ross asked.

"Well, together to have sex, as it turned out. But I wanted to live happily-ever-after. And he did say he'd be divorcing his wife. Soon."

"Hmm. Did you ever ask yourself if you could bear that feeling of quivering and having an enlarged heart forever?"

"I supposed it wouldn't feel like that forever, that it would calm down and become a warm and comfortable feeling of love and trust and dependability."

"That sounds very nice. Tell me what love looks like."

The picture that came to mind was one of Hadley standing on the front porch with his wife, kissing her deeply and running a hand over her swollen tummy, proud of the baby his wife carried. Tears came to her eyes. "I always wanted to be in love. You know, that love that's sure and strong and beyond doubt. And of course, filled with helpless passion."

Ross leaned back in her chair and crossed her hands over her chest. "I was in love with my husband," she said. "I was in love with him so much my eyes crossed. Then he hit me and terrified me and begged for forgiveness and promised to never do it again, and all that lightheadedness came back and I loved him desperately again. And then we fought and made up and it wasn't long before he hit me again."

"Oh, Ross," Addie said, sympathetic.

"I was so high on emotion I couldn't see daylight. I was either afraid or maybe just cautious and nervous or helplessly in love, because when he wasn't cruel he was so loving and sweet. It was the most terrible roller coaster. It took me such a long time to realize it wasn't love at all. It was addiction and abuse and control and maybe a lot of things that weren't healthy. Because, Adele, real love doesn't always sparkle and rain glitter on your head. Real love can be a little like warm milk—not all that tasty but soothing and predictable. Real love is feeling trust and kindness toward someone who isn't a prince all the time but is never a beast. Real love can be a little boring sometimes. Or at least not so pretty. Real love sits in the steam bath with a baby with the croup or changes the oil in your car before you go off on a long drive. Real love is someone you can call when you have the flu and he brings home chicken soup and changes the sheets on the bed. Real love sits by you on the couch while you weep at a silly chick flick… Or maybe real love endures yet one more football game and even throws some wings in the oven for him because he deserves it."

"And if you get bored and just don't feel that jazz anymore?"

"I guess that's an individual thing," Ross said. "I had an awful lot of jazz with my abusive husband. He used to say the best part of a good fight was the making up afterward. Eventually I began to really resent what I had to endure to get that good lovin'. It took me a long while to realize that all that sparkle wasn't really love. It was infatuation, and it wouldn't turn into the calm, strong, enduring and dependable trust that could last."

"I think, Adele, you have to figure out what love looks like to you. Can you imagine a life with the professor? Or do you think you'd just uncover a lot of lies and manipulation? Or, let me ask you this—how would it feel to not have Jake, your closest friend, in your life anymore?"

"That would be a terrible loss," she said. "But I'm not sure I really love him."

"Has there ever been a time in your relationship when you were uncomfortable with him?"

"No," Adele said. "But what do I know? In spite of the agony of loss, I still thought I was in love with Hadley. He broke my heart, but I probably would have taken him back if he'd said all the right words."

"You still haven't decided what you really want your life to look like. Maybe you're more like me and you just want your independence. I don't really want to be married again. I don't want some man's rowing machine under my bed. I get my oil changed at the station on the corner, and I can install a ceiling fan just fine."

"Thanks for the chat, Ross," Adele said. One thing was sure—Ross always made Adele smile. And think.

Justine had asked her daughters if they were planning to be home for dinner. Both said yes. When they got home from school at nearly five, she was in the kitchen slicing and dicing vegetables. She had a skirt steak marinating in soy sauce, white wine and ginger. It was Friday. She had left work just a little early and was preparing a special dinner.

And the table was set for five.

"I've invited a friend for dinner so please, don't throw your stuff around the living room and kitchen."

"Who's coming?" Amber asked, tossing her backpack and coat on the sofa.

Justine scowled at the backpack and coat, and Amber reluctantly picked them up. "Who?"

"Well, a friend. A man I know. I went to dinner with him a few times and talked to him on the phone several times, and I thought you might like to meet him. In the interest of transparency," she added in her best lawyer tone.

"You've been dating him? Without saying a word?"

"Here's the deal. I met him through a colleague in the San Jose office, and I had a drink with him. I wasn't about to trot him home to my daughters after one drink. I wanted to get to know him first. I thought if we dated a little and I liked him, I'd introduce you. I'm not good at secrets, but this isn't necessarily serious. For right now, we've had a good time and seem to have plenty in common. He's nice."

"You're dating?" Olivia asked.

"I guess that's what I'm doing," she admitted.

"Without saying anything to us first?" Amber asked.

Justine went back to the island in the kitchen and resumed her chopping. "I was a little torn about that. The thing is, I have never done this before. I met your dad in college and was with him and only him from that moment on. This is a whole new experience for me—going on a date after a divorce. A divorce I didn't want, at that. His name is Logan, he's very interesting, he has a good sense of humor and is respectful. He not only has a good reputation, he's a former police officer and a licensed private investigator, so you can be relatively sure he's up to scrutiny.

"I like him," she went on. "But let's be clear—I'm not looking for a new husband. I have no intention of getting married again or even living with a guy. The only people I'm interested in living with are you two and Addie. And with Addie for as long as it works for her. Some days I get the impression we're crowding her."

"It's just the remodel," Livvie said. "You know how long it takes Addie to make some decisions. And you make them fast."

"Not this time," she said. "I talked to Logan on the phone for weeks, maybe a couple of months, before I agreed to meet him for dinner."

The doorbell rang. Justine felt a jab of panic.

"Okay, look—I just want to introduce him to you so you are completely aware of who I'm going out with. And I'm not going out that much. You are and always will be my priority. You don't have to like him, you don't have to approve of him, you only have to be nice to him."

The doorbell rang again.

"We can be nice," Amber said. "You better let him in."

"Right," Justine said.

"Does Addie know he's coming over?" Livvie asked.

"I called her and told her. She didn't seem that happy about it. I promised he wouldn't stay late." She smoothed her supershort hair and went to the door.

Logan stood there, two bottles of wine and a bouquet of flowers in his hands. "I was starting to think you changed your mind," he said.

"No, just briefing the girls."

He handed her the wine. "Am I allowed in?"

"Of course. Come in." She stepped aside and said, "Logan, this is Amber and this is Olivia. Girls, this is Logan."

"You're my mom's boyfriend?" Amber asked.

"I am," he said.

"Well, now…" Justine began.

"Lighten up, Justine, we've spent months on the phone and have been out for drinks, coffee, dinner and even a town fair. I didn't say fiancé, life partner or future wife, but if it takes more to make me a boyfriend…" He whistled. He looked at the girls and winked. "It's early in the relationship. I might be pushing it to claim boyfriend, but I'm up to the job. Nice to meet you."

"I'll pour you a glass of wine," Justine said. "Red or white?"

He asked for red and then looked at the table. "Nice," he

said, handing the flowers to Amber. Then he looked around the living room, dining room and kitchen. "Just like you described it," he said. "This looks like a good old house."

"It's at least old," Amber said.

"I live in an old house, renovated and turned into four apartments," he said. "It's small but perfect for one person, and I can hear the ocean from my patio."

"Mom said you're a cop or something," Amber said.

"Or something. I was a cop, a detective actually. Robbery. Retired. Now I work as an investigator." He watched as Amber put the flowers in a vase, then he accepted a glass of wine from Justine. He wandered into the living room and sat on the far end of the sectional. Livvie was wedged into the opposite corner. "Now I do similar work but as a civilian rather than a civil servant. So, which one of you is the senior and which one is the junior?"

"I'm the senior," Amber said, joining them in the living room. "I'll graduate this year."

"Planning on college?" he asked.

"Cal State Berkeley," Amber said.

"Are you looking forward to it?" he asked.

"I think so," she said. "I'm glad to be staying in California, but I hope to live on campus eventually. We're going to need another car. Livvie will still go to our old high school in San Jose, and we won't be able to ride together anymore."

"And I'm thinking about the community college for my first year," Livvie put it. "A lot of people are doing that."

"Do either of you know what you want to do after college? I had three majors in my first couple of years and still turned out to be a cop, so it's definitely not required."

"I have no idea," Livvie said. "I've been saying librarian for a long time because I love to read, but things change. Amber likes clothes."

"I wish I could find a job wearing them," she said, making him laugh.

Justine couldn't have choreographed it any better. He got them talking about themselves first and then before long they were asking him what it was like to be a cop. He spoke freely and openly about some of his experiences while keeping the conversation and stories age appropriate. He told them about a robbery he'd working—the robber had a weapon and forced his way into an occupied home and there was no indication he'd left, yet they couldn't find him. He was hiding inside the dirty old furnace in the basement and gave himself away, very loudly, when the homeowner turned on the heat. Then there was a bank robbery where the thief made a wrong turn, right into the safe.

"But really my favorite of all time was the thief who led us on a chase and didn't get very far because he took a turn too tight, drove through a neighborhood backyard wall and landed, car and all, in the homeowner's swimming pool. I think I have a picture if you want to see."

They wanted to see and he got out his phone, scrolling through the pictures.

Justine was just about to give up on Addie when she walked in. Introductions were made, and they all sat down so dinner could be served.

Justine didn't exactly find Addie's regard for Logan to be cool, but it took ten or fifteen minutes for her to warm up while Justine served dinner. Once everyone was eating, Addie became fully engaged in the conversation.

"When did you two first meet?" Addie asked.

"Hmm," he said, pausing before answering. "I was doing some work for Justine's company last winter. I think it was a workman's comp claim or something like that. Then I was recommended to her for one of her own cases."

"You worked together?" Addie asked.

"I'm a detective for hire. I investigate everything under the sun, including corporate background checks, bankruptcies, potential hires, anything and everything. So, I met her, found out she was divorced, asked her to meet me for a drink." He shrugged. "That has to be six months ago or so."

"Almost five," Justine said. "We met for coffee, had a few phone chats, went to Carmel for a town art fair... Eventually we had dinner."

"I have good references," he said.

"And there were coincidences. He was moving to Carmel, I was leaving the company and taking a job here."

"My office is in San Francisco, but I usually work in the field. I'm only in my office a couple of days a week..."

"In the field?" Addie asked.

"Research, interviews, surveillance, whatever case I'm working on."

"Is it like top secret stuff?" Amber asked.

"Nah. Most of the information is easy to find in public records. But public records or not, it's always privileged. I can't tell any details. You know," he said, giving Addie a nod.

Maybe that was the point on which they bonded—Addie also collected personal stories she couldn't share.

After dinner, Logan helped clear the table, clean up the kitchen and had a cup of coffee. The girls wandered off, Addie chatted with them for a while then went to her room, kind of obviously leaving them alone. It was ten when Logan left. Justine walked him to his car.

"That couldn't have gone better if I'd scripted it," she said to him.

"This isn't my first rodeo," he said. "By the time you're

my age, the women I date have kids. Usually teens. I hate to sound arrogant, but I think I do all right with teens."

"You do all right," she said with a laugh. "That was a very good intro."

"Some advice?" he said. Without waiting for an answer he continued. "Reassure them that I won't be sleeping over now. Tell them your holiday gatherings still belong to you. Tell them I have a family, too, even though I don't have kids. A good first meeting doesn't commit them. Believe me, they'll be glad to hear it."

"But I think they liked you," she said.

"I appreciate that. They need time even if they like me. And so do you."

"I do," she admitted. "But I've been honest, Logan. I like you. I love spending time with you. And I'm committed to only one man—I'm the ridiculously faithful type. But I don't see another marriage in my crystal ball. Nor anything close to marriage."

He grinned at her. "You've been very clear. And I don't blame you."

"Still, that was so much easier than I expected."

He gave her a kiss on the forehead. "Go in now, get the debrief. I'm sure they have opinions and questions."

"I'm sure," she laughed.

She went inside and found Addie waiting for her. The girls were not in sight.

"I expected to be questioned about Logan," she said.

"I think Livvie is on the phone with her boyfriend, and Amber wandered off. So, Logan seems very nice. How long have you been keeping him a secret?"

Justine sat down on the sectional. "I don't really know how this dating business goes," Justine said. "I didn't mean to keep him secret. After a few months of seeing him, I thought I'd better come clean. I'm completely surprised to be dating. Not only didn't I expect to, I wasn't looking to."

"No surprise to me," Addie said. "You always land on your feet."

Justine held her tongue. Was that how Adele really saw it? That after what had happened to her, a few dates with a nice guy was landing on her feet? It was going to take a lot more than that to erase the agony of having the man you'd loved and relied on for so long betray you.

She tilted her head slightly, listening. "What's that sound?" she asked.

Adele shrugged. "Maybe Olivia on the phone?"

"I'm going to check."

She went up the stairs and listened at Livvie's door. She heard her talk, then laugh. And still there was that sound. She pushed open Amber's door.

Her daughter was facedown on her bed, her cries muffled in the pillow. Justine sat on the edge of the bed and gently touched her back. "Hey, bunny rabbit. What's the matter? Did something happen? Did something someone say upset you?"

She shook her head, rolled over and wiped her eyes. She sat up on her bed.

"What is it? Did meeting Logan upset you? Did I make a mistake?"

"No," she said with a hiccup of emotion. "He's nice."

"So why are you crying?"

Her face contorted. "It's like I lost my dad!"

"Because of Logan? Honey, I'm not going to trade your dad for Logan. Logan is just a new friend."

"But my dad is gone," she whimpered. "It's almost Thanksgiving. He moved in with her last March. He won't see us without including her and she's a creep. Why does she even want to be around us? We don't want to know her at all. And he'll never come home!"

"Oh honey, honey… Listen, there's something you have to understand—your dad left me, not you. Your dad and I won't be a married couple again. I can't. I just can't. I don't understand this business of him insisting you include his girlfriend—it's crazy to me. Your dad and I won't be getting back together. But it's not because of Logan. It's because your dad loves another woman. He walked away from everything we built together. He crushed my heart and yours and Livvie's. I can't let him do that again."

She thought about the things she'd tried to keep from the kids—the early mornings of throwing up, the nights she couldn't sleep or woke up every hour, the mornings of struggling with her makeup so the sleepless nights wouldn't show on her face. She lost so much weight, she looked emaciated. A doctor friend asked her if she could do with some Xanax, but she was afraid of becoming dependent.

In retrospect, that black hole had passed relatively quickly—a few months. But she had thought about nothing else but her husband and his mistress, obsessed with the betrayal. She thought about all those women who caught their husbands in an affair and didn't have careers, couldn't afford to break free.

"We lost him forever," Amber said. "It's not our fault, but we lost him."

"Not really, honey. I think your dad somehow lost himself. He wasn't feeling strong or important, I guess. And the woman he found made him feel important."

"But she's a creep! She's weird and kind of mean."

Justine was shaking her head. "I can't do anything about that. He made his choice. I think in time he might discover he made a bad choice, but it's a final choice."

"And you won't ever take him back? Ever?"

"What if I did and it happened again?" Justine asked. "Listen, we haven't come to the end of this story yet. This is all new. Many things could change. Your dad has a new business—maybe that will help him feel better about himself. Maybe..."

"Mom, everyone in town knows that kayak shack is a loser! It's gone out of business a bunch of times!"

"Here's what I hope," Justine said. "Your dad was a good dad, and I always thought of him as a good man. Maybe he'll come around enough so you and Livvie can spend time with him, have a good relationship with him. Maybe the woman he's with will become more likable in time, who knows? I just want you to remember that very few things are forever. Maybe it seems like your dad is gone now, but maybe that changes in a few months or years."

"The counselor said something like that, but it still hurts. It hurts that he left us."

"What did the counselor say, honey?"

"Something like keep an open mind, but I'm allowed to have boundaries. Like I don't have to go out to dinner with her. I don't know what's wrong with my dad. I can tell she's not a good person."

Justine felt at once relieved and guilty—her daughters didn't know the half of it. She was hitting him! Scott was not a skinny, weak little man and Cat was small, though strong. Was Scott letting her hit him? Was he not fighting back? Oh God, imagine if they were beating up each other! She had that scrappy look about her.

"I had that same feeling, Amber. That suddenly I didn't know my own husband. I'm hoping it's temporary insanity."

"But you won't take him back?"

"Listen, we can still have good lives, your dad and me.

We can be good parents and find a way to get along. Your dad is a smart man, he can work and make a living just like me. He just has to make some good choices."

"He hasn't so far," Amber said, taking a final sniff. "And now you have a boyfriend."

"If that worries you, I can tell Logan we can't see each other anymore. I told you—you come first."

"But you like him," she said.

"Of course! So do you. I think he's a good guy. But Amber, we're not in love or engaged or planning a future together. Logan is not in the way of you having a good relationship with your dad. That can still happen if he just gets his head on straight."

"I don't like our chances," Amber said. "I've never seen my dad act so stupid."

She had to concentrate to keep from saying, *If only you knew.*

CHAPTER SIXTEEN

Adele enrolled in a couple of classes for the spring semester at Berkeley. When she was admitted to the master's program, those classes would be applied to her transcript. One was from six to eight in the evening three nights a week, and the other was every Saturday, online.

The only person she wanted to tell was Jake. She dropped by the store, picked through some fresh produce, then went looking for him. She finally asked one of the produce managers.

"The last time I saw him he was hosing down the receiving dock out back."

"I'll go there," she said.

"Well, since you're not supposed to, leave your groceries with me and be very careful. It could be slick."

She knew her way around the store, of course. It was one of her regular outings the entire time she lived in her parents' house. She knew the store, the office, the dock, the storeroom, even the dumpsters. She found Jake in the shipping area, wielding his high-powered hose. She stood back, waiting for him to see her. He turned off the water.

"Adele Descaro, as I live and breathe."

"Yes, Jake, it's me. I left my cart in the vegetable aisle. How are you?"

"Doing fine, Addie. But how about you?"

She walked toward him. "I saw Bobby Jo at the Walmart the other day, and you'll never believe what she asked me. She asked if we'd had a falling out. A fight."

"Is that so? She never asked me," he said.

"Well, you are the boss. Maybe she didn't want to seem nosy."

"That never bothered her before," he said with a laugh.

"So, there's been some drama, and I thought you'd want to hear about it," she said.

"Absolutely, if it's at all interesting, which most of the drama in this town is not. Whatcha got?"

"Justine is dating someone."

"No kidding? Do you like him?"

"I guess," she said with a shrug. "He seems perfectly nice. But it made me see that we never actually dated even if we went out on a few dates here and there, and now we're not seeing each other at all."

"Not true," he argued. "I brought over a bottle of wine and some artichoke spinach dip from the deli. Bobby Jo is well-known for it, and I don't really know your diet restrictions, but if you can have wine and ice cream, you can have a little of the dip sometimes."

"That was a week ago and I haven't seen you since."

"Well, Addie, that's because we had a little bit of a stand-off about who we are to each other. Last thing I heard—you were thinking about it."

"I'm thinking about it a lot. You are important to me. How about if I cook for you tonight at your place?"

He had a look of genuine disappointment on his face. "I'm sorry, Addie, I can't. I offered to help a friend with some wiring. Simple job. It shouldn't take more than a couple of hours, but I made a commitment and she's feeding me dinner for it."

"She?" Adele asked.

"Jeannie Spicer. You know her."

"Oh, I know her all right. But really, dinner for a chore?" Jeannie was divorced with three kids, and while Jake had helped her out a few times before, this particular time it bothered her.

"It's what she always does," Jake said. "I don't mind helping her if I can. That worthless ex of hers sure doesn't help much."

"Hmm," Addie said.

"So, tell me about Justine's new man. What's he do?"

"He's a private investigator," she said. "I guess I better go so you can finish up and get over to Jeannie's."

"I'd take it as a good sign that you're acting a little jealous, if I didn't know you better. You're never jealous."

She got her groceries and went home. She was surprised to find that despite the evening before when Logan's dinner had stirred up some emotions, Justine and the girls were in good spirits. They were going out for pizza and a movie, and she joined them. She could've called to invite Jake to dinner the next day, Sunday, but instead she waited to see if she'd hear from him.

She didn't.

On Monday at work she made sure she had time to meet at least briefly with Ross. "I feel like I'm losing control of my life. My house is full of new furniture, not to mention people. Justine's trying to be patient, but she wants to remodel the house immediately after the holidays and she keeps trying to get me to make decorating decisions. I'm afraid of losing my best friend, Jake, because he's ready to move forward with our relationship. And I'm not ready for any of it!"

"You did have a lot of control before, didn't you?" Ross said.

"Before when?" Addie asked.

"Before your mom passed away and you were expected to finally get on with your life."

"And I did! I got this job and enrolled in school. But really, one thing at a time!"

"You came to this office for reentry help and were mistaken for a job applicant. I think you handled that very well, but Adele—that was a fluke," Ross gently pointed out. "At some point you'll have to take initiative."

"I enrolled in school!"

"You did, indeed. You have some choices to make with the rest. You can tell your sister you're just not ready to remodel. Pick a time—how much do you need? Two months? Three? Because you said she's driven but very reasonable. Right?"

"Yes. That's true. I just hate the thought..."

"Adele, do you have trouble telling people no?"

"Obviously," she said, grumbling.

"That's a very grown-up thing to learn how to do. It's not always easy. But if you don't, you have to suffer the consequences."

"What consequences?" Adele asked.

"You tell me, Adele. If you don't say no to Justine or at least give her some boundaries, what will you be living with? You'll have a muddled-up house that's half old and half new, and things will continue to be disrupted. Or, you can move forward and give her some room and maybe things get remodeled. And what about this friend of yours,

Jake? What if you came right out and told him you don't love him?"

"But of course I love him!" she said. "I've always loved Jake. He's my best friend in the world. It's just that… I don't know if I love him in the way I should to make a commitment of some kind. What if I discover in a few years that it just wasn't a passionate enough love?"

"Welcome to the real world," Ross said. "I think it's fair to say people discover that all the time. God knows why—maybe they change and it turns out your partner isn't the man you thought he was. Maybe you get bored. The hard truth is, very few couples stay passionately in love for decades. They usually fall in love, get married, learn that love relaxes into a dependable partnership and work at staying together. Love tends to ebb and flow."

"Then how do people stay together for fifty years?" she asked.

"Some people stay in bad relationships because they feel they have no options," Ross said. "I did that for about ten years. I had no job, no money, very little education…and I couldn't see my way out. But oh did I have passion. On the good days I had piles of passion."

"So I guess you're saying passion isn't the answer?" Adele said.

Ross folded her hands on her desk. "People travel the world looking for the perfect mate. Some go through a hundred partners in search of true love. That's why I told you to figure out what love is to you. I know what it is to me."

"Please," Adele said. "Tell me."

"It may not be the same to you. But to me, number one is respect. He would have to respect my feelings, my opinions, my space. He doesn't have to agree with me, just respect me. And he has to be willing to stay in balance with me—in other words, we have to help each other out. Regularly. There's got to be compromise—a way to share the load. And if a man ever says a mean word, for me that's a big red flag. But girl, I am not looking for some man with a good line that makes my toes tingle. I'd rather have the real damn thing."

"If I could just figure out what is the real thing."

"There's a good description in the Bible. Love is not jealous or mean, it is kind and thoughtful—something along those lines. Good relationships seem to boil down to people who are good to each other and thoughtful of their partner's feelings and needs. I have this friend I met in group when I was getting divorced. She was leaving her husband and she loved him madly, though he didn't deserve it and he treated her badly. He cheated, he lied, he was mean and had a foul temper, but she had the hardest time letting him go. But she did. Her survival depended on it. After that she wanted nothing to do with love—I think she felt love had cheated her, tricked her. A few years later she married again, this time to a man who treated her with respect, cared about her, was faithful and kind. He wasn't anything like the first husband and he wasn't flashy, but his feelings for her were dependable. She trusted him and relied on him. And she fell in love then, once she knew he was the real deal."

"Jake is all of those things," Adele said. "Why do I have doubts?"

"Hell if I know, cupcake. But that isn't my question to answer. That's on you. For right now, why don't you try to figure out what it's going to take to accept your sister's help fixing up that house that hasn't seen a fresh coat of paint in at least ten years. Seems like a good place to start. Because I think your issue is being indecisive. You would drive me out of my mind with that."

"I don't mean to be indecisive," she said. "I just want to be sure."

"Like I said, that would drive me crazy. I'm much too busy to wait around on someone like you, being sure."

"Don't you ever make a mistake?"

"Sure I do, but I'd rather redo a mistake than spend days on end waffling. Lord, I do hate waffling."

"I think I've made that a habit…"

"We have a time management workshop. I suggest you fit it in your schedule because you have a special case. You are quick and efficient in this office, but I think when it comes to things to do for yourself, you just can't make up your mind. And that's going to rob you of the happiness you've earned."

Adele took what Ross said to her to heart. The older woman was right. When Adele needed to do her job, serve the clients in the office who needed her help, she never hesitated. When it came to deciding what she wanted for herself, she felt confused and sluggish.

Inexplicably, she found herself parked in front of the house that had once belonged to her professor. Maybe it still did belong to him, but he was now divorced. She was just giving herself a memory check—that had been a terrible day. He'd sent her off with instructions to have an abortion, promised he was getting a divorce and then she'd seen him with his wife.

And now, as if history was repeating itself, she saw Hadley coming out of the house. He was wearing biking shorts and a fitted shirt, carrying his helmet. He walked around the side of the house and came back steering two bikes with his hands. In just a moment, a beautiful blonde woman came out of the house wearing biking attire, as well. She waved to the kids and a teenage babysitter, then claimed one of the bikes, put on her helmet and off they went.

Adele wasn't positive, but that woman looked like his wife, the same one she had seen about eight years ago. He wasn't divorced at all. Didn't he know she would find out eventually? Had she given in to his advances, it would have been very soon. But why was he pursuing her so ardently? Why was he so contrite and apologetic about their affair and its damages? What was going through his head? Was he simply a predator, going after as many young college women as he could fit in his schedule? It made no sense!

For a moment she wanted to follow them, maybe pull up alongside and ask, "Do you know what your husband does for sport?" Would Mrs. Hutchinson appreciate the tip or was she happy with her denial?

And why do I care? Adele asked herself.

Because she wanted the real thing. She wanted it to sparkle, and when the sparkle ceased to glitter, she wanted it to be secure. She wanted to trust a man who was worthy of trust. At one time she had thought the classy, sophisticated professor had whatever that was, but it had been a sham. Maybe she was too young and inexperienced; maybe he was just that good. He was, in the end, the naked emperor.

She watched them ride away and thought she was very lucky that hadn't gone according to her plans. It could have been a long and painful relationship.

Her only regret was losing her baby.

"I'd like to meet you for a drink," Logan said over the phone to Justine. "Maybe that little pub called Sheep Herder's in Half Moon Bay. I wouldn't bother you, but I have to tell you something."

"Are you breaking up with me?" she asked, half kidding.

The other half had been thinking no one was this lucky, to be humiliated by a wayward husband only to find a delightful man to fill in the empty spots in her life.

"Absolutely not," he said. But he didn't laugh. "When are you off work?"

"No one has late appointments today so we'll close up shop at five." She would take some work home, of course. She always did. She didn't always get to it, but she was diligent in her effort.

"I'll plan to be there by five thirty. Take your time."

Because she smelled an ill wind, she didn't waste any time. She phoned her girls to tell them she'd be home to cook dinner but first she was meeting Logan for a glass of wine. She promised not to be late and hoped she'd be able to keep the promise. Something in his voice seemed ominous.

He was already at the pub when she got there, sitting at a small table in the corner. The place boasted a good crowd at five thirty and would probably be packed by seven. This little pub and a number of quaint little eateries and shops were in the newer section of town, closer to the ocean. When she approached him, he stood and gave her a friendly peck on the cheek.

"How are you?" he asked.

"I have a feeling you're going to tell me how I am. What's up? Are you all right?"

"I'm fine. Sit. Would you like a glass of wine?"

The waiter was at their table before she could even answer. When he left, she just looked at Logan with her eyes full of questions.

"I'd like you to understand, I wasn't actively searching for more information on your ex or his new partner. It's pretty routine for us to go through police calls and reports to see if any clients or their problems appear there. A few days ago there was a call for paramedics at your ex's house. The police were called. Your... Scott was hurt, and though he insisted he'd had a little too much to drink and took a header down the stairs, he also had some scratches on his neck and so medical contacted the police before transporting him. He now has a line of stitches across his forehead. And it was a suspicious setting."

She was stunned. This drama of Scott and his woman was growing by the day. "Suspicious?" Justine repeated.

"There was evidence of a fight. Things were messed up in their house. The sofa was slashed and the stuffing was popping out."

"The sofa? Why on earth...?"

"My opinion? Someone had a temper tantrum. And I don't think it was Scott. He was transported and admitted. I read the police report—the officer suggested to Scott that he not allow his girlfriend to visit. They couldn't press any charges because they didn't see any battery, and neither of them would admit to it."

"You said he had stitches..."

"Split his head open and had to have a CT scan to make sure he's okay. They kept him overnight for observation. He had a mild concussion. He's been released. He'll be fine— this time. But I think his problems are ongoing."

"Oh God, this is terrible. I wished so many horrible things on him, but I didn't really mean it. I just wanted him to be sorry. I wouldn't go back in time a day, that's impossible. But I don't want him to be beat up!"

"Well, I'm going to have a talk with him," Logan said. "I don't think you should. That might send the wrong message. But I'll base a visit on what we saw in the parking lot that night. I'll round up a list of support groups. This is more common than you think. Some statistics put it at one in three domestics involve the man as the victim. I already knew a few things about battered husbands—"

"They're not married, are they?"

"Not to my knowledge, but they are a couple. I know a few things. Men as victims suffer a lot of shame—they're very embarrassed. The women who abuse them sometimes beat them up while they sleep, destroy their property, get insanely jealous, carry out vindictive plots. Maybe throw a hissy fit and tear up their sofa."

"The sofa! Listen, I don't know anything. I haven't really looked into these cases when the man is the victim, and I don't really know much about Scott and this Cat person. But I know this—when we met in San Jose to divide our property, it was very clear she wanted my couch. He asked for it specifically, and he had never liked it that much. I'm sure she's been in my house, though not since the divorce. Maybe she was acting out, showing him what she thought of the couch she ended up with. I don't know. Maybe I should—"

"No, you shouldn't. Didn't you already tell me you reached out to him, worried, after that parking lot scene? Your regular presence and interference could exacerbate the problem. But there is one thing you do have to do. And you have to do it very well. You must talk to your daughters and sister. You're going to have to tell them that despite Scott's denial and evasion, he is being battered by his girlfriend. They have to know it's a volatile situation. They shouldn't go to Scott's until this is satisfactorily resolved. They probably shouldn't let him in your house unless there's someone around who can make sure you're all safe. In an ideal world, I'd want you to have a restraining order, but that's not a simple process. You have to be threatened for a judge to sign off on that, and you haven't been personally threatened. Just tell the girls the truth and all of you give him space."

"And meanwhile you're going to stick your nose in?"

"Yes, as someone who knows a little about this and has a few resources. I'm going to give him the names of a few counselors and some support groups for men. I don't know if it'll help him, but I'm going to try. Then I'm going to leave it the hell alone. If you get involved, it could make matters worse. In the simplest of terms, the girlfriend is very threatened by you."

"Why?" she asked indignantly. "I lost him! He chose her over me."

"Listen, I have no idea what her mental and emotional impression of you is, but she obviously wanted what you had. She wanted the couch, for God's sake. Scott managed your home and I bet she saw it. I bet she looked in your closet and kitchen. I bet she saw you before you first saw her. It's human nature. It's typical of her type. Scott, though married, looked like a sure thing—money, savings, investments, capable, resourceful and available."

"He was married! He wasn't available!"

"He was if the woman could manipulate him into thinking he could do a lot better. These affairs? They're usually little more than motivation and opportunity. She supplied the motivation and the opportunity was built in—you were working. She probably made him feel like a god."

I do have a degree, you know. How many times had he said that? Had he been feeling less than her because she had a law degree? But he was the one who pushed her, who said he didn't want to work and she'd be capable of supporting them well! It was his idea.

"God, no good turn ever goes unpunished. I didn't want to be a lawyer. That wasn't my dream. I was teaching. I liked my job. Scott's dream was having plenty of money without having to work for it. I did everything he said I should do! Everything was about us."

"Come on, it's not like you were victimized with a good education and excellent job. But let me tell you about men. Most men, anyway. They don't play second fiddle well, and they're very susceptible to high praise and power. If he didn't feel important enough, that wasn't your fault. He could've applied himself to being useful, to elevating his status. But he was offered a shortcut to feeling important. And he took it.

"Justine, you have to talk to your daughters, and all of you have to stay away for now. At least until Scott gets some help."

"He's never going to get help," she said.

Logan, being an expert in surveillance, watched the house he knew to be Scott's as well as the kayak shack. He had identified the make and model of the vehicle Cat drove, and when it was not in evidence, he parked and went to the door. It was a nice, new, modern neighborhood south of the bay, and many of the houses there had a nice view of the ocean.

Scott's car was parked in the drive, and Logan knocked on the door. There was no response so he knocked again. Scott could be sleeping. After all, it had been less than a week since his head injury.

Finally the door opened and Logan said, "Hey, Scott."

"What do you want?"

"I wanted to talk to you for just a minute." He touched his forehead, indicating Scott's stitches. "How's that doing? Healing?"

"I'm fine," he said. "What can I do for you?"

"Well, if it's not an inconvenient time, you could invite me in. So we can talk."

"About what?"

"Your many injuries, for starters."

"I don't have anything to discuss with you," he said. "Did Justine send you?"

Logan shook his head. Of course he remembered that Justine identified him as former law enforcement. "No, I'm here on my own. Justine doesn't even know I'm here." At least, not at the moment, though she did know he planned to talk to Scott. "Listen, I've seen things like this before, and you're not the only person shit like this happens to."

"You don't know anything about it."

"But I do. And you spent the night in the hospital, the same night someone took a sharp implement to your couch. Knife? Scissors? Something else? Because women who beat up their partners tend to do things like damage the man's property or hit them in their sleep or, God forbid, take that knife to them when they're defenseless. I've only met your girls once, but they seem like nice girls—this is not the way you want to be remembered by them."

Scott took a step toward him. "What do the girls know about this?"

"I don't know," Logan said. "I honestly don't know. But my advice to them would be to stay away from you as long as you're mixed up with this woman. She has a history, you know. It's a matter of public record."

"She was the victim of abuse," Scott said.

"Actually, she and her last husband were accusing each other of battery. My guess is, this isn't a sudden affliction. This has been going on a while. Most victims are reluctant to break away, at least at first, but I want to tell you a few things. Thanksgiving is getting close. Then Christmas comes barreling at you. These situations heat up during the holidays. I'd suggest you break it off with her because she's poison—she's going to push you down the stairs again."

"She didn't," he said, but he said it more calmly, a little emotionally.

"Whatever, Scott. I brought you a couple of things." He reached into his jacket pocket. "Here's a list of a few counselors not near you. They happen to be men. They have experience in this sort of thing. And here's a list of locations, dates and times of support groups for men. This happens more often than you think. You're not alone. Google it, if you haven't already." Logan tried looking past Scott. "She's not here?"

"Not right now, no."

"Buddy, she's got red flags all over the place. Do yourself a favor…"

"This really isn't your business. You can let it go now. And if you talk to Justine, just tell her no one is hitting me. No one is battering me."

"Take this information, Scott," he said, holding out the paper and the business card. "At least take it and think about it."

"I don't want it."

Scott backed into his house and closed the door.

Logan stood for a moment as if anticipating the door might open and the conversation could continue. He was the wrong person to confront Scott, he could see that. But there was no right person. Justine couldn't do it—Scott would have too much pride at stake to come clean with her.

Scott had made a mistake, and now he was just going to have to either solve it himself or live with it.

CHAPTER SEVENTEEN

Thanksgiving was at the end of the week, and Adele and Justine had decided on a quiet day with the girls. They were going to cook; it had been a long time since they'd done that together, possibly ten years back when their mother was not only alive but able-bodied and spry.

"Are you going to invite Logan?" Adele asked.

"No," she said. "I think that would be premature. He's going to be with his family, I'll be with mine. I did ask him if he wanted to go for a bike ride on Friday, however. What about Jake?"

"I asked him if he wants to stop by," Adele said. "He'll be with his mother, and his brother is going to have his kids for the day. With two ex-wives they juggle the holidays. Jake said he'll stick close by, help his mother with the cooking and clean up and distract her from the chaos that usually comes with Marty. After all that, he said he'd love to stop by for a slice of pie."

There was nothing at all off about the day—it was perfectly calm and relaxing, the food was wonderful, soft music played in the background. They turned on the space heater in the living room and after dinner played some gin rummy. Justine excused herself to talk to Logan on the phone for a little while. But Jake didn't show up until nine. And he was exhausted.

"Marty and his kids would wear down a stronger man," he said. "And didn't he just bring a girl. Angie something. She's a looker, but it was pretty obvious he wanted someone to chase after his kids."

"And she didn't see through that?" Justine asked.

"She's young," Jake said. "So young. I think she might be twenty-two."

"Sheesh," she said. "At least she's old enough to vote. What's the matter with young women these days? Doesn't the fact that he's had two wives and multiple girlfriends make her wonder if he's reliable?"

"Apparently not," Jake said with a laugh. "Not yet, anyway."

"So, tomorrow Justine and the girls are going for a long bike ride with Logan, her new boyfriend. We could do something."

"Sorry, Addie. It's a big day at the store."

"But Thanksgiving is over. Shouldn't it be quiet?"

"It's Black Friday. Everyone is shopping. We'll have some sales, like the rest of the world. And I promised Jeannie I'd stop by after work to have a look at her plans. You know, her remodel plans."

"Why?" she asked.

"I have some experience," he said. "And she knows I have no interest in taking advantage of her."

"You're talking about her a lot," Adele said.

Jake smiled at her. "I'd think you were jealous if I hadn't already waited a long time for you to even notice me."

"Now you're being silly. I've more than noticed you. I'm just the slow moving, cautious type."

"If you don't pick up a little speed, we'll both be too old to enjoy life by the time you get into the passing lane."

"Now you're teasing me," she said.

"No. I'm not. We've been over this."

He gave her a kiss on the forehead and walked down the sidewalk.

She noticed his wide shoulders under his leather jacket; his narrow waist. He had his hands in the pockets of his jeans and took long strides down the sidewalk. Jake wasn't just well built and strong, he was also handsome. But above all, he was kind and honest. For all that Marty was a player, Jake was steadfast.

It was just that he had been her best friend for her entire adult life. Could your best friend also be your passion? Because when she thought about being in love, the image that came to mind was someone exciting. Someone irresistible. Not someone she was already so comfortable with. It would be like dating her brother.

Yet she loved him. She couldn't imagine life without him.

Justine was sitting on the sofa, idly reading or texting on her phone. The girls were not in evidence, but Addie could hear the distant sound of the TV upstairs.

"I have a question, Justine. If it's too personal..."

Justine rested her phone in her lap. "I don't think I have anything too personal left. Go ahead, try me."

"Were you madly in love with Scott when you decided to marry him?"

She shook her head. "No. We'd been steadies for three years or so. The madly in love part had pretty much settled into mutual respect and affection. It did come back now and then, briefly, when we'd be all over each other like a couple of teenagers, but that in-love part was fleeting. I loved him, though. I always felt pretty secure. Now, looking back, I wonder if he strayed before and was just clever enough to get away with it. Why are you asking me this?"

"Was he your best friend?" Addie asked.

"Sometimes," she said. "What's going on?"

"It's Jake," she said. "I'd be lost without him. I love him, I do. But I just don't know if it's the kind of love that has the power of endurance. Know what I mean? What if I tell him I love him and want to be with him forever and it turns out I really just love him as a good friend?"

"What about physical attraction? What about idiosyncrasies that drive you batshit crazy? Like bad breath or he's a lousy kisser or he doesn't like anything you like?"

"I can't think of anything," she said. "We even watch *Downton Abbey* together, though he'd probably rather watch something with a gunfight or something."

"Then why don't you take him out for a spin?"

"What if it doesn't go well? What if I discover it's not okay? That it won't work?"

"Then you tell him."

"So, are you in love with Logan?"

"A little bit," she said. "But at this stage in my life, I'm not looking for another husband, and he knows that. He doesn't blame me. He's not looking for another wife—he was married and has been divorced for years. But we both agree we like what we have. It could last." Justine smiled. "When I found out about Scott and that woman, I thought my world ended. All I wanted was to survive it. I was worried about the house, about losing it, about not being able to feel confident again. Look what happened. The girls are so happy here. My workload is better and more interesting. I know the whole town. They know me. I thought this would be temporary. I love it. I don't remember even liking this house when I was growing up. It was just a house. I'll move if it's too much for you, but…"

"It's not too much for me," Addie said. "I just can't believe you're happy in this old house and in this old town. You had a mansion before!"

"It was a nice house, but hardly a mansion. It was Scott's choice, anyway. I want a quieter life than I had with a big, demanding firm. This is a little like coming home."

Adele laughed. "Justine, you did come home."

"Here's the surprise—I find myself, not even a year after my divorce, genuinely happy. Happier than I was. I didn't know I wasn't happy before, but I like that no one tells me what we should do, what I should do. Oh, I'm still pissed off. Scott's a fool and he made some bad choices, but he's stuck with it. I'm working on making the choices that work for me. And the girls, of course.

"Addie, you should think about Jake. If he's a good man and you feel good with him, you don't want him to get away. Trust me, there isn't a surplus of guys like that. I don't think you need a guy to be happy, but the right one can flesh out your life. Just make sure he's going to support what you want to do and not tell you what you should do."

December brought out all the Christmas decorations in Half Moon Bay, and the town glittered. Justine helped decorate the front window of the law practice. People were a little friendlier and happier, if possible. Justine finally got Adele's agreement on all the tiles and colors and paint; they went together to the appliance store to get new appliances as the ones in the house now were withering with age. They even had time to sit down with a couple of contractors and attempt to plot out the remodel to begin early in January.

Justine had brought Christmas decorations from the

San Jose house to adorn the old house, and they put up a tree early. The days grew shorter and the sun was setting by five. And all the lights in town were illuminating the streets.

Justine was just coming out of the law office at five when she heard her name. "Justine," Scott said. "Hi."

"Hi, Scott. What brings you to my part of town?"

"I wonder if we could have a talk," he said, shivering either from the cold or from anxiety. "Would you have a drink with me?"

She looked around nervously. "Is your girlfriend lurking somewhere?"

"No. Just me. Let's go to Tony's Oyster Bar. We can walk. Just for a quick drink."

"Is this about Christmas plans? Because we can discuss that—"

"I'd like to talk about that, yes, but that's not what this is about. I think I probably should say I'm sorry or something…"

A huff of laughter came out of her. "Ya think?" she said.

"Let's get a beer or something. Please."

Justine dreaded whatever was to come. She noticed the fine white scar along his hairline and frowned.

"You're not planning to clear the air, are you, Scott? Because I really don't need another long list of reasons how I somehow drove you to another woman."

"Nothing like that, I promise."

"All right," she said, taking off down the street at a brisk pace. "Just a glass of wine. That's all. I have plans for dinner."

"Oh? That guy? Logan?" he asked.

"No, my sister and daughters. I'm making a rotini pesto

tonight. And salad. And bread. Logan is working, and I have some work to do later."

"That sounds really good," he said, struggling to keep up.

"Thank you. You're not invited."

It took them only minutes to reach Tony's. The place was crowded for happy hour, but most of the patrons were gathered around the bar. Justine found a table in the back near the kitchen door, and she sat down. She put her briefcase on the chair beside her and quickly texted her daughters that she was stopping for a glass of wine and wouldn't be long. She ordered a chardonnay and waited in silence until it arrived. She didn't ask "How you doin'?" or make small talk. When her wine arrived, she took a sip and said, "What is it, Scott?"

"Boy, you don't make it easy," he said.

"If anyone on earth hasn't earned easy, it's you. What did you want to talk about?"

"Well, I don't know how to say this, Justine." He stopped and looked down into his beer. Then he looked up with the soulful eyes she had once loved. "I made a mistake. I was wrong about everything."

"Is that so," Justine said. "And what has that got to do with me? Or Christmas?"

"It has nothing to do with Christmas!" he said angrily. "It has everything to do with you. Didn't you hear me? I was wrong! I regret leaving the marriage. I regret having an affair. I was manipulated and fool enough to fall for it."

"She beat you up again? Or just leave you?"

"She never beat me up!" he insisted. "We had a disagreement. It happens. Justine, I never stopped loving you. You're the mother of my children, of course I always loved you. I thought… I don't know what I thought. I made a mistake. I should never have strayed, should never have…"

"Strayed?" she asked, drawing out the word. "Scott, you engaged in a complicated and destructive series of lies for months if not years and destroyed our family! You betrayed us all. So you made a mistake. I guess you'll have to live with that."

"Be reasonable, Justine. I'm sorry. I recognize where I went wrong and I've learned. I learned way more than I wanted to. We can put it back together."

"No," she said. "We can't."

"I realize it could take time…"

"It would take a miracle," she said. "You said you didn't love me anymore. After my heart stopped ripping apart, I stopped loving you. You took what you wanted and rented a fancy house to live in with a woman who hadn't given you years, sacrificed for your marriage, helped raise your children, trusted you and—" She paused and sipped her wine. "Let me ask you something. You want your marriage back?"

"If humanly possible."

"Why?"

"Because I can see now that I was confused! Wrong! Misled and used! You were right and I was crazy! Call it a midlife crisis, but in a way it illuminated all the things I took for granted. We deserve a second chance. We had a good marriage."

"Everything you took in that settlement," she said. "Are you prepared to return it to our joint retirement and savings accounts?"

He dropped his chin and looked down into his beer. "Just give me a chance and I'll make it up to you," he said. And he said it quietly.

"She got it, didn't she?" Justine said. "How'd she get it?"

"She didn't exactly get it," he said.

"Yet you don't have it," Justine said. "She tricked you."

"She misled me. We were going to be partners. Now I have no money and a failing business. I thought we were going to be partners. I thought I was going to save the business for her, help her out. I thought she'd be grateful, but—" He cleared his throat. "She was very convincing."

"Until she coldcocked you," Justine said.

He didn't respond. He did wince, and she thought the scar on his forehead got whiter.

"I told you that was going to happen," she said.

"Because I'm so completely undesirable? Because who, besides you, could possibly want me? Because I'm *nothing*?"

"No! Because she played to your ego and won! You weren't nothing. You were everything to your wife and daughters! But you walked away from the real thing—loyalty and love and commitment—for a chance to be a big shot! She played you! What made her finally leave? Did you run out of money?"

"No. I told her I would never marry again!"

She leaned away from him, actually surprised that he said that. She thought he was a goner, that he'd fall for anything. She wanted to know how much she'd gotten out of him for that kayak shack, but on the other hand, she'd rather not know. Besides, she could find out. Anything that involved a sale and a filed document could be traced.

"What about you, Justine? Are you into this Logan all the way? Serious?"

"Oh, I'm serious about Logan. I'm not seeing anyone else. We don't have any plans. It's new."

"Then there's still hope for me," he said, his face brightening just the smallest bit.

Here she was, about nine months since catching Scott in an affair. She knew women who caught their husbands' cheating more than once, yet kept their marriage intact and even seemed content. Justine couldn't do that. As she looked at Scott now, after what he'd done, she wondered why she'd loved him at all. He'd always wanted as much as he could get with as little effort as possible.

And then he blamed her for working such long hours. Blamed the failure of their marriage on her not being perpetually available to stroke his ego.

All this talk of second chances and regrets—Justine was much too cynical for that. He'd probably be back with his other woman by the end of the week.

"No, Scott. I'm not at all open to the idea of reconciling. Not remotely. In fact, I'm not sure we'll even be friends."

"How can you say that? After thirty years together?"

She shook her head, and remarkably, she felt the sting of tears. She'd felt for a long time if she could only break down and give out a big, sobbing cry it would release some pressure. "That's the thing," she said quietly. "After that many years, after all that love and trust, what you did to me was unconscionable. I doubt any other human being could have wounded me so deeply."

She pushed back her wineglass, then her chair. She picked up her briefcase and walked out of the bar.

The night was cold and dark, but for the twinkling of the Christmas lights. She was aware that the betrayal was not over for her yet. In fact, his desire to come back to her seemed only to make it worse. She had no idea she could hurt so much.

But then she had a vision of Scott with nothing left after

taking everything he could from her. Scott, homeless and bereft. It was a very sad vision. Then the tears coursed down her cheeks.

Adele hadn't seen much of Jake since that last big talk they'd had. It was almost a showdown. She'd given things a lot of thought and decided she would find a way to convince him they should get back on track, spend as much time together as possible and let their relationship evolve naturally. She felt they had missed a step in the development of their relationship.

She had to make Jake understand that after being friends for so long, it was awkward to her to change *love* to *in love* when she wasn't sure exactly what that meant in the grand scheme of things. She cared for him, cared deeply. If she were to make a list of all the attributes she thought were important in someone she could be devoted to, Jake had them all. Tenderness, strength, integrity, honesty, kindness, wisdom…oh, the list was long and impressive. All that was lacking was that zing of passion she recalled from years ago when she fell hard for the useless professor.

She had come to learn that feeling wasn't worth much without all the other things, but that wasn't helping her right now.

She had tried explaining that to Ross who said, "Sounds to me like you're taking him completely for granted."

But of course she didn't think she was doing that. She thought it was more probable he was trying to motivate her with his frequent trips to Jeannie's house to look at her remodel plans or her tile choices. She had tile choices and remodel plans he could look at!

With that in mind, she fluffed and buffed, fixing her hair and makeup, and took off from her house to the market. If she found that Jake was once again heading to Jeannie's, she just might scream. Justine and the girls were going to San Jose to a high school choir concert tonight, and Adele decided it was the right time to give Jake a piece of her mind. He was clearly avoiding her and trying to make her jealous. That was no way to lay the groundwork for a romantic relationship.

She had rehearsed what she'd say many times and did so again as she walked through the cold, foggy night to the market. *Jake, I've had so many changes this year, my new job that will lead to a new career, my sister and nieces moving in, not to mention that I lost forty pounds and have a completely new lifestyle...and now I feel that I'm losing you! This isn't the time to put restrictions or demands on our—*

She stopped suddenly as the market came into view and outside the front entrance was a paramedic's truck, a big fire rig and an ambulance. Lights flashed against the low hanging winter clouds. Had someone slipped and fallen? She picked up her pace. Then she saw a gurney wheeled out of the market. The paramedics appeared to be rushed, and one was holding up an IV bag.

She ran. Someone had stretched yellow crime scene tape across the street. A crime? she asked herself. The police were there, but they seemed to be working crowd control. She had a sudden horrible fear that it was Jake. Jake, whose father died of a heart attack at a relatively young age. She couldn't remember offhand just how old he'd been. She raced up to the gurney just as they reached the ambulance's back door.

"Who is it?" she asked the first person she came to. "Who's hurt?"

Bobby Jo, the deli manager, and Lee, the assistant manager, were there. She heard Lee say, "I'll go fetch his mother. Where are you taking him?"

"We'll go to Sutter, but no guarantee he'll stay there. He might need a specialist in the Bay Area."

"Jake!" she cried, rushing to the gurney. "Jake!"

"Please stand back, ma'am," a firefighter said. "Are you family?"

"No," she said. "I mean yes, yes. I'm his best friend! What happened?"

Lee interceded, grasping her elbow to keep her from clambering into the ambulance just behind the gurney.

"Hang on, Addie," Lee said. "Let them get him to the hospital."

"What happened?"

"A whole wall of boxes crashed down on him. I don't know how. Nothing like that has ever happened before. Knocked him out cold," Lee said. "I wonder if he had a heart attack or something and ran the forklift right into the boxes? They were mostly canned goods. His head is bleeding. You can't go with him. I'll give you a ride after I pick up Beverly if you want—"

Addie took off at a dead run back to her house, back home where she could grab her car. Without a thought of anyone else, she rushed to get to Jake. She paused in her panic only for a second to remind herself that Lee would make sure Beverly got to the hospital. But at the moment all she could think about was making sure Jake knew she was there, knew she loved him, knew that the greatest loss of her life would be if she lost him.

How could I have wondered for a second? she thought miserably.

By the time she got to Sutter Hospital, he had been seen by a doctor and was having tests—a head CT, an EKG, a few other things, and they were considering sending him to UCSF.

"For surgery?" she asked the nurse. "Heart surgery?"

"Are you aware of some heart condition we should know about?" the nurse asked.

"No, only that his father died of a heart attack, and he wasn't very old. Did you ask him about that?"

"He's talking to the nurses and they'll get a medical history. I'm afraid that's all I can tell you," the admissions nurse said. "He hasn't named you as a family member."

"Is he conscious?" she asked.

"He was fully conscious when he came in and was talking."

"Can I see him? For just a second?"

She shook her head. "I'm sorry. This isn't a good time for visitors. I'll check with the doctor, but I'm sure the answer will be no. At least until they can figure out his injuries."

"Please check, will you? And if I can't see him, can you give him a message from me, from Addie?"

"I can try, but understand, he's been medicated and they don't want to get him excited."

"Just tell him Addie is here and that I love him. That's all. But that's important, okay?"

"I'll see what I can do. You can sit in this waiting room."

"His mother," Addie said. "Someone is bringing his mother…"

"Yes, there was a call. She's on her way. This would be the best place to wait for her."

"I'll wait."

It seemed a long wait, with Addie looking at her watch constantly. Every five minutes it seemed like twenty had passed. Then Beverly rushed into the ER and Addie embraced her. "Is he all right?" Beverly asked.

"I haven't been able to see him. They're running tests of some kind. On his head, I think."

"Lee said heavy boxes fell on him and the forklift tilted onto its side. Let me see what the nurse will tell me."

But aside from saying Jake seemed to be doing fine, the nurse didn't have anything to report. Finally, after a half hour, Beverly was allowed to see her son. When she came out, she was smiling. "He has a big bandage on his noggin, and he said while he waits for test results, he'd like to see you. If you're still here, he said." And then her smile broadened.

"As if I'd leave," Addie said, walking into the patient area. She found his name on the white board outside the drawn curtains and rather sheepishly peeked inside. He sat up in bed, blood splattered on his shirt and a big white bandage wrapped around his head. "Aw, Jake. God."

"I know. Pretty dramatic, right? I have to stay the night. To make sure I don't walk in my sleep."

"Really?"

He laughed. "No, not really. To be sure I'm not brain damaged, probably."

"Jake, what the heck happened?"

"I tried to move too many boxes and hit the gas instead of the brake, a few boxes fell forward and I upended the forklift. Kaboom. I was never very coordinated." He smiled a lopsided smile. "Just to be sure I'm not delirious, the nurse said some pretty girl loves me."

"And you assume it was me?"

"I assumed it was Jeannie, but I'm giving you a chance here. I could die before morning."

She put a hand on his cheek. "I've always loved you, Jake. I was worried about the right kind of love. Then you crashed into the canned goods, and all at once I realized there are lots of kinds of love. And I feel them all. I've wasted so much time overthinking things! I don't want to ever be without you. Not ever."

"Then that's how you will have it. You're my girl. From now on."

"Wow, that was easy."

"It won't always be easy," he said. "Now we have to live up to it. I'm looking forward to that."

"Jake, do you think if I promised to sit up all night, watching you, the doctor would let me take you home?"

"It's worth a try," he said, beaming.

Justine wasn't expecting anyone when the doorbell rang the Saturday before Christmas. In fact, she was just about to hop in the shower—she'd been cleaning, organizing and cooking all day and looked a mess. The girls were off doing some last-minute Christmas shopping, and she used the time to straighten up the house and make a lasagna for dinner. Livvie had invited her boyfriend, Jared, and often when Jared came over he would bring a pal along, maybe for Amber to look over.

When she opened the door Scott stood there, his arms laden with gifts. "Scott," she said, absently smoothing her hair. "This is unexpected."

"I hope you don't mind," he said. "I'll just leave these and go. Unless…"

She waited for him to finish. "Unless?"

"Do you have a minute?"

"Sure. Let me take these." She took the packages, six of them, and put them under the tree.

"The girls aren't here?" he asked. He stepped just inside the door.

"Shopping. They'll be home before long but really, Scott. You can't get in the habit of dropping in."

"What about Addie?"

"She's been looking after Jake full-time, though I don't think he needs much looking after anymore. He hurt his head at work."

"I'm sorry to hear that," Scott said. "I just wanted you to know—Cat is gone. She's not coming back."

"Left the sinking ship, did she?" Justine said before she could stop herself.

"Not quite," he said. "Though she did get away with a bundle. I told her it was over and that the next time she came around, I'd have to call the police. I believe she already has a record of some kind. She must. She left willingly, and she knows I'm not completely flat broke yet. She was working on me to go after you in court to try to get more money."

"She'd have been disappointed. The courts would never side with you. Our settlement was by the book."

"I made a mistake," he said. "I admit it. She didn't turn out to be the woman I thought she was."

Justine looked at that thin scar at his hairline. "I'm sure that must have come as a surprise."

"I'm sorry, Justine. You'll never know how sorry. If you ever want to give me any kind of chance…"

"No," she said, shaking her head. "I couldn't possibly take the chance that you'd hurt me like that again. You really don't know how deeply hurt I was."

"You seem to have recovered," he said.

"That's what you wanted," she said. "After only two months, before we were officially divorced, you said you thought I'd be over it by then." She sighed. "That was the biggest shock. I was surprised by the lying and the cheating, but that happens to a lot of people. It's a surprise, but not a cold, heart-stopping shock. It was your cruelty." She shook her head. "The man I married was imperfect, as I am, but you were never cruel. You walked away from me as if it was your right. As if it didn't matter what happened to the rest of us as long as you were happy. And you weren't kind."

"I'm sorry. I guess I'm too late. That Logan guy "

"Logan is a very special man, but the reason I won't consider taking you back is you, Scott. Your selfishness and meanness. And you found yourself a woman twice as selfish and cruel."

He nodded. "Well, you're strong. You've always been strong."

"I am strong. I'm glad I'm strong. But my strength doesn't mean you or anyone has the right to treat me with such terrible, heartless malice. Let's call it done."

"Well, I had hoped we'd at least be friends…"

She laughed. "Do you even know what a friend is? A friend is someone you can depend on, someone who has your back, someone you share your confidences with, your fears and dreams. A friend is there for you and doesn't betray you. A friend stays in balance with the give-and-take of life, doesn't just take and then take more and then more."

"You have absolutely no love for me, is that it? After all those years and two beautiful kids."

"It's not the kind of love that would allow me to be a fool, Scott."

He was quiet for a long moment. "What are your plans for Christmas?" he asked.

"A quiet Christmas for us. Jake and Addie will be cooking for Christmas Eve. Christmas will be a quiet day with the girls. And you?"

"I suppose I'll check in with the folks…"

"You should do that," she said. "And thank you for bringing the girls gifts."

"There's one for you, too," he said.

"I wish you hadn't. I'll give it back to you unopened. I hope you and the girls can work out a relationship, but you and I?" She shook her head. "We are now something that might have been and didn't make it."

Christmas morning began what Justine had come to think of as a new normal. She put on a comfortable, fleecy sweat suit and got about the business of making brunch. Addie had stayed the night at Jake's, something that Justine imagined would become routine, but they were planning to come over for brunch and gifts. The bacon had been cooked, the sausage was frying on the stove, potatoes were ready to go, a large fruit salad was prepared and in the refrigerator. The coffee was brewed, and while Justine had a cup, she tried not to think of all the lovely Christmases they'd had as a family, nostalgic holidays that seemed more perfect in retrospect than they probably were.

Amber was the first to wander into the living room where the fire blazed in the old fireplace. Next came Livvie, who walked into her mother's arms.

And then there was a knock at the front door. "Why would Addie knock at her own front door?" Justine mused, heading that way.

"It might be Daddy," Livvie said. "I invited him."

"Oh Livvie, you should have checked with me!"

"It'll be all right, Mom. He brought our presents yesterday. We have presents for him. I told him not to stay too long, and I told him no girlfriends were invited. I think there are things we should be openminded about. If he acts like a fool, he won't be invited back."

"Still…"

"You don't want us to go to his house, do you? Let's take one for the team. He's pathetic right now."

"Did he call you and ask?"

"No. I did it. I checked with Amber and she's okay. We were pretty mean to him all last summer. I just want him to know we can still be a family, if a weird and broken family, but everyone has to play by the rules. Rule number one—respect the boundaries of the others. That means no mistress at our Christmas brunch. He said that wouldn't be an issue."

He knocked again. Justine looked skeptical. "As I've been told, she is no longer in the picture. But I told him no stopping by on a whim. This isn't his house and we're not a couple."

"Fair enough," Livvie said.

Justine thought, *I can do this*. And she smiled at her daughters, thinking, *We somehow raised two very bright, intuitive girls*.

EPILOGUE

One Year Later

Adele and Justine went for a long walk on the beach at dawn on Christmas morning before the events of the day would begin. These early-morning walks had become a cherished part of their daily routine over the past year.

Addie was deep into her master's program and still working, but she was learning about transition following a divorce and making adjustments, entering a new relationship in her own family. She had moved in with Jake this past spring, and she was loving it 90 percent of the time. There was that 10 percent when one of them was grumpy or needed space or when they disagreed on things, both major and minor. But they both agreed they were in for the long haul, and they were planning a June wedding.

Justine completed the remodel of the old house, and it came as no surprise that it was stunning. For a while Addie was filled with envy; it had seemed like an old hovel while she lived there. But Jake's house was beautiful, as well, so it didn't trouble her for long. Amber was attending Berkeley, so Addie saw her fairly often, and Livvie had switched over to the high school in Half Moon Bay for her senior year. That's where her friends were now.

Justine was happier than Addie had ever seen her. She realized with some surprise that Justine wasn't naturally tense, wired for sound. It might have been the corporate career; it might have been the marriage; it might have been both. But now she was relaxed, self-confident and content. Her humor was sharp and her laugh was frequent. She was still seeing Logan, and they seemed to have a solid, romantic relationship, yet Justine held fiercely to her independence.

Scott had some trouble letting go of the girlfriend for the first few months of the new year but finally appeared to have broken free for good. He was stuck with a money-losing kayak shack but was in the process of turning it into a bar with a modest food service. He'd spent the fall enlarging the shack, laid a patio, got his food service licenses and would be ready to go by spring. It would serve as a good place to relax and watch a Pacific sunset, watch the whales when they were migrating, and he could provide picnic box lunches for people on their way to the beach. He kept a few kayaks, but he added rollerblades, bicycles, windsurfers and a few other beach accoutrements.

Of course, he had a girlfriend, but this one seemed sane and did not have a record. Neither did any mysterious bruises pop up unexpectedly. He did not drop in on Justine and the girls without permission.

So on this Christmas morning, one year and nine months since Addie saw Scott kissing Cat, they were coexisting without much trouble. Scott was invited to the Christmas morning unwrapping and brunch, but Logan was coming over Christmas evening. Amber's and Olivia's boyfriends were also dropping by. Addie and Jake were in and out through the holidays; there were too many desserts and board games ready to be played.

Addie was truly in love. There was no longer any question of whether it was the right kind of love. She'd taken a healthy look around and realized Jake was the man for her. Always had been. Had she not been a brokenhearted grieving mother or an overworked caregiver, their romance might have happened earlier. But the fact that they'd always maintained their closeness through all of those trials only made their love stronger and more steadfast. Practically every woman in town wanted to trade places with Addie.

As they watched the sun rise through the fog, they discussed how different but so much better their lives were. The new normal was working out, it seemed, for everyone involved.

"I agree," Justine told Addie. "I never would have believed we would all be doing so well after everything that happened. But it would be better if Scott suffered a little more," she said with a grin.

"True," Addie said, "but maybe we should actually thank him. His bad choices forced us to make good ones."

"I'll never thank him for being such an idiot," Justine said. "But I am happier than I've been for a long time, and they do say living well is the best revenge."

"Here's to living well!" Addie said as they both laughed.

* * * * *

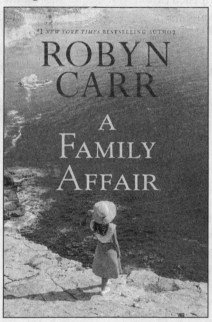

Escape to Virgin River and read the books that everyone is talking about!

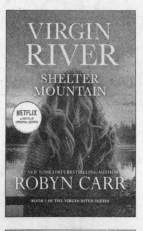
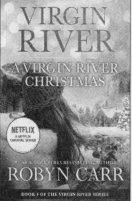

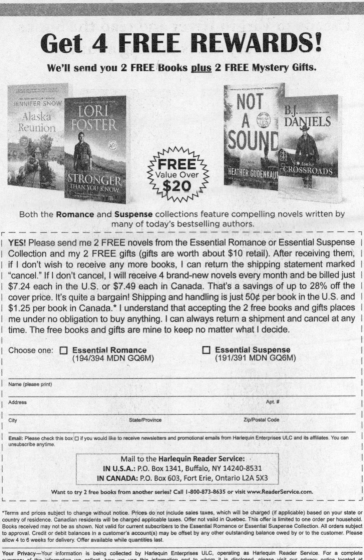